A.
W9-AFH-164
GEORGE

Praise for The Morganville Vampire Novels

"An electrifying, enthralling coming-of-age supernatural tale." —The Best Reviews

"A solid, utterly compelling story that you will find addictive and hypnotic. If Rachel Caine is not on your auto-buy list, put her there immediately, if not sooner." —The Eternal Night

"Rachel Caine brings her brilliant ability to blend witty dialogue, engaging characters, and an intriguing plot." —Romance Reviews Today

"A rousing horror thriller that adds a new dimension to the vampire mythos." —*Midwest Book Review*

Praise for Rachel Caine's Weather Warden Series

"You'll never watch the Weather Channel the same way again." —Jim Butcher

"The Weather Warden series is fun reading . . . more engaging than most TV." —*Booklist*

continued . . .

"A kick-butt heroine who will appeal strongly to fans of Tanya Huff, Kelley Armstrong, and Charlaine Harris."　　　　　　　　　　—*Romantic Times*

"Hugely entertaining."　　　　　　　—SF Crowsnest

"A fast-paced thrill ride [that] brings new meaning to stormy weather."　　　　　　　　　　—*Locus*

"An appealing heroine with a wry sense of humor that enlivens even the darkest encounters."　　—SF Site

"I dare you to put this book down."
　　　　　　—*University City Review* (Philadelphia)

"Rachel Caine takes the Weather Wardens to places the Weather Channel never imagined!"
　　　　　　　　　　—Mary Jo Putney

"A spellbinding . . . thought-provoking, action-packed thriller."　　　　　　　—*Midwest Book Review*

THE MORGANVILLE VAMPIRE NOVELS

Glass Houses
The Dead Girls' Dance
Midnight Alley

MIDNIGHT ALLEY

THE MORGANVILLE VAMPIRES, BOOK THREE

RACHEL CAINE

nal
JAM
books

NAL Jam
Published by New American Library, a division of
Penguin Group (USA) Inc., 375 Hudson Street,
New York, New York 10014, USA
Penguin Group (Canada), 90 Eglinton Avenue East, Suite 700, Toronto,
Ontario M4P 2Y3, Canada (a division of Pearson Penguin Canada Inc.)
Penguin Books Ltd., 80 Strand, London WC2R 0RL, England
Penguin Ireland, 25 St. Stephen's Green, Dublin 2,
Ireland (a division of Penguin Books Ltd.)
Penguin Group (Australia), 250 Camberwell Road, Camberwell, Victoria 3124,
Australia (a division of Pearson Australia Group Pty. Ltd.)
Penguin Books India Pvt. Ltd., 11 Community Centre, Panchsheel Park,
New Delhi - 110 017, India
Penguin Group (NZ), 67 Apollo Drive, Rosedale, North Shore 0632,
New Zealand (a division of Pearson New Zealand Ltd.)
Penguin Books (South Africa) (Pty.) Ltd., 24 Sturdee Avenue,
Rosebank, Johannesburg 2196, South Africa

Penguin Books Ltd., Registered Offices:
80 Strand, London WC2R 0RL, England

First published by NAL Jam, an imprint of New American Library,
a division of Penguin Group (USA) Inc.

First Printing, October 2007
10 9 8 7 6 5 4 3

Copyright © Roxanne Longstreet Conrad, 2007
All rights reserved

NAL JAM and logo are trademarks of Penguin Group (USA) Inc.

Printed in the United States of America

Without limiting the rights under copyright reserved above, no part of this
publication may be reproduced, stored in or introduced into a retrieval system, or transmitted, in any form, or by any means (electronic, mechanical,
photocopying, recording, or otherwise), without the prior written permission
of both the copyright owner and the above publisher of this book.

PUBLISHER'S NOTE
This is a work of fiction. Names, characters, places, and incidents either are
the product of the author's imagination or are used fictitiously, and any resem-
blance to actual persons, living or dead, business establishments, events, or
locales is entirely coincidental.
  The publisher does not have any control over and does not assume any
responsibility for author or third-party Web sites or their content.

If you purchased this book without a cover, you should be aware that this
book is stolen property. It was reported as "unsold and destroyed" to the
publisher, and neither the author nor the publisher has received any payment
for this "stripped book."

The scanning, uploading, and distribution of this book via the Internet or via
any other means without the permission of the publisher is illegal and punish-
able by law. Please purchase only authorized electronic editions, and do not
participate in or encourage electronic piracy of copyrighted materials. Your
support of the author's rights is appreciated.

CF
C123m

For the people who got me through my own personal Morganville years: Elizabeth Sandlin, Andy Sealy, Mona Fluitt, Bruce Tinsley, Luis Hernandez, Gary Wiley, Scott Chase, Marsha McNeill, Rachel Scarbrough, and many more who made the days bright. Also to the memory of sitting next to Stevie Ray Vaughn, hearing him make magic when few people were even listening.

For the people who are getting me through *these* Morganville years: Cat Conrad, Kelley Walters, Marla Stair, Katy Hendricks, Claire Wilkins and Baby Griff, Becky Rocha, Laurie Andrews and her lovely girls, P. N. Elrod, Jackie Leaf, Bill Leaf, Joanne Madge, Irene Ferris, Ter Matthies, the Alphas, ORAC, Douglas Joseph, Sharon Sams and her son Boardman, Ann Jackson and her son Trey, and literally too many LiveJournal and MySpace friends to even attempt to list. Every one of them a special, undeserved gift.

And to Charles Armitage and Kevin Cleary, for making Morganville an even more exciting place.

ACKNOWLEDGMENTS

Fast turnaround reading and commenting from a select group of people, including (but probably not limited to) Jackie, Sharon, Donna, and Lisa. Especially Donna, who reminded me that if you put a knife on the table in the first act, you'd better not switch it to a gun in the third . . . thanks, Donna!

1

The instant the phone rang at the Glass House, Claire knew with a psychic flash that it had to be her mother.

Well, it wasn't so much a psychic flash as simple logic. She'd told Mom that she would call days ago, which she hadn't, and now, of course, it could only be her mother calling at the most inopportune moment.

Hence: had to be a call from Mom.

"Don't," her boyfriend—she couldn't believe she could actually call him that, *boyfriend,* not a boy friend—Shane murmured without taking his mouth off of hers. "Michael will get it." And he was giving her a very good argument in favor of ignoring the phone, too. But somewhere in the back of her mind that little voice just wouldn't shut up.

She slid off of his lap with a regretful sigh, licked her damp, tingling lips, and dashed off in the direction of the kitchen door.

Michael was just rising from the kitchen table to head for the phone. She beat him to it, mouthing a silent apology, and said, "Hello?"

"Claire! Oh my goodness, I've been worried sick, honey. We've been trying to call you on your cell for days, and—"

Crap. Claire rubbed her forehead in frustration. "Mom, I sent you guys an e-mail, remember? My cell got lost; I'm still working on getting another one." Best not to mention how it had gotten lost. Best not to mention anything about how dangerous her life had become since she'd moved to Morganville, Texas.

"Oh," Mom said, and then, more slowly, "Oh. Well, your father forgot to tell me about that. You know, he's the one who checks the e-mail. I don't like computers."

"Yes, Mom, I know." Mom really wasn't *that* bad, but she was notoriously nervous with computers, and for good reason; they had a tendency to short out around her.

Mom was still talking. "Is everything going all right? How are classes? Interesting?"

Claire opened the refrigerator door and retrieved a can of Coke, which she popped open and chugged to give herself time to think what, if anything, to tell her parents. *Mom, there was a little trouble. See, my boyfriend's dad came to town with some bikers and killed people, and nearly killed us, too. Oh, and the vampires are angry about it. So to save my friends, I had to sign a contract, so now I'm basically the slave of the most badass vampire in town.*

Yeah, that wouldn't go over well.

Besides, even if she said it, Mom wouldn't understand it. Mom had been to Morganville, but she hadn't really *seen*. People usually didn't. And if they did, they either never left town or had their memories wiped on the way out.

And if by some chance they started to remember, bad things could happen to them. Terminally bad things.

So instead, Claire said, "Classes are great, Mom. I aced all my exams last week."

"Of course you did. Don't you always?"

Yeah, but last week I had to take my exams while worrying that somebody was going to stick a knife in my back. It could have had an effect on my GPA. Stupid to be proud of that . . . "Everything's fine here. I'll let you know when I get the new cell phone, okay?" Claire hesitated, then asked, "How are you? How's Dad?"

"Oh, we're fine, honey. We miss you is all. But your father's still not happy about your living in that place, off campus, with those older kids. . . ."

Of all the things for Mom to remember, she had to remember *that*. And of course Claire couldn't tell her *why* she was living off campus with eighteen-year-olds, especially when two of them were boys. Mom hadn't gotten around to mentioning the boys yet, but it was just a matter of time.

"Mom, I told you how mean the girls were to me in the dorm. It's better here. They're my friends. And really, they're great."

Mom didn't sound too convinced. "You're being careful, though. About those boys."

Well, that hadn't taken long. "Yes, I'm being careful about the boys." She was even being careful about Shane, though that was mostly because Shane never forgot that Claire was not quite seventeen, and he was not quite nineteen. Not a huge age difference, but legally? Huger than huge, if her parents got upset about it. Which they definitely would. "Everybody here says hello, by the way. Ah, Michael's waving."

Michael Glass, the second boy in the house, had settled down at the kitchen table and was reading a newspaper. He looked up and gave her a wide-eyed, *no-you-don't* shake of his head. He'd had a bad enough time of it with her parents the last time, and now . . . well, things were even worse, if that was possible. At least when he'd met them, Michael had been half-normal: fully human by night, an incorporeal ghost by day, and trapped in the house twenty-four/ seven.

For Morganville, that *was* half-normal.

In order to help get Shane out of trouble, Michael had made a terrible choice—he'd gained his freedom from the house and obtained physical form at the time, but now he was a vampire. Claire couldn't tell if it bothered him. It had to, right? But he seemed so . . . normal.

Maybe a little too normal.

Claire listened to her mother's voice, and then held out the phone to Michael. "She wants to talk to you," she said.

"No! I'm not here!" he stage-whispered, and made waving-off motions. Claire wiggled the phone insistently.

"You're the responsible one," she reminded him. "Just try not to talk about the—" She mimed fangs in the neck.

Michael shot her a dirty look, took the phone, and turned on the charm. He had a lot of it, Claire knew; it wasn't just parents who liked him, it was . . . well, everybody. Michael was smart, cute, hot, talented, respectful . . . nothing not to love, except the whole undead aspect. He assured her mother that everything was fine, that Claire was behaving herself—his eye roll made Claire snort cola up her nose—and that he was watching out for Mrs. Danvers's little girl. That last part was true, at least. Michael was taking his self-appointed older-brother duties way too seriously. He hardly let Claire out of his sight, except when privacy was required or Claire slipped off to class without an escort—which was as often as possible.

"Yes ma'am," Michael said. He was starting to look a little strained. "No ma'am. I won't let her do that. Yes. Yes."

Claire had pity on him, and reclaimed the phone. "Mom, we've got to go. I love you both."

Mom still sounded anxious. "Claire, are you sure you don't want to come home? Maybe I was wrong about letting you go to MIT early. You could take the year off, study, and we'd love to have you back home again. . . ."

Weird. Usually she calmed right down, especially when Michael talked to her. Claire had a bad flash of Shane telling her about his own mother, how her memories of Morganville had started to surface. How the vampires had come after her to kill her because the conditioning didn't stick.

Her parents were in the same boat now. They'd been to town, but she still wasn't sure just how much they really knew or understood about that visit—it could be enough to put them in mortal danger. She had to do everything she could to keep them safe. That meant not following her dreams to MIT, because if she left Morganville—assuming she could even get out of town—the vampires would follow her, and they'd either bring her back or kill her. And the rest of her family, too.

Besides, Claire *had* to stay now, because she'd signed a contract pledging herself directly to Amelie, the town's Founder. The biggest, scariest vampire of them all, even if she rarely showed that side. At the time, she'd been Claire's only real hope to keep herself and her friends alive.

So far signing the contract hadn't meant a whole lot—no announcements in the local paper, and Amelie hadn't shown up to collect on her soul or anything. So maybe it would just pass by . . . quietly.

Mom was still talking about MIT, and Claire didn't want to think about it. She'd dreamed of going to a school like MIT or CalTech her whole life, and she'd been smart enough to do it. She'd even gotten early acceptance. It was drastically unfair that she was stuck in Morganville now, like a fly in a spider's web, and for a few seconds she let herself feel bitter and angry about that.

Nice, the brutally honest part of her mocked. *You'd sacrifice Shane's life for what you want, because you know that's what would happen. Eventually, the vampires would find an excuse to kill him. You're not any better than the vampires if you don't do everything you can to prevent that.*

The bitterness left, but regret wasn't following bitterness any time soon. She hoped Shane never knew how she felt about it, deep down.

"Mom, sorry, I've got to go; I have class. I love you—tell Dad I love him, too, will you?"

Claire hung up on her mother's protests, heaved a sigh, and glanced at Michael, who was looking a little sympathetic.

"That's not easy, talking to the folks," he offered. "Sorry."

"Don't you ever talk to your parents?" Claire asked, and slid into the chair at the small breakfast table across from him. Michael had a cup of something; she was afraid it was blood for a second, but then she smelled coffee. Hazelnut. Vampires could, and did, enjoy food; it just didn't sustain them.

Michael looked suspiciously good this morning—a little color in his face, an energy to his movements that hadn't been there last night.

He'd had more than coffee this morning. How did that happen, exactly? Did he sneak off to the blood bank? Was there some kind of home delivery service?

Claire made a mental note to check into it. Quietly.

"Yeah, I call my folks sometimes," Michael said. He folded the newspaper—the local rag, run by vampires—and picked up a smaller, rolled bundle of letter-sized pages secured by a rubber band. "They're Morganville exiles, so they have a lot to forget. It's better if I don't keep in contact too much; it could make trouble. I mostly write. The mail and e-mail get read before they're sent; you know that, right? And most of the phone calls get monitored, especially long-distance."

He stripped off the rubber band and unfolded the cheap pages of the second newspaper. Claire read the masthead upside down: *The Fang Report.* The logo was two stakes at right angles making up a cross. Wild.

"What's that?"

"This?" Michael rattled the paper and shrugged. "Captain Obvious."

"What?"

"Captain Obvious. That's his handle. He's been doing these papers every week for about two years now. It's an underground thing."

Underground in Morganville had a lot of meanings.

Claire raised her eyebrows. "So . . . Captain Obvious is a vampire?"

"Not unless he's got a serious self-image problem," Michael said. "Captain Obvious hates vampires. If somebody steps out of line, he documents it—" Michael froze, reading the headline, and his mouth opened, then closed. His face set like stone, and his blue eyes looked stricken.

Claire reached over and took the newspaper from his hands, turned it, and read.

NEW BLOODSUCKER IN TOWN

Michael Glass, once a rising musical star with too much talent for this twisted town, has fallen to the Dark Side. Details are sketchy, but Glass, who's been keeping to himself for the past year, has definitely joined the Fang Gang.

Nobody knows how or where it happened, and I doubt Glass will be talking, but we should all be worried. Does this mean more vamps, fewer humans? After all, he is the first newly risen undead in generations.

Beware, boys and girls: Glass may look like an angel, but he's got a demon inside now. Memorize the face, kibbles. He's the newest addition to the Better-Off-Dead club!

"The *Better-Off-Dead* club?" Claire repeated aloud, horrified. "He's kidding, right?" There was Michael's picture, probably directly out of the Morganville High yearbook, inset as a graphic into a tombstone.

With crudely drawn-in fangs.

"Captain Obvious never comes out and tells anyone to kill," Michael said. "He's pretty careful about how he phrases things." Her friend was angry, Claire saw. And scared. "He's got our address listed. And all your names, too, though at least he points out none of you are vampires. Still. That's not good." Michael was getting past the shock of seeing himself outed in the paper, and was getting worried. Claire was already there.

"Well . . . why don't the vampires do something about him? Stop him?"

"They've tried. They've arrested three people in the last two years who said they were Captain Obvious. Turned out they didn't know anything. The captain could teach the CIA a thing or two about running a secret operation."

"So he's not that obvious," Claire said.

"I think he means it in the ironic sense." Michael swallowed a quick gulp of coffee. "Claire, I don't like this. Not like we didn't have enough trouble without this kind of—"

Eve slammed in through the kitchen door, which hit the wall with a thunderous boom, startling both of them. She clomped across the kitchen floor and leaned on the breakfast table. She wasn't very Goth today; her hair was still matte-black, but it was worn back in a simple ponytail, and the plain knit shirt and black pants didn't have a skull anywhere in view. No makeup, either. She almost looked . . . normal. Which was so *wrong*.

"All right," she said, and slapped down a second copy of *The Fang Report* in front of Michael. "Please tell me you have a snappy comeback for this."

"I'll make sure the three of you are safe."

"Oh, *so* not what I was looking for! Look, I'm not worried about us! We're not the ones Photoshopped into tombstones!" Eve looked at the picture again. "Although yes, better dead than that hairdo . . . God, was that your prom photo?"

Michael grabbed the paper back and put it face-down on the table. "Eve, nothing is going to happen. Captain Obvious just loves to talk. Nobody's going to come after me."

"Right," a new voice said. It was Shane. He'd come in behind Eve, clearly wanting to watch the fireworks, and now he leaned against the wall next to the stove and crossed his arms. "By all means, let's keep on shoveling the bull," he said. "It's trouble, and you know it." Claire waited for him to come over to the table and join the three of them, the way things used to be.

He didn't. Shane hadn't willingly stayed long in the same room with Michael since . . . the change. And he wouldn't look at him, except in angles and side glances. He'd also taken to wearing one of Eve's silver crosses, although just now it was hidden beneath the neck of the gray T-shirt he was wearing. Claire found her eyes fixing on its just-visible outline.

Eve ignored Shane; her big, dark eyes were fixed on Michael. "You know they'll all be gunning for you now, right? All the would-be Buffys?" Claire had seen *Buffy the Vampire Slayer,* but she had no idea how Eve had managed; it was contraband in Morganville, along with every other movie or book featuring vampires. Or vampire killing, more to the point. Internet downloads were strictly controlled, too, though no doubt there was a hot black market in those kinds of things that Eve had tapped into.

"Like you?" Michael said. He still hadn't forgotten the arsenal of stakes and crosses that Eve kept hidden in her room. In the old days, that had seemed like good sense, living in Morganville. Now, it seemed like a recipe for domestic violence.

Eve looked stricken. "I'd never—"

"I know." He took her hand gently in his. "I know."

She softened, but then she shook it off and went back to frowning at him. "Look, this is *dangerous.* They know you're an easier target than those other guys, and they're going to hate you even more, because you're one of us. *Our* age."

"Maybe," Michael said. "Eve, come on, sit. Sit down."

She did, but it was more like a collapse, and she didn't stop jittering her heel up and down in agitation, or drumming her black-painted fingernails on the table. "This is bad," she said. "You know that, right?

Nine point five on the ten point scale of make-me-yak."

"Compared to what?" Shane asked. "We're already living with the enemy. What does that score? Not to mention you probably get extra points for banging him—"

Michael stood up so fast his chair tipped and hit the floor with a clatter. Shane straightened, ready for trouble, fists clenched.

"Shut up, Shane," Michael said, deathly quiet. "I mean it."

Shane stared past him at Eve. "He's going to bite you. He can't help it, and once he starts, he won't stop; he'll *kill* you. But you know that, right? What is that, some freak-ass Goth idea of romantic suicide? You turning into a fang-banger?"

"Butt out, Shane. What you know about Goth culture you got from old episodes of *The Munsters* and your Aryan Brotherhood dad." Great, now Eve was angry, too. That left Claire the only sane one in the room.

Michael made an effort to dial it back. "Come on, Shane. Leave her alone. *You're* the one hurting her, not me."

Shane's gaze snapped to Michael and focused. Hard. "I don't hurt girls. You say I do, and you'd better back it up, asshole."

Shane pushed away from the wall, because Michael was taking steps in his direction. Claire watched, wide-eyed and frozen.

Eve got between them, hands outstretched to hold both of them back. "Come on, guys, you don't want to do this."

"Kinda do," Shane said coolly.

"Fine. Either hit each other or get a room," she snapped, and stepped out of the middle. "Just don't pretend it's all about protecting the itty-widdle girl, because it isn't. It's about the two of you. So get it together, or leave; I don't care which."

Shane stared at her for a second, eyes gone wide

and oddly hurt, then looked at Claire. She didn't move.

"I'm out," he said. He turned and walked through the kitchen door. It swung shut behind him.

Eve let out a little gasp. "I didn't think he'd go," she said, so unsteadily that for a second Claire thought she was going to cry. "What a freaking *idiot*."

Claire reached over and took her hand. Eve squeezed, hard, and then leaned back into Michael's embrace. Vampire or not, the two of them seemed happy, and anyway, this was *Michael*. She just couldn't understand Shane's anger. It seemed to bubble up when she least expected it, for no reason at all.

"I'd better . . ." she ventured. Michael nodded.

Claire slipped out of her chair and went to find Shane. Not like it was difficult; he was slumped on the couch, staring at the PlayStation screen and working the controls on yet another zombie-killing adventure. "You taking his side?" Shane asked, and splattered the head of an attacking undead monster.

"No," Claire said and settled in carefully next to him, with enough open space between so he didn't feel pressured. "Why are there sides, anyway?"

"What?"

"Michael's your friend; he's our housemate. Why do there have to be sides?"

He snapped his fingers. "Um, wait, I've got this one . . . because he's a bloodsucking, night-crawling leech who *used* to be my friend?"

"Shane—"

"You think you know, but you don't. He's going to change. They all change. Maybe it'll take time, I don't know. Right now, he thinks he's just human plus, but that's not what it is. He's human *minus*. And you'd better not forget it."

She stared at him, a little bit stunned and a whole lot saddened. "Eve's right. That sounds like your father talking."

Shane flinched, paused the game, and threw the controller down. "Low, Claire." He wasn't exactly his dad's biggest fan at the best of times—he couldn't be, with the number of cruel things his dad had done to him.

"No, it's just true. Look, it's *Michael.* Can't you give him the benefit of the doubt? He hasn't hurt anybody, has he? And you have to admit, having a vampire on our side, *really* on our side, couldn't hurt. Not in Morganville."

He just glared at the screen, jaw set. Claire was trying to think of another way to get through to him, but she was derailed by the ringing of the doorbell. Shane didn't move. "I'll get it," she sighed, and went down the hall to open the front door. It was safe enough—midmorning, sunny, and relatively mild. Summer was finally starting a slide toward fall, now that it had burned all the green out of the Texas landscape.

Claire squinted against the brilliance. For a second she thought that there was something deeply wrong with her eyes.

Because her archenemy, Queen Bitch Monica Morrell, flanked by her ever-present harpies Gina and Jennifer, was standing on the doorstep. It was like seeing Barbie and her friends, blown up life-sized and dressed like Old Navy mannequins. Tanned, toned, and perfect, from lip gloss to toenail polish. Monica had on a forced, pleasant expression. Gina and Jennifer were trying, but they looked like they were smelling something rotten.

"Hi!" Monica said brightly. "Got plans today, Claire? I was thinking we could hang."

That's it, Claire thought. *I'm dreaming. Only this is a nightmare, right? Monica pretending to be my friend? Definitely a nightmare.*

"I—what do you want?" Claire asked, because her relationship with Monica, Gina, and Jennifer had started with being pushed down the stairs at the dorm, and hadn't improved since. She was a crawling bug to the Cool Girls. At best. Or . . . a tool. *Was this about Michael?* Because his status had changed from "her-mit musician" to "hottie vampire" in one night, and Monica was definitely a fang-banger, right? "You want to talk to Michael?"

Monica gave her an odd look. "Why would I want to do that? Can he go shopping in broad daylight?"

"Oh." She had no idea what else to say to that.

"I thought a little retail therapy, and then we all go study," Monica said. "We're going to check out that new place, not Common Grounds. Common Grounds is so last century. Like I *want* to be under Oliver's thumb all the time. Now that he's taken over as Protector for our family, he's been all hands-on, wanting to see my grades. Sucks, right?"

"I—"

"C'mon, save my life. I really need help with economics, and these two are boneheads." Monica dismissed her two closest friends with an offhand wave. "Seriously. Come with. Please? I could really use your brainpower. And I think we should get to know each other a little better, don't you? Seeing as how things have changed?"

Claire opened her mouth, then closed it without saying anything. The last two times she'd gone anywhere with Monica, she'd been flat on her back on the floor of a van, getting beaten and terrorized.

She managed to stammer, "I know this is going to sound rude, but—what the hell are you doing?"

Monica sighed and looked—how weird was this?— contrite. "I know what you're thinking. Yes, I was a bitch to you, and I hurt you. And I'm sorry." Gina and Jennifer, her constant Greek chorus, nodded and repeated *sorry* in whispers. "Water under the bridge, all right? All is forgiven?"

Claire was, if anything, even more mystified. "Why are you doing this?"

Monica pursed her glossy lips, leaned forward, and dropped her voice to a low, confidential tone. "Well . . . all right, yeah, it's not like I had a head injury or something and woke up thinking you were cool. But you're different now. I can help. I can introduce you around to all the people you really need to know."

"You're kidding. I'm different *how*?"

Monica leaned even closer. "You signed."

So . . . this wasn't about Michael. Claire had just become . . . popular. Because she'd become Amelie's property.

And that was terrifying.

"Oh," she managed, and then, more slowly, "Oh."

"Trust me," Monica said. "You need somebody in the know. Somebody to show you the ropes."

If the only other person left on the planet was Jack the Ripper, Claire would have trusted him first. "Sorry," she said. "I have plans. But—thank you. Maybe some other time."

She shut the door on Monica's surprised face, then locked it. She jumped when she turned to find Shane standing right behind her, staring at her as though he'd never seen her before.

"Thank you?" he mimicked. "You're thanking that bitch? For what, Claire? For beating you? For trying to kill you? For killing my sister? Christ. First Michael, then you. I don't know any of you anymore."

In true Shane fashion, he just took off. She listened to the heavy tread of his footsteps cross the living room and then go up the stairs. Heard the familiar slam of his door.

"Hey!" she shouted after him. "I was just being polite!"

2

"So," Eve said as she drove Claire to school, "what was up with the Monica thing? I mean, maybe you ought to watch your back with her. Even more than you already do."

"She sounded like she really kind of meant it. It took a lot for her to come eat crow like that."

Eve shot her a look. One of *those* looks, doubly effective coming from a girl wearing rice-powder makeup and flawless eye liner and black-cherry lips. "In Monica's world, being friends means doing whatever Monica wants, when Monica wants to do it. Somehow, I can't see you as one of her brain-dead backup singers."

"No! That's not—I didn't say I was *going* to be her friend, just—you asked." Claire crossed her arms and settled back in the bucket seat of Eve's ancient black Caddy, shooting for a stubborn look. "She's not my friend, okay? You're my friend."

"So when Monica starts bringing the in-crowd to hang at your study table, you'll get up and leave? No way. You're too nice. Before you know it, you're tagging along with them, and then you start to actually feel sorry for them. You'll tell me how Monica's not bad, she's just misunderstood, and before you know it you're braiding each others' hair and giggling over boy bands."

Claire made a retching sound. "I wouldn't do that."

"Please. You like everybody. You even like me.

You like *Shane,* and let's face it, Shane's kind of an idiot, at least right now." Eve's eyes narrowed as she thought about that. "And about Shane, I swear, if he doesn't snap out of it, I'm going to punch him in the face. Well, punch him in the face and then run like hell."

Claire played that out in her head and nearly laughed. Eve's best possible punch wouldn't do more than surprise Shane, she figured, but she could just picture the wounded look of confusion on his face. *What the hell did I do?*

"I'm not popular," she declared. "Monica's not my friend, and I'm not hanging with her, ever, end of story."

"Swear?"

Claire held up her hand. "Swear."

"Huh." Eve didn't sound convinced. "Whatev."

"Look, if we're friends, how about buying me a mocha?"

"Mooch."

"You're the one with the job."

Midafternoon, and it was raining, which was kind of a rarity—a cold, early-fall rain that came down in glittering sheets. Claire, like about 90 percent of the other students, hadn't thought to bring an umbrella, so she sloshed along miserably along the Quadrangle, past the empty benches and rain-soaked message boards, toward her chem lab. She loved Chem Lab. She hated rain. She hated being soaked to the skin, and frankly, living in this part of Texas made it usually not that much of a risk. There was no room in her backpack for anything frivolous, like a raincoat. She worried her books were getting soggy, but the back-pack was supposed to be waterproof. . . .

"You look cold," said a voice from behind her, and then the rain cut off, and she heard the hollow thump of raindrops hitting the thin skin of an umbrella. Claire looked up, blinked water out of her eyes, and saw she was walking under a golf umbrella big enough for four or five of her . . . or one of her, plus the guy holding the umbrella. Because he was *huge.* Also cute, in that big-boned football player kind of way. He would have made Shane look small. Well proportioned, though, so the height (had to be at least six feet five, Claire thought) and weight just seemed right on him. He had chocolate brown skin and gorgeous brown eyes, and he seemed . . . kind of nice.

"I'm Jerome," he said. "Hey."

"Hey," she said back, still amazed that somebody who was clearly *somebody* would stop to hang an umbrella over her head. "Thanks. Um, I'm Claire. Hi."

She juggled her dripping backpack to her other hand and offered him her right. He took it and shook. His was about three times as large, big enough (she bet) to cup most of an entire football.

He was wearing a TPU athletic department T-shirt. No mystery about his major.

"Where're you heading, Claire?"

"Chem Lab," she said, and pointed at the building, which was about a football field–length away, on the other side of the Quad. He nodded and steered that direction. "Look, it's nice of you, but you don't have to—"

"It's no problem." He smiled at her. He had dimples. "I hear the Science Building is nice this time of year. And anything for a friend."

"But I'm not—"

Jerome nodded to a group of girls standing huddled together under the awning of the Language Arts Building. Pretty girls. In the center of them was Monica Morrell, and she blew Jerome a flirty sort of kiss.

"Oh," Claire said. "*That* friend." Her estimate of Jerome fell by several dozen notches, hit bottom, and started digging for China. "Look, I appreciate it, but I'm not sugar. I won't melt."

She veered away and walked fast. Jerome took about two long strides and put the umbrella over her again without comment. She glared at him.

He lifted an eyebrow. "I can play this game all day."

"Fine," she said. "But I don't need favors from Monica."

"Girl, it's an umbrella, not a Lamborghini," he pointed out. Way too reasonably. "I'm not even lending it to you. It's not really that much of a favor."

She kept her mouth shut, head down, and walked fast. Jerome stopped at the foot of the Science Building's stairs, and she bounded up and darted under the concrete porch, which was already choked with other students hiding from the rain. She looked back down. Jerome smiled and waved, and a bronze or copper bracelet caught her eye.

He was Protected. Probably a native of Morganville.

"I'm not her friend. That was not my fault," she complained, defending herself to an Eve who wasn't even there.

And then she sneezed, sniffled, and dragged her soggy butt to class.

The rain kept up all day and all night, but the next day dawned bright and shiny, with a pale silver sun not quite as fierce as Claire expected. Kind of nice, actually. She'd already showered by the time Eve stumbled into the bathroom, looking more like the walking dead than most vampires. Eve mumbled something and ignored Claire as she started up the shower again. Claire finished at the sink and hurried downstairs. She found Michael at the coffeepot, emptying the filter of cold grounds. Deeply weird that he was *more* of a morning person as a vampire. Maybe he was just enjoying having a morning again, instead of becoming a floaty ghost at dawn.

"Eve's up. You'd better make it so dark the spoon melts."

Michael shot her a half smile, still almost lethal enough to stop a girl's heart. Luckily he knew just how much current to use on his charm. "That bad, huh?"

She thought about it for a second as she took down a bowl and the box of Rice Krispies, and found the milk behind the bottles of beer—contraband, from Shane—in the fridge. "You've seen that movie where the zombies eat people's brains?"

"*Night of the Living Dead*?"

"The zombies would run if they got a look at her."

Michael spooned extra coffee into the fresh filter. He looked good, she thought. Strong, tall, confident. He had on a nice blue shirt and some not-so-ratty blue jeans, and he was wearing shoes. Running shoes, sure, but shoes. Claire stared at his feet. "You're going out," she said.

"Got a job," Michael said. "Working at JT's Music over on Third Street, ten to close. Mostly I'll be demo-ing guitars and selling them, but JT said he'd let me do some private lessons if I wanted."

That was so . . . normal. *Really* normal. And he sounded happy, too. Claire bit her lip and tried to organize the explosion of questions in her brain. "Ah—what about the sun?" she asked. Because that seemed to be the first hurdle.

"They issued me a car," Michael said. "It's in the garage. Fully sunproofed. And there's underground parking at JT's. There is most places."

"Issued—who issued you a car?" He shot her a *you're not stupid* look. "The town? Amelie?"

He didn't answer directly as he slid the filter com-partment shut and turned on the *brew* switch. The machine began wheezing and trickling into the pot. "They tell me it's standard procedure," he said. "For new vampires."

"Not that there have been any for fifty years, right?"

He shrugged. It was obvious that she was making him uncomfortable with the questions, but Claire couldn't help herself. "Did you ever find out why— why there haven't been any in so long?"

"I don't think it's a great idea to be too curious right now."

She understood that—and understood he meant it

for her as well—but she couldn't stop asking questions, somehow. "Michael—did they get you the job, too?"

"No. I know JT. I got the job all by myself. They offered—" He stopped, clearly thinking he'd already said too much.

Claire finished it out, guessing. "They offered you some kind of job in the vampire community. Right? Or—" Oh God. "Or they offered to make you a Protector?"

"Not right off the bat," he said, still staring at the coffeemaker. "You have to work up to that. So they say."

Michael. Owning people. Skimming off their wages like some Mafia don. She tried not to let him see how sick that idea made her feel, that he'd ever really consider doing it.

His eyes suddenly cut toward her, as if he'd read her mind. "I didn't do it. I found the job at JT's, Claire," Michael said, and suddenly moved toward her. She flinched, and he took a deep breath and held out his hand in clear apology. "Sorry. I forget sometimes—it's hard, okay, learning how to move around people when I can go so much faster. But I wouldn't hurt you, Claire. No way."

"Shane thinks—"

Light caught and flared in Michael's eyes, eerie and frightening, and then he blinked and it was gone. He obviously made a real effort to keep his voice quiet. "Shane's wrong," he said. "I'm not changing, Claire. I'm still your friend. I'll look after you. All of you. Even Shane."

She didn't answer him. Truthfully, as much as she liked him—and it verged on love—she felt something different about him today. Something complicated and agitated and strange.

Was he . . . hungry? He was staring at her. No, he was staring at the thin skin of her neck, wasn't he? Claire put her hand to it, involuntary but irresistible.

and Michael got a very slight pink flush in his pale cheeks and looked away.

"I wouldn't," he said, in a far different tone than before. It almost sounded scared to her. "I wouldn't, Claire. You have to believe me. But—this is hard. It's so hard."

She did believe him, mostly because she could hear all the heartbreak and sorrow in his voice. She took a breath, stepped forward, and hugged him. He was tall; the top of her head only brushed his chin. His arms felt strong and comforting, and she told herself that he wasn't warm because it was chilly in the kitchen. It wasn't really true, but that helped.

"I wouldn't hurt you," he murmured. "But I've got to admit, I want to. I spent all my life hating vampires, and now—now look at me."

"You had to," Claire said. "You didn't have a choice."

She felt his sigh go through both of them. "Not true," he said. "Shane's right—I did have a choice. But this is the choice I made, and now I have to live with it."

He let go when she stepped back. Neither of them knew what to say, so Claire busied herself by opening kitchen cabinets to get down the four mismatched cups they used in the morning. Michael's was plain chunky stoneware, oversized, like a diner cup on steroids. Eve's was a petite black thing with a yawning cartoon vampire on it. Shane's had a happy face with a bloody bullet hole in the center of its forehead. Claire had taken one with Goofy and Mickey on it.

"How's school?" Michael asked. Neutral subjects. He didn't want to talk it out; he wanted to keep it inside. She wasn't too surprised. Michael had always been too self-contained for his own good, as far as she could tell.

"Too easy," she sighed, and poured coffee.

They were sitting down and sipping from their mugs when the kitchen door opened, and Shane—wearing pajama bottoms and a ratty old faded T-shirt—came into the kitchen. He avoided Michael, picked up his cup off the counter, and filled it to the brim. He left without a word.

Michael watched him go, face set and hard.

Claire felt the need to apologize. "He's just—"

"I know," Michael said. "Believe me. I know exactly how Shane is. Doesn't mean I have to like it right now."

I really need to stop being the Glass Goodwill Ambassador, Claire thought, but she knew she'd keep on doing it. Somebody had to, after all. So after she'd finished her coffee, she went to talk to Shane.

Shane's door was unlocked and slightly open. Claire pushed it and stepped inside, then stopped short. All her carefully prepared speeches flew right out of her head, because Shane was getting dressed.

The sight of him short-circuited her thought processes and completely grounded her better judgment. He'd already hauled on his blue jeans, and his back was to her. No shirt yet. She was spellbound by the ripples of muscles on his back, the gorgeous smoothness of his skin, the way his shaggy hair brushed the tops of his shoulders and begged to be smoothed back. . . .

The sound of his zipper being pulled up snapped her back to sanity. She stepped hastily back, out into the hall, and pulled the door almost shut, then knocked.

"What?" It wasn't a friendly response.

"It's me," she said. "Can I come in?"

She heard something halfway between a grunt and a sigh, and opened the door to find him dragging a dark gray, form-fitting shirt over his head. It looked very good on him. Not as good as the no-shirt thing, but she was trying hard not to think about that. It had made her warm and fluttery inside.

"Is that a new shirt?" she asked, desperate to get her mind off the vivid mental pictures that kept bubbling up. That got another indefinite grunt. "It looks nice."

Shane gave her an ironic look. "We're talking clothes now? Wait, let me get my *Fashion for Dummies* book."

"I—never mind. About Michael—"

"Stop." Shane stepped forward and kissed her on the forehead. "I know, you don't want me ripping him, but I can't help it. Give me some time, okay? I need to figure some things out."

Claire tipped her head back, and this time he found her lips. It was, she thought, supposed to be a fast and sweet little kiss, but somehow it slowed down, got warmer and deeper. His lips were damp and soft as silk, and that was such a contrast to the hard lines of his body pressed against her, the strength of his hands sliding around her waist and pulling her even closer. She heard him growl low in his throat, a wild and hungry sound that made her go weak and faint.

He broke the kiss and leaned against her, breathing hard. "Good morning to you, too. Man, I just can't stay mad when you do that."

"Do what?" she asked innocently. She didn't feel innocent. She also didn't feel sixteen-nearly-seventeen, not at all. Shane always made her feel older. Much older. Ready for anything. It was a good thing Shane wasn't as dumb as her hormones seemed to be.

"Unless you want to stay home and cut class, we don't really have time to talk about it," he said, and waggled his eyebrows. "So. Wanna cut class and make out?"

She socked him on the arm. "No."

"You are such a strange girl. Ow," he said, in the way that meant he hadn't felt it at all. "You riding with Eve?"

"When she passes the snarling cannibal phase, yeah. Another two cups of coffee, probably."

"You sure you don't want a bodyguard?" He meant it. Shane didn't have a job—she wasn't really sure he could get one, after what his dad had been up to in

Morganville recently. Probably better he kept it low profile for a while. The fewer vampires—and vampire loyalists—he came in contact with right now, the better. He was still thought of as an unindicted coconspirator to his dad's revenge rampage, and even though the mayor had officially signed his pardon, nobody had much liked it.

Accidents happened.

"I don't need a bodyguard," Claire said. "Nobody's out to get me. Even Monica's gotten all friends-making with me."

That earned her a too-sharp look, which didn't go well with his reddened, kissable lips. "Yeah. Why is that?"

She shrugged and avoided his eyes. "I don't know."

He tipped her chin up with one finger. "So, are we at the lying part of the relationship already? Usually that comes after the exciting, hot and sexy honeymoon period."

She stuck out her tongue at him, and he leaned forward and—to her horror—licked it. "Ewwww!"

"Then don't stick it out." Shane smiled. "If you're going to hang out in my room and tempt me, there's a penalty. One item of clothing per minute comes off."

"Perv."

He pointed to himself. "Male and eighteen. What's your point?"

"You are *so*—"

"Say, you got any pleated miniskirts and kneesocks? I really get off on—"

She squealed and dodged his grabby hands, then checked her watch. "Oh, crap—I really do have to go. I'm sorry. Look, you'll be—you're okay, right?"

The smile disappeared, leaving only a trace in his dark, secretive eyes. "Yeah," Shane said. "I'll be okay. Watch your back, Claire."

"You too." Claire started for the door, but she heard his footsteps behind her and turned; he moved her back to the wall, tipped up her chin, and kissed her so thoroughly that she felt her head fill with light and her knees turn to rubber.

When she could breathe again, and he pulled back to give her just an inch or so of space between their lips, she gasped, "Was that a good-bye?"

"That was a come-home-soon," he said, and pushed off from the wall. "Seriously, Claire. Watch yourself. I worry."

"I know," she said, and smiled. Her knees were still weak, and the chorusing light in her head just didn't seem to be fading. "Best kiss so far, by the way."

His eyebrows rose. "You're keeping score?"

"Hey, you raised the bar. I don't grade on a curve."

She left him, reluctantly, to grab her backpack and see if Eve was in the mood to eat brains, or to give her a ride to school.

3

Morning classes went pretty well, and Claire spent her breaks hanging at the coffee bar at the University Center, where Eve barista'd her way through the day. Eve was good at it—calm, efficient, seemingly impervious to the pissy demands and bitchiness of a lot of the students. Claire had figured out that the rude ones were mostly Protected, so it was a class thing; Eve had elected not to sign up with a vampire for protection, and those who had looked down on her.

Or else they were just bitchy. Which was equally possible. People didn't have to have a vampire connection to be arrogant jerks.

Eve was working today with another girl, somebody Claire didn't know; she had long, straight brown hair that shimmered like a curtain when she moved. She wore it loose around her shoulders, which Claire guessed was okay because she wasn't working directly with the drinks or anything, just taking orders and cash. Her name tag said AMY, and she looked cheerful and sweet. She and Eve were talking like friends, which was good; Eve needed that. Claire killed time between classes by skimming through her English Lit—boring—and reading a book she'd checked out from the library on advanced string theory—not boring. She liked the whole idea of vibrating strings being the basis of everything, that there were all kinds of surfaces that vibrated. It made the world more . . . exciting. Always in motion.

Her watch beeped to let her know she was going to be late for class if she didn't hurry, so she packed it up, waved to Amy and Eve, and jogged out of the UC and into the warm afternoon sunshine.

As she was blinking in the glare, she ran into Monica. Literally, as Monica was coming up the steps while she was going down. Claire automatically reached out to steady the other girl when she wavered, and then thought, *What am I doing?* Because Monica had once laughed as Claire tumbled down the stairs and cracked her head halfway open.

"Hey, *watch it,* bitch!" Monica snapped, and then did a double take. "Claire? Oh, hi. Cute shirt!"

Claire looked down at herself, mystified. It wasn't. She didn't really own any clothes she'd classify as cute, and even the best of them would never match Monica's standards, which were much higher.

"You on your way to class?" Monica continued brightly. "Too bad, I'd buy you a mocha or something."

"I—uh—yeah, I've got class." Claire edged around and tried to descend the steps, but Monica got in her way. Monica's smile was friendly, but it didn't really warm up her big, pretty eyes. "I'll be late."

"One thing," Monica said, and lowered her voice. It occurred to Claire that it was almost the first time she'd seen Monica alone, not flanked by Gina and Jennifer, not trailing an entourage of the Popular. "I'm having a party on Friday night. Can you come? It's at my parents' house. Here's the address." Before Claire could react, Monica pressed a slip of paper into her hand. "Keep it quiet, all right? I'm asking only the best people. Oh, and wear something nice; it's formal."

And then Monica was gone, breezing by her up the steps, where she fell in with a group of girls and went into the UC's glass atrium, chatting and laughing.

The best people? Claire eyed the slip of paper, thought about throwing it away, and then shoved it in her pocket.

Maybe this was a golden opportunity to convince Monica that she wasn't ever going to be anything like a friend.

She headed out for class, moving quickly, but keeping her eyes peeled. When she spotted the guys she was looking for, she veered off the sidewalk and onto the grass.

Gamers. Nerds. They sat around outside most of the afternoon moving counters around on complicated-looking boards and rolling dice. She'd seen them every day for weeks, and in all that time she'd never seen any kind of girl with them, or even approach them. In fact, when she cleared her throat they stared at her as though she were an alien from one of the planets on their game board.

"Hi," she said, and thrust out the slip of paper. "My name's Monica. I'm having a party on Friday night. If you guys want to come. Tell your friends."

One of them reached out and gingerly took the slip of paper. Another snatched it away from him, read it, and said, "Wow. Really?"

"Really."

"Mind if we invite some other people?"

"Knock yourself out."

Claire headed off to class.

"Claire Danvers?"

Last class of the day, and Claire, startled, looked up from writing the date in her notebook. The professor didn't usually take roll. In fact, he seemed pretty much indifferent to who showed up, which was sometimes next to nobody. Like today—she was one of about twelve people. Showing up was really kind of useless in this particular course, since Professor What's-His-Name lectured from PowerPoint slides, bullet by bullet, and then made them available on his Web site right after the lecture. No wonder most people skipped.

She raised her hand, wondering what was going on. She had a guilty flash of handing over the party invitation to the Nerd Squad, but no, how could they find out so soon? And besides, who'd care, besides Monica?

The professor—gray, wrinkled, tired, and unenthusiastic—stared at her for a second without recognition, then said, "You're wanted in Administration, room three-seventeen. Go now."

"But—" Claire started to ask what was going on, but he'd already dismissed her and turned back to his PowerPoint, droning on in a monotone. She stuffed books into her bag, wondered again what was going on, and left without much regret.

She'd been in the Administration Building exactly three times—once to register, once to file the official paperwork to move off campus, once to do add/drop. It looked just like any administration building at any school—grubby and utilitarian, with tired, crabby employees and desks piled high with file folders. She avoided the first-floor Registrar's Office and went up the steps. The second floor was quieter, but still full of people talking, keys clicking on computers, printers running.

The third floor was whisper-quiet. Claire started down the hallway, and the silence sank deeper. She couldn't even hear sounds from outside the windows, although she could clearly see people out there walking and talking, and cars tooling around the street below. Room 317 was at the end of the hall. All of the glossy wooden doors were firmly closed.

She knocked on 317, and thought she heard someone say "Come in," so she turned the knob and stepped inside . . . into darkness. Complete, velvety darkness that disoriented her immediately. The knob slipped out of her hand and the door clicked shut, and she couldn't find it again. Her hand moved over what felt like a featureless, smooth wall.

A light bloomed behind her and she turned to see the flare of a match, and a candle wick catching fire. In the glow, Amelie's face shone like perfect ivory.

The elder vampire looked exactly the same as before: cool, queenly, pale, with her white-blond hair twisted back in an elegant updo that must have required servants to achieve. She was wearing a white silk suit, and her skin was flawless. If she wore makeup, Claire couldn't tell. Her eyes were eerie in the near-dark . . . luminous and not quite human, and very beautiful.

"My apologies for the dramatics," Amelie said, and smiled at her. It was a very nice smile, cool and polite. Claire's mother had always loved the Hitchcock movie *Rear Window*, and Claire was struck by the thought that if Grace Kelly had ended up a vampire, this was how she'd have looked. Icy and perfect. "Don't bother looking for the door. It's gone until I wish it to be there again."

Claire's heartbeat sped up, and she knew Amelie could tell, though the vampire didn't comment on it; she just shook out the match and dropped it in a silver dish on the table next to the candle. Claire's eyes adjusted gradually to the dimness. She was standing in a fairly small room, some kind of library crammed with books. *Crammed* was an understatement—the books were double-stacked on the shelves, leaning in towers on the top of the bookcases, filling the corners in untidy ziggurats. So many books that the whole room smelled like ancient paper. There wasn't any wall space, except where Claire had come in, that wasn't blocked up by packed, groaning shelves.

"Hi," Claire said awkwardly. She hadn't seen Amelie since signing the Protection papers and putting them, as instructed, in the mailbox outside. She'd expected some kind of visit, but . . . nothing. "Um— what should I call you?"

Amelie's delicate brows rose, pale on pale. "I know that the concept of manners has declined, but I should think you would know at least some polite form of address that would be appropriate."

"Ma'am," Claire stammered. Amelie nodded.

"That will do." She lit another candle. The light

strengthened, flickering but casting a warm and welcome glow. Claire spotted another door in the shadows, small and fitted with an antique-style doorknob. There was a big skeleton key in the massive lock.

Nobody else in the room, just she and Amelie.

"I have called you to discuss your studies," Amelie said, and sat down in a chair on the other side of the table. There wasn't any seat on Claire's side, so she stood there, awkwardly. She put her backpack down and folded her hands.

"Yes ma'am," she said. "Aren't my grades okay?" Because usually a 4.0 GPA was okay by most standards.

Amelie dismissed it with a wave. "I did not say classes; I said studies. No doubt you are finding the local college beneath your abilities. You are said to be quite exceptional."

Claire didn't know what to say to that, so she didn't say anything. She wished she had a chair. She wished she could say something nice and get back to class and never, ever see Amelie again, because as superficially polite and kind as the old vampire was, there was something ice-cold about her. Something unsettlingly *not human.*

"I would like you to study privately with a friend of mine," Amelie said. "For credit, of course." She looked around, smiling very slightly. "This is his library. Mine is far more orderly."

Claire's throat felt tight and uncomfortable. "A . . . uh . . . vampire friend?"

"Is that an issue?" Amelie folded her white hands together on the table. The candlelight flickered in her eyes.

"N-no ma'am." *Yes.* God, she couldn't imagine what Shane was going to say.

"I believe you will find him most interesting, Claire. He is indeed one of the most brilliant minds I have ever encountered in my long life, and he has learned so much through his lifetime that he could never teach it all. Still, he has much to pass along. I have been seeking the right pupil, one who can quickly grasp the discoveries he has made, and assist him in his research."

"Oh," Claire whispered faintly. *So . . .* an old vampire. Her experience wasn't so good with the older ones. Like Amelie, they were cold and strange, and most of them were cruel, too. Like Oliver. Oh God, she wasn't talking about Oliver, was she? "Who—?"

Amelie looked down. Just for an instant, and then she met Claire's eyes and smiled. "You have not met," she said. "Not formally, at any rate. His name is Myrnin. He is one of my oldest friends and allies. Understand, Claire, that your actions since you came to Morganville, including your agreement with me, have won my trust. I would not grant this honor to any but those I found worthy."

Flattery. Claire recognized it, and knew the slight warmth in Amelie's voice was probably calculated, but it still worked. It made her feel less scared. "Myrnin," she repeated.

"It is an old name," Amelie agreed, in response to the question in Claire's tone. "Old and forgotten, now. But once he was a great scholar, known and revered. His works should not be forgotten as well."

There was something strange in that, but Claire was too nervous to figure out what Amelie could be trying to say. Or not say. She was working hard to swallow a lump in her throat, but it was about the size of a poisoned apple and seemed to be growing larger. She could only nod.

Amelie smiled. It looked kind of artificial, like an expression she'd practiced in a mirror rather than learned as a child. Smiling was something her face just didn't naturally do, Claire decided. And sure enough, the smile was gone in seconds, without a trace.

"If you're ready . . . ?"

"Now?" Claire cast an involuntary, helpless look at the blank wall behind her. There wasn't a door, and that meant there was no way to retreat. So she didn't really have a choice.

Amelie wasn't waiting for her answer, anyway. The

ice queen stood up and walked—oh so very undead Grace Kelly— to another small, low doorway with the key in the lock. She turned the key, withdrew it, and looked down at it for a moment before holding it out to Claire. "Keep it," she said. "Leave your book bag here, please. I shouldn't want you to forget it. You will leave through the same door that brought you."

Claire's fingers closed around the key, registering rough, cold, heavy metal. She shoved it in the pocket of her blue jeans as Amelie swung open the door, and leaned her backpack against a convenient bookcase.

"Myrnin?" Amelie's voice was low and gentle. "Myrnin, I've brought the girl I told you about. Her name is Claire."

Claire knew that tone of voice. You used it with old, sick people, people who didn't really understand what was happening anymore. People you didn't think were really going to be around for long. Coming from Amelie, it was really odd, because she could also hear the love in that low voice. Could vampires love? Well, sure, she guessed; Michael could, right? So why not Amelie, too?

Claire stepped out from behind Amelie at the vampire's imperative gesture, and anxiously scanned the room. It was big, full of the weirdest mixture of equipment and junk she'd ever seen. A brand-new wide-screen laptop computer with a shimmying belly dancer as a screen saver. An abacus. A chemistry set that looked straight out of some old Sherlock Holmes movie. More books, carelessly piled around as trip hazards, leaning in columns on every table. Lamps— some electric, some oil. Candles. Bottles and jars and shadows and angles and . . .

And a man.

Claire blinked, because she was expecting an old, sick person; expecting it so much she looked around again, trying to find him. But the only man in the room sat in a chair, peacefully reading a book. He marked the spot with a finger, closed it, and looked up at Amelie.

He was young, or at least he looked it. Shoulder-length curly brown hair, big, dark puppy-dog eyes, flawless, faintly golden skin. Frozen at the age of maybe twenty-five, just enough for creases to be forming at the corners of his eyes. Also, he was really, really . . . *pretty*.

And he didn't look sick. Not at all.

"Ah, good, I've been waiting for you," he said. He spoke English, but with some kind of accent, nothing that Claire could identify. It sounded a little bit like Irish, a little bit like Scottish, but more . . . liquid, somehow. Welsh? "Claire, is it? Well, come forward, girl, I won't bite." He smiled, and unlike Amelie's cool attempt, it was a warm, genuine expression, full of merriment. Claire took a couple of steps toward him. She sensed Amelie tensing behind her, and wondered why. Myrnin seemed okay. Seemed more okay than any vampire she'd seen so far, except maybe Sam, Michael's grandfather—and Michael, the youngest vampire in Morganville.

"Hello," she said, and got an even wider smile.

"She speaks! Excellent. I have no use for someone without a backbone. Tell me, young Claire, do you like the sciences?"

That was an antique way of saying it . . . *the sciences.* People usually said *science* or mentioned a specific thing, like biology or nuclear studies or chemistry. Still, she knew the right answer. "Yes, sir. I love the sciences."

His dark eyes glittered, full of slightly wicked humor. "So very polite, you are. And philosophy?"

"I—I don't know. We didn't study it in high school. I just got to college."

"Science without philosophy is nonsense," he said, very seriously. "And alchemy? Do you know anything of it?"

She just shook her head to that one. She knew what it meant, but wasn't it all about turning lead into gold or something like that? Sort of con-man science?

Myrnin looked tragically disappointed. She almost

wanted to lie to him and tell him that she'd gotten an A in Alchemy 101.

"Don't be difficult, Myrnin," Amelie said. "I told you, this age doesn't regard the subject with much respect. You won't find anyone with a working knowledge of the Hermetic arts, so you'll have to use what's available. From all accounts, this girl is quite gifted. She should be able to understand what you have to teach, if you are patient."

Myrnin nodded soberly and put the book aside. He stood up—and up—and up. He was tall, gawky, with long legs and arms—like a human stick bug. He was wearing a weird mixture of clothes, too—not homeless-guy weird, but definitely funky. A vertically striped knit shirt under what looked like some kind of frock coat, and blue jeans, old ones, with holes in the knees. And flip-flops. Claire stared at his exposed toes. Somehow, with that outfit, flip-flops looked almost indecent.

But he had pretty feet.

He extended his hand to Claire, bending over to do it. She carefully took it and shook. Myrnin looked surprised, then delighted. He pumped the handshake enthusiastically enough to make her shoulder ache. "A handshake, is that the correct way to greet these days?" he asked. "Even for such a lovely young woman? I know it's common among men, but among women it seems quite a violent gesture—"

"Yes," Claire said quickly. "It's fine. Everybody does it." God, he wasn't going to try to kiss her hand or anything, was he? No, he was letting go and crossing his arms. Studying her.

"Quickly," he said. "What's the elemental designation for rubidium?"

"Um . . . Rb."

"Atomic number?"

Claire frantically called to mind the periodic table. She'd played with it the same way other kids played with puzzles, back when she was young; she'd known every detail. "Thirty-seven."

"Group number?"

She could see the square on the table now, as real as if it were a card in her hand. "Group one," she said confidently. "Alkali metal. The period number is five."

"And what are the dangers of working with rubidium, young Claire?"

"It spontaneously burns when exposed to air. It also reacts violently to water."

"Solid, liquid, gas, plasma?"

"Solid to forty degrees centigrade. That's the melting point." She waited for the next question, but Myrnin only cocked his head and watched her. "How did I do?"

"Adequately," he said. "You've memorized well. But memorization is not science, and science is not knowledge." Myrnin stalked over to a leaning stack of books, tossed some carelessly to the floor, and found a threadbare volume that he flipped open without much regard for the fragile pages. "Ah! Here. What is this, then?"

He held the book out to her. Claire squinted at the dim illustration. It looked a little like a small square sail, full of wind. She frowned and shook her head. Myrnin snapped the book closed with a sharp clap, making her jump.

"Too much to teach her," he said to Amelie. He began to pace, then got distracted and fiddled with a glass retort full of some noxious green liquid. "I don't have time to coddle infants, Amelie. Bring me someone who at least understands the basics of what I am trying to—"

"I've told you before, there is no one available who would recognize that symbol, and in any case, the field has never attracted the most trustworthy of characters. Give Claire a chance. She's a quick study." Her voice cooled to a measured, icy tone. "Do not force me to make it an order, Myrnin."

He stopped moving, but he didn't raise his head. "I don't want another student." He sounded resentful.

"Nevertheless, you must have one."

"Have you explained the risks?"

"I leave that to you. She is yours, Myrnin. But make no mistake, I will hold you responsible for her performance, and for her safety."

Claire heard the click of metal, and when she looked behind her, Amelie was . . . gone.

She'd left her alone. With *him*.

When Claire turned back to him, Myrnin had raised his head and was staring straight at her. Warm, brown eyes no longer amused. Very serious.

"It seems neither of us has much choice," he said. "We'll just have to make the best of it, then." He fumbled through the stacks of books and came up with one that looked just as threadbare and fragile as the first one he'd mishandled, but this one was much thinner. He thrust it toward her, and Claire took it. The inscription on the cover was in English. *Metals in Egyptian Inscriptions.*

"The symbol I showed you is for copper," Myrnin said. "Know the rest when you come back tomorrow. I will also expect you to read Basil Valentine's *Last Will and Testament.* I have a copy here . . . ." He shoved books around, almost frantic, and located something with a cry of satisfaction. He held that out to her as well. "Pay special attention to the alchemical symbols. You'll be expected to copy them out until you know them by heart."

"But—"

"Take them! Take them and get out! Out! I'm busy!"

Myrnin rushed past her, bowling over stacks of books in his haste, to fling open the door through which Amelie had disappeared. He was at least a foot taller than the door itself, like a human in a hobbit house. He stood there, jittering his foot in impatience, the flip-flop making plastic slaps between flesh and floor.

"Did you hear me?" he snapped. "Go. No time now. Get out. Come tomorrow."

"But—I don't know how to get home. Or back here."

He stared for a second, and then he laughed. "Someone will have to bring you. I can't configure the system just for you!"

Configure the system? Claire stopped, staring back. "What system? These—doorways?" The implications were dizzying. If Myrnin understood the doorways, controlled the doorways, the ones that appeared and disappeared out of nowhere in Morganville . . . *I need to know. I need to know how that works.*

"Yes, I am responsible for that, among many other things, though it's hardly the most important thing right now," he said. "Later, Claire. Go now. Talk tomorrow."

He took hold of her, bodily shoved her through the doorway, and slammed it behind her. She heard his hand hit the wood with stunning force.

"Lock it!" he shouted. Claire dug the key out of her pocket. She could barely get it in the lock; the light was bad here, and her hands were shaking. But she managed, and heard the solid click as the tumblers fell. "Take the key!" Myrnin yelled.

"But—"

"You're responsible for me now, Claire. You must keep me safe." Myrnin's voice had fallen lower now, as if he'd gotten tired. "Keep me safe from everyone."

And then he started . . . crying.

"Myrnin?" Claire said, bending closer to the door. "Are you okay? Should I come in and—"

The whole door vibrated with the force of his blow. Claire scrambled backward, shocked.

And the crying continued. Lost, little-boy crying.

Claire hesitated for a few seconds, then turned to see that Amelie hadn't left after all. She was standing quietly by the desk, in the glow of the single candle, and her expression was composed, but sad.

"Myrnin's mind is not what it once was. He has periods of lucidity, however. And at all costs, you must take full advantage of these to learn what he has to teach. It can't be lost, Claire. It *must not* be lost. There are things he does that—" Amelie shook her head. "There are projects in motion that must continue."

Claire's heart was racing, her whole body shaking. "He's crazy, he's a vampire, and you want me to be his student."

"No," Amelie said. "I *require* you to be his student. You will comply, Claire, by the rules of the contract you signed of your own free will. This is valuable work. I would not risk you unnecessarily."

Have you explained to her the risks? Myrnin had asked that. "What are the risks?" Claire demanded.

Amelie merely pointed to the bookcase, where her backpack still leaned. Claire grabbed it and hauled it to her shoulder—and paused, because a doorway had formed in the blank area of the wall. A solid wooden door, with a plain knob. Identical to those at the university. "Open it," Amelie said.

"But—"

"Open the door, Claire."

Claire did, and the glare of fluorescent lights and the dead, air-conditioned smell of the Administration Building swept over her in a rush.

Amelie blew out the light. In the darkness, Claire couldn't see her anymore.

"Be ready at four o'clock tomorrow in the University Center," Amelie said. "Sam will fetch you. I suggest you do the reading Myrnin requires of you. And Claire—tell no one what you're doing here. Absolutely no one."

It wasn't until Claire was in the hall, with the door shut, that she realized Amelie hadn't answered her question. She opened the door again, but—there was just a room piled with discarded, broken furniture. Something moved furtively in the corner. There was a window with crooked blinds, but no Amelie. No cave of books. No Myrnin.

"He's sick," Claire said aloud, to whatever was rustling in the corner behind a three-legged desk. "That's why she talked to him like that. He's old, and he's sick. Maybe even dying." Vampires could get sick. Vampires could *die*? Somehow she'd never even considered that.

She shut the door gently, adjusted the weight of her backpack, and looked down at the two ancient books in her hand.

Last Will and Testament.

She hoped that wasn't a sign of her future.

Eve chattered on about her day on the drive back, talking about some boy who had totally tried to ask her out, and Amy's boyfriend, Chad, who'd come by to help clean up and was a total sweetheart, and how her boss was a toerag, but at least he'd given her a twenty-cent-an-hour raise. "I think that's just for not quitting in the first couple of weeks," Eve said, but she sounded pretty jacked about it, and Claire was pleased for her. "Yeah, it's only a couple more dollars a week, but—"

"But it's something." Claire nodded. "Congratulations, Eve. You deserve it. You're really good at this. I'll bet you could run the whole thing if you wanted."

"Me? Manager?" Eve laughed so hard she snorted. "Yeah, like I want to become Tinpot Dictator of the coffee bar. Get serious."

"No, I mean it. You're nice, people like you; you know what you're doing. You could. You'd be good at it."

Eve shot her a sideways look that was almost a frown. "You're serious."

"Yep."

"I don't know if I'm ready for management. Don't you have to wear a tie for that?"

"You've got one," Claire said solemnly.

"Only one with the Grim Reaper on it. Hey, wait. That could be my management style! Screw up and I'll kill you, maggot." Eve grinned. "They ought to teach that in business school."

"They probably do here," Claire sighed.

"What's up with you, CB?" CB stood for Claire Bear, which was Eve's funny nickname for her. Claire didn't think she much resembled a bear, not even the stuffed Gund variety. "You seem really, I don't know, thoughtful."

"Yeah, well—" She couldn't talk to Eve about Myrnin. "Homework and stuff." Yeah, it was just that she'd never had quite *this* kind of pass/fail pressure before. She'd flipped through the book on Egyptian inscriptions. That was pretty straightforward, though she wasn't sure how actually Egyptian it all was. Interesting, though. The other one, *Last Will and Testament,* was lots tougher. Tons of symbols in some weird notation she didn't understand. She'd be up all night trying to make sure she remembered even the basics. "Eve . . . has anybody ever broken their contract in Morganville? I mean, and lived?"

"Contract?" Eve shot her yet another look, this one definitely coming with a side order of frowning. "You're talking about a vamp contract? Sure. People have tried everything, at one time or another. But not very successfully."

"What happened?"

"Back in the old days, they got hanged. These days, I think they just throw 'em in jail until they rot, if the vampires don't eat 'em. But hey, not like you and me have to worry about it, right? Live free or die!" Eve held up her hand. "High five!"

Claire slapped it, without much enthusiasm. She was thinking about the way the pen had felt in her hand, moving across that stiff paper. Signing her life away. And she felt ashamed.

"Why?" Eve asked.

"Huh?"

"Why are you asking?" Eve made the turn onto Lot Street, and the glow of the windows of the Glass House—home—spilled out into the street. "C'mon, Claire. Someone you know thinking about it?"

"Um . . . there's this guy at school. I just heard him say—I wondered, that's all."

"Well, quit wondering. His problem, not yours. Ready for the fire drill? Quick like a bunny. Go!" Eve braked the black Caddy hard, Claire threw open her passenger-side door and jogged around the back of the car, banged open the white picket gate, and raced up the walk to the steps with her house keys in her hand. She heard the engine die, and the noisy clatter of Eve's shoes behind her.

Eve's steps stopped. Stopped dead. Claire whirled, scared and expecting to see a vampire on the prowl, but Eve was just checking the mailbox, grabbing a small handful of stuff, and then hurrying up the steps as she sorted through it. Claire stepped over the threshold, and Eve followed, hip-bumping the door shut behind them and shooting the bolt with her elbow, a feat Claire would never have tried—or been able to accomplish with half that grace.

"Electric bill, water bill—Internet bill. Oh, and something for you." Eve pulled out a small bubble-padded mailer from the pile and handed it over. "No return address."

Who'd send her anything? Well, Mom and Dad, sure, and the occasional card from another relative. Her former BFF Elizabeth had sent a postcard from Texas A&M, but only the one. Claire didn't recognize the neat handwriting on the outside of the envelope. Eve left her to it and walked down the hallway, yelling to let Shane and Michael know they were back, to which Michael yelled back, "Get in here and make me some dinner—now, woman."

"News flash, Michael, you're supposed to have turned evil, not redneck!"

Claire ripped open the package and upended it, and a small jewelry box slid into her hand. A nice one—red velvet, with some kind of gold crest embossed into it. She felt the skin tighten up on the back of her neck. *Oh no.*

Her suspicions were confirmed as she flipped up the lid and saw the gold bracelet nestled on bloodred velvet. It was pretty, and it wasn't too big; delicate enough to circle one of her small wrists.

The Founder's Symbol was embossed discreetly in a small gold cartouche.

Oh no.

Claire bit her lip and stared at the bracelet for a long time, then snapped the lid shut, put it back in the envelope, and went to join Eve and Michael in the kitchen.

"So?" Eve was getting down pots, and Michael was rummaging in the refrigerator. "Spaghetti okay with you?"

"Fine," Claire said. She wondered if she looked spooked. She hoped not, but even if she did, Eve was looking at Michael, and he was looking back, and she was safe from any kind of major inspection while they were making eyes at each other.

Until she turned, and ran into Shane, who'd come in the kitchen door behind her. The package felt hot and heavy in her right hand, and she took an involuntary step back.

Which hurt him. She saw the flash of it in his eyes. "Hey," he said. "You all right?"

She nodded, unable to speak, because if she said anything, it would have to be a lie. Shane stepped closer and put a warm hand on her face; it felt good, so very good that she leaned into it, then further, into his arms. He made her feel small and loved, and for just a second, what was in the package in her hand didn't matter.

"You're working too hard," he said. "You look pale. School okay?"

"School's fine," she said. That wasn't a lie, school was definitely not what scared her anymore. "I guess I need more sleep."

"Just a few more days until the weekend." He kissed the top of her head, bent closer, and whispered, "My room. I need to talk to you."

She blinked, but he was already stepping back and heading out the door. She looked over her shoulder at Eve and Michael, but they were happily talking as

Eve adjusted the flame under the pots, and they hadn't noticed anything.

Claire shoved the package into her backpack, zipped it up, and followed Shane upstairs.

Shane's room was very utilitarian—his bed was never made, though he made an attempt as she came in to straighten out the sheets and toss the blanket over it. A couple of posters on the wall, nothing special. No photos, no mementos. He didn't spend a lot of time here, except to sleep. Most of his stuff was crammed into the closet.

Claire leaned her backpack against the wall and sat down next to him on the bed. "What?" she asked. If she'd expected a wild predinner make-out session, she was disappointed. He didn't even put his arm around her.

"I'm thinking of leaving," he said.

"Leaving? But Eve's making dinner—"

He turned and made eye contact. "Leaving Morganville."

She felt a surge of utter panic. "No. You can't!"

"Done it before. Look, this place, it's—I didn't come back here because I missed it. I came back because my dad sent me, and now that he's been and gone and I'm not doing his dirty work anymore . . ." Shane's eyes were begging her to understand. "I want a life, Claire. And you don't belong here. You can't stay. They'll kill you. No, worse. They'll make you into one of them, one of the walking dead. I'm not talking about the vampires, either. Nobody who lives here has a pulse, not really."

"Shane—"

He kissed her, and his lips were warm and damp and soft and urgent. "Please," he whispered. "We need to leave this town. It's going to get bad. I can feel it."

God, *why* was he doing this? Why now? "I can't," she said. "I—school, and—I just can't, Shane. I can't leave." Her signature on a piece of paper. Her soul on a platter. It had been the price to keep them safe, but she'd have to keep on paying, right? As apprentice to Myrnin. And she guessed that wouldn't be a long-distance study course.

"Please." It was barely a whisper from him, his lips brushing hers, and honestly, she would have done almost anything for him when he used that tone, but this time . . .

"What happened?" she asked.

"What?"

"Was it something with Michael? Did he—did you—?" She didn't even know what she was asking, but something had deeply disturbed Shane, and she had no idea what it was.

He looked at her for a long few seconds, then pulled away, stood up, and walked to his window to look down on the backyard they never really used. "My dad called," he said. "He told me that he was coming back, and he wanted me to be prepared to take out some vampires. If I stay, I'm going to have to kill Michael. I don't want to be here, Claire. I can't."

He didn't want to make the choice, not again. Claire bit her lip, hard; she could hear the pain in his voice, although he wasn't going to let her see it in his expression. "You really think your dad will come back?"

"Yeah. Eventually. Maybe not this month, maybe not this year, but . . . someday. And next time, he'll have what he needs to start a real war around here." Shane shivered; she saw the muscles in his back tense up under the tight gray shirt he was wearing. "I need to get you out of here before you get hurt."

Claire got up, walked to him, and put her arms around him from behind. She leaned against him, her head on his back, and sighed. "I'm more worried about you," she said. "You and trouble . . ."

"Yeah." She heard the smile in his voice. "We're like that."

4

The spaghetti was good, and a little pleading got Shane to sit down and eat. He sat across from Michael, but they didn't talk, and they didn't make eye contact. All in all, pretty polite. Claire was just starting to relax when Shane asked, blandly, "You put extra garlic in this, Eve? You know how I like the garlic."

She shot him a dirty look. "Oh, the *neighborhood* knows." And then an apologetic one toward Michael. "It's okay, right? Not too much?" Because garlic wasn't something vampires were especially fond of. That was why Shane tended to use it as garnish on everything he ate.

"It's fine," Michael said, but he was picking at his food, and he looked a little pale. "Monica stopped by today. Looking for you, Claire."

Both Shane and Eve groaned. For once, all three of her housemates were entirely in agreement. And they were all looking at her.

"What?" she asked. "I swear, it's not—I'm not sucking up to her or anything! She's just—crazy, okay? I'm not her friend. I don't know why she's coming around."

"She's probably going to set you up again," Eve said, and scooped more spaghetti into her bowl. "Like she did at the frat dance. Hey, she's throwing a party this Friday, did you hear? Superexclusive, flying in out of towners and everything. I guess it's her birthday, or Daddy-gave-me-money day, or whatever. We should crash."

"I like the sound of that," Shane said. "Crashing Monica's party." He glanced at Michael, then quickly away. "What about you? That break some kind of vampire rules of conduct or something?"

"Blow me, Shane."

"Boys," Eve said primly. "Language. Minor at the table."

"Well," Shane said, "I wasn't actually planning to do it."

Claire rolled her eyes. "Not like it's the first time I've heard it. Or said it."

"You shouldn't say it," Michael said, all seriousness. "No, I mean it. Girls should say 'eat me,' not 'blow me.' Wouldn't recommend 'bite me,' though. Not around here."

Eve choked on her spaghetti. Shane pounded her on the back, but he was laughing, too, and so was Michael, and Claire glared at them for a little bit before giving in and admitting it was funny, after all.

Everything was all right.

"So. Friday night?" Eve asked, wiping her eyes and gasping through her giggles. "Par-tay? Because I could so use a good blowout."

"I'm in," Michael said, and took a manful bite of spaghetti. Claire wondered if it burned him. "I think if I'm with you, there's no way she can keep us out. Vampire VIP status. Might as well be good for something."

Shane looked at him, and for a second there was that warmth that Claire missed so much, but then it was gone again, and the wall was back firmly in place between the two of them.

"Must be nice," he said. "We should all go, if it's going to ruin Monica's night."

They finished the rest of the meal in uncomfortable silence. Claire realized that she kept thinking about that red velvet box sitting upstairs in her room, and struggled not to look guilty. Probably didn't succeed. She caught Michael watching her with a strange intensity; whether he was picking up on her discomfort or still wondering about why she didn't jump at the chance to go to Monica's party.

She ate too fast, cleaned her dishes, and dashed upstairs with a mumbled excuse about homework. Well, it wasn't as though they weren't used to her studying. It was Shane's turn for dishes, so that would keep him busy for a while. . . .

The box was right where she'd left it, sitting on the dresser. She grabbed it, put her back against the wall, and slid down to a cross-legged sitting position as she weighed the box in her hand.

"You're wondering whether or not to wear it," Amelie said, and Claire yelped in surprise. The elegant older vampire, completely at her ease, was seated in the antique old velvet chair in the corner, her hands folded primly in her lap. She looked like a painting, not a person; there was something about her—now more than ever—that seemed antique and cold as marble.

Claire scrambled to her feet, feeling stupid about it, but you just didn't sit like that in Amelie's presence. Amelie acknowledged the courtesy with a graceful nod, but didn't otherwise move.

"I apologize for surprising you, Claire, but I needed to speak with you alone," she said.

"How can you get in here? I mean, this is our house; aren't vampires . . . ?"

"Prevented from entry? Not into another vampire's home, and even were you all human, this house ultimately belongs to me. I built it, as I built all of the Founder Houses. The house knows me, and so I need no permissions to enter." Amelie's eyes glinted in the dark. "Does that disturb you?"

Claire swallowed and didn't answer. "What did you want?"

Amelie raised one long, slender finger and pointed

at the velvet box in Claire's hand. "I want you to put that on."

"But—"

"I am not asking. I am instructing."

Claire shivered, because although Amelie's voice stayed level, it sounded . . . hard. She opened the box and shook the bracelet out. It felt heavy and warm in her hand, and she peered at it carefully.

There wasn't a catch, but it was clearly too small to fit over her hand. "I don't know how—"

She saw a flash in her peripheral vision, and by the time she looked up, Amelie was taking the bracelet out of her palm, and cold strong fingers were holding her arm.

"It's made for you," Amelie said. "*Hold still.* Unlike the bracelets most of the other children wear, yours cannot be removed. The contract you signed gives me this right, do you understand?"

"But—no, I don't want—"

Too late. Amelie moved, and the bracelet seemed to pass *through* Claire's skin and bone, and settle heavily around her wrist. Claire tried to yank free, but there was no way, not as strong as Amelie was. Amelie smiled and held her still for another second, just to make the point, before she let go. Claire turned the bracelet frantically, pressing, looking for the trick.

It looked seamless, and it wasn't coming off.

"It must be done this way, the old way," Amelie said. "This bracelet will save your life, Claire. Mark me. It is a favor I have given rarely in my life. You should be grateful."

Grateful? Claire felt like a dog on a leash, and she hated it. She glared at Amelie, and the vampire's smile intensified. She couldn't really say it brightened—there was something in it that undermined the whole concept of comfort.

"Perhaps you'll be grateful at a later date," Amelie said, and raised her eyebrows. "Very well. I'll leave you now. No doubt you have studies."

"How am I supposed to hide this from my friends?" Claire blurted, as the vampire walked toward the door.

"You aren't," Amelie said, and opened the door without unlocking it. "Don't forget. You should be well prepared for Myrnin tomorrow." She stepped out into the hall and closed it behind her. Claire lunged forward and turned the knob, but it refused to open. By the time she twisted the thumb lock and swung it back, Amelie was gone. The hall was empty. Claire stood there, listening to the clatter of dishes from downstairs, the distant laughter, and wanted to cry.

She scrubbed at her eyes, took a deep breath, and went to her desk to try to study.

The next day was a busy whirl of classes, quizzes, and discussion groups, and Claire was grateful for the afternoon break when it finally arrived. She felt stupid, dressed in her long-sleeved T, but it was the only thing she had that could hide the bracelet, and she desperately wanted to hide it. So far, so good. Eve hadn't noticed, Shane hadn't been awake when they'd left for school. No sign of Michael, either. She'd gotten desperate last night and tried a couple of ways to break the gold band—scissors, then a pair of rusty old bolt-cutters from the basement—but she broke the blade on the scissors, and the bolt-cutters were clumsy and slid right off the metal. She couldn't do it alone, and she couldn't ask for help.

Can't hide it forever.

Well, she could try.

Claire headed for the UC and the coffee bar, and she found Eve harassed, pink-cheeked under the rice-powder makeup, all alone behind the counter. "Where's Amy?" Claire asked, and handed over three dollars for a mocha. "I thought she was working all week?"

"Yeah, no kidding, me too. I called my boss, but he's sick and so's Kim, so it's just me today. Not enough coffee in the world to make this easy." Eve blew hair from her sweaty forehead and zipped over to the espresso machine, where she pulled shots. "Ever have one of those dreams where you're running and everybody else is standing still, but you can't catch up?"

"No," Claire said. "Usually mine are about being naked in class."

Eve grinned. "For that, you get a free caramel shot. Go sit down. I don't need you hovering like the rest of these vultures."

Claire claimed a study desk and spread out her books, got her mocha when Eve called her name, and yawned as she cracked open *Last Will and Testament* again. She'd spent most of the night memorizing the symbols, but they were tricky. She'd gotten all of the Egyptian ones down, but these were a whole lot less straightforward, and she had the sense that Myrnin wouldn't be too forgiving of mistakes.

A shadow fell over her book. She looked up and saw Detective Travis Lowe, and his partner, Joe Hess, standing close behind him. She knew both of them pretty well; they'd helped her during that crazy time when Shane's dad had been skulking around Morganville, trying to kill vampires (and succeeding). They didn't wear bracelets, and they weren't Protected; as she understood it, they'd earned some kind of special status. She wasn't sure how they'd managed that, but it had to be something really brave.

"Morning, Claire," Hess said, and pulled up a chair. Lowe did the same. They weren't all that similar in body types—Hess was tall and kind of wiry, with a long face; Lowe was chubby and balding. But the expressions in their eyes were identical—careful, hidden, wary. "How have you been?"

"Fine," she said, and resisted the nearly overwhelming urge to touch her bracelet, fiddle with it. She looked from one to the other, feeling less secure all the time. "What's going on? Is something wrong?"

"Yeah," Lowe said. "You could say that. Look, Claire, there's—I'm sorry to tell you this, but there was a dead girl out back of your house. She was found this morning by the trash collectors."

A dead girl? Claire swallowed hard. "Who is she?"

"Amy Callum," Hess said. "She's a local girl. Family lives just a few blocks from you. Her people are pretty broken up about it." He shifted his gaze toward the coffee bar. "She worked here."

Amy? Coffee Bar Amy? Oh no . . . "I knew her," Claire said faintly. "She worked with Eve. She was supposed to be here today. Eve was saying—" Eve. Claire looked over and saw that Eve was still chattering away brightly, filling orders, taking cash. They hadn't told her yet. "You're sure it was our house?"

"Claire . . ." The two detectives exchanged a look, not a good one. "Her body was stuffed inside your trash can. We're sure."

Claire felt faint. That close . . . she'd put out trash just two days ago, right? Dumped garbage bags into the can. Amy had been alive then. And now . . .

"Did you see anything last night?" Hess continued.

"No, I was—it was dark when I got home. And then I studied all night."

"Hear anything, maybe some racket out by the garbage cans?"

"No, sir. I had headphones on. I'm sorry."

Shane had been looking out the window, she remembered. Maybe he'd seen someone. But he'd have said, right? He wouldn't hide something like that.

An awful thought struck her, and she looked up into Joe Hess's calm, impartial eyes. "Was it—" Too many people around. She mimed fangs in the neck. He shook his head.

"It's the same as the last one we found," Lowe said. "Can't rule out our toothy friends, but it doesn't fit their style. You know whose style it fits, though?"

"Jason's," Claire said numbly. "Eve's brother. He's still out?"

"Haven't caught him doing anything illegal yet. But we will. He's too crazy to live sane." Lowe studied her. "Haven't seen him, have you?"

"No."

"Good." Like there'd been some signal between

them, Hess and Lowe got up from their chairs. "We'd better go tell Eve. Look, you think of anything, you call, all right? And don't go out alone. Protection doesn't cover this." Lowe cast a significant look at her wrist, and she felt herself blush, as though he'd guessed what color panties she had on. "You need to go out, you go with one of your friends, all right? Same goes for Eve. We'll try to keep an eye on you, but caution is your best defense."

Claire watched as the cops walked away. They exchanged nods with a tallish young man who was coming in her direction. For a second she thought it was Michael—he had the same walk, the same basic shape—but then his hair caught the light. Red hair, not blond like Michael's.

Sam. Sam Glass, Michael's grandfather. Amelie had told her that Sam would escort her to see Myrnin; she'd just forgotten about it. Well, that was okay. Claire liked Sam. He was quiet and kind and didn't seem much like a vampire at all, except for the pale skin and the slight weird shine to his eyes. Exactly like Michael, now that she thought of it. But then, they were the two youngest, and—weirdly—related. Maybe the older the vampires got, the farther they moved from normal.

"Hey, Claire," Sam said, as if they'd just talked five minutes before, although she hadn't seen him for nearly a week, at least. She supposed that time was different for vampires. "What'd they want?" He was wearing a TPU T-shirt and jeans, and it made him look kind of hot. Hot for a redheaded vampire, anyway. And he had a nice, if absent, smile. She wasn't his type. As far as Claire knew, Sam was still totally in love with Amelie, a concept she found harder to wrap her brain around than curved-surface string theory.

He was still waiting for an answer. She scrambled to put one together. "There's a dead girl. She was found in our garbage cans. Amy. Amy Callum?"

Sam's mobile, earnest face took on a grim look.

"Dammit. I know the family, they're good folks. I'll stop by and see them." He sat down and leaned closer, dropping his volume. "She wasn't a vampire kill, I know that much. I'd have heard by now if someone had stepped out of line."

"No," Claire agreed. "It sounded as though she was killed by one of us." She realized, with a rush of horror, that he wasn't *us*, exactly, and blushed. "I mean— one of the—humans."

Sam smiled at her, but his eyes were a little sad. "That's all right, Claire; I'm used to it by now. It's an us-and-them town." He looked down at his hands, loose and relaxed on the tabletop. "I'm supposed to take you to your appointment."

"Yeah." She hastily closed up her books and began loading her backpack. "Sorry, I didn't realize what time it was."

"No rush," he said. Still not looking at her. Very softly, he continued, "Claire. Are you sure you know what you're doing?"

"What?"

His hand flashed out and grabbed her wrist—the one with the bracelet hidden under the long sleeve. It dug painfully into her skin. "You know what."

"Ow," she whispered, and he let go. "I had to. I didn't have a choice. I had to sign if I wanted to keep my friends safe."

Sam didn't say anything to that; he was looking at her now, but she didn't dare meet his eyes. She didn't like him knowing about her agreement with Amelie. What if he told Michael? What if Michael told Shane? *He's going to find out, sooner or later.* Well, she'd much rather it be later.

Sam said, "I know that. I wish you wouldn't do this other thing. With Myrnin. It's—not safe."

"I know. He's sick or something. But he won't hurt me. Amelie—"

"*Amelie* isn't in the business of worrying about individuals." That, for Sam, was surprisingly bitter, especially when it came to Amelie. "She's using you the way she uses all humans. It's not personal, but it's not in your best interest, either."

"Why? What is it you're not telling me?"

Sam looked at her for a long time, clearly trying to decide, and finally said, "Myrnin's had five apprentices in the past few years. Two of them were vampires."

Claire blinked, surprised, as Sam got to his feet. "Five? What happened to them?"

"You're asking the right questions. Now ask the right people."

He walked away. Claire gasped, grabbed her bag, and followed.

Over at the coffee bar, the two detectives were breaking the news to Eve. As Claire looked back, she saw the precise second that Eve realized her friend was dead. Even from across the room, it hurt to see the pain in her face, quickly masked and locked away. In Morganville, losing someone was something you got used to, Claire supposed.

God, this town *sucked* sometimes.

Sam had a car, a sleek, dark red sedan with dark-tinted windows. It was parked in the underground garage beneath the UC, in a reserved spot marked SPONSORS ONLY, with a graphic of a sticker that had to appear in the corner of the windshield for the parking to be legal.

A sticker that Sam, of course, had. "So that means what, you donate money or something?"

Sam opened the passenger door for her, a bit of chivalry she wasn't really used to, and Claire climbed inside. "Not exactly," he said. "Amelie gives them to vampires who have campus business."

Once he was in the car, turning the key, Claire said, "You have campus business?"

"I teach night classes," Sam said, and grinned. He looked about twelve, when he did that. She had the feeling it wasn't something vampires were into, looking that endearingly goofy. Maybe if they were, they'd be more popular with the local breathing population. "Sort of an outreach program."

"Cool." The tinting was so dark it was like midnight outside. "You can see through this?"

"Like daylight," Sam said, and she gave up, buckled her seat belt, and let him drive. It wasn't a long trip—nothing in Morganville was—but she had time to notice some things about Sam's car. It was clean. *Really* clean. No trash at all. (Well, he wouldn't be chowing down on burgers in the car, now, would he? Wait. He could . . .) It also didn't smell like most cars. It smelled new and kind of sterile. "How are classes going?"

Oh, Sam was going to do the interested-adult thing now. "Fine," Claire said. Nobody ever wanted to really hear the truth, to a question like that, but *fine* wasn't a lie, either. "They're not very hard." Also not a lie.

Sam shot her a glance, or so she thought, in the dim lights from the dashboard. "Maybe you're not getting all you can out of them," he said. "Ever thought of that?"

She shrugged. "I've always been ahead. It's better than high school, but I was hoping for something harder."

"Like working for Myrnin?" Sam's voice had gone dry. "That's a challenge, all right. Claire—"

"Amelie didn't exactly give me a choice."

"But you still want to do it, don't you?"

She did. She had to admit that. Myrnin had been scary, but there had been something so bright in him, too. She knew that spark. She felt it herself, and she was always looking for someone, something to feed it. "Maybe he just needs someone to talk to," she said.

Sam made a noncommittal noise that somehow sounded amused, too, and pulled the car to a stop. "I have to move fast," he said. "It's the door at the end of the alley; I'll meet you there in the shade."

He opened his door and just . . . vanished. The door slammed shut, but it did it on its own. Claire gaped, unbuckled her seat belt, and got out, but there was no sign of Sam at all on the street, in the brilliant sunlight. The car was parked at the curb of a cul-de-sac, and it took her a second, but then she recognized the house in front of her. A big Gothic ramble of a house, nearly a mirror image of the Glass House where she lived, but this one belonged to a lady named Katherine Day and her granddaughter.

Gramma Day was on her porch, rocking peacefully and stirring the warm air with a paper fan. Claire raised her hand and waved, and Gramma waved back. "You come to see me, girl?" Gramma called. "Come on up; I'll get some lemonade!"

"Maybe later!" Claire called back. "I have to go—"

She realized, with a jolt of horror, where Sam had told her to go.

Into the alley. The alley where everybody, Gramma Day included, had told her *not* to go. The alley with the trap-door spider vampire who'd tried before to lure her inside.

Gramma pulled herself to her feet. She was a tiny, wrinkled woman who looked as dry and tough as old leather. Had to be tough, to be old in Morganville, Claire thought. "You all right, girl?" she asked.

"Yeah," Claire said. "Thanks. I'll—I'll be back."

She headed off down the alley. Behind her, Gramma Day called out, "Girl, what you playin' at? Ain't you got good sense?"

Probably not.

The alley was narrow, with fences on both sides, and it seemed to get even more narrow the farther she went, like a funnel. She didn't feel any strange attraction, though, or hear voices.

She also didn't see Sam.

"Here," a voice said, as she turned a slight corner. And there he was, leaning back in a patch of black shade next to an overhanging doorway, which was attached to what looked like a shack. Not a really well-made shack, either. Claire wondered if it was supposed to lean like that.

"It's Myrnin," she said. "He's the trap-door spider."

Sam looked thoughtful at that, and then nodded. "Most people know not to come down this way," he said. "He only takes Unprotecteds. He can tell the difference, so he wouldn't try it with you. Not now."

Cheery. Sam opened the door, which didn't look sturdy enough to keep out a cool breeze, and stepped inside. A smell washed out into the still air, something old and bitter. Chemicals. Ancient paper. Unwashed clothes.

Well?

Claire sucked in a breath that tasted of all those things, and stepped into Myrnin's lair.

5

Myrnin was in a mood. A *good* mood.

"Claire!" As she came down the steps—the only thing in the shack itself were the steps leading down—into his main chamber, he flashed across the room in a blur and stopped just an inch away from her, close enough that she flinched back into Sam's broad chest and he steadied her. Myrnin's eyes were wide, blazing with enthusiasm. "I've been waiting! Late, late, late, you're very late, you know. Come on, come on, we haven't got time for nonsense. Did you bring the books? Good. What about *Last Will and Testament*? Are you familiar with the symbols? Here, take this." Chalk, pressed into her hand. Myrnin moved again, fast as a grasshopper, and rolled an ancient stained chalkboard closer. He had to shove over some stacks of books to do it, which he did with cheerful disregard for how much of a mess he was making.

Sam, almost inaudibly, whispered, "Be careful. He's dangerous when he's like this."

Yeah, no kidding. Claire nodded, swallowed, and smiled as Myrnin turned toward her with those crazy, delighted eyes. She wanted to ask what came after the manic phase, but she didn't dare.

"I'll be in the other room," Sam said. Myrnin waved him off impatiently, barely sparing him a glance.

"Yes, yes, fine, go. Here. First let's start with the Egyptian inscription for *asem. Asem.* You know what element that represents?"

"Electrum," Claire said, and carefully chalked the symbol. Sort of a bowl, with a big staff through the middle. "How's that?"

"Excellent! Yes, that's it. Now, something difficult. *Chesbet.*"

Sapphire. That was a hard one. Claire bit her lip for a second, getting the order in her mind, and then drew it out. Circle above a double-slashed line, next to a leg, next to a thing that looked kind of like a car with no wheels over two separated circles.

"No, no, no," Myrnin said, grabbed an eraser, and rubbed out the car. "Too modern. Look."

He drew it again, this time more roughly, and it still looked like a car to her. She copied it, twice, until he was satisfied.

There were a lot of symbols, and he quizzed her on just about all of them, growing more and more excited. Her arm ached from holding up the chalk to the board, especially when, after she screwed up the symbol for lead, he made her repeat it a hundred times.

"We should do this on computer," she said, chalking it carefully for the eighty-ninth time. "With a drawing pad."

"Nonsense. You're lucky I don't make you inscribe it with a stylus on a wax tablet, like the old days," Myrnin snorted. "Children. Spoiled children, always playing with the shiniest toy."

"Computers are more efficient!"

"I can perform calculations on that abacus faster than you can solve them on your computer," Myrnin sneered.

Okay, now he was pissing her off. "Prove it!"

"What?"

"Prove it." She backed off on her tone, but Myrnin wasn't looking angry; he was looking strangely interested. He stared at her for a second in silence, and then he broke into the biggest, oddest smile she'd ever seen on the face of a vampire.

"All right," he said. "A contest. Computer versus abacus."

She wasn't at all sure now that was a good idea, even if it had been *her* idea, essentially. "Um—what do I win?" *More importantly, what do I lose?* Making bargains was a way of life in Morganville, and it was a lot like making deals with man-eating fairies. Better be careful what you ask for.

"Your freedom," he said solemnly. His eyes were wide and guileless, his too-young face shining with honesty. "I will tell Amelie you were not suited to the work. She'll let you go about your life, such as it is."

Good prize. *Too* good. Claire swallowed hard. "And if I lose?"

"Then I eat you," Myrnin said.

With absolutely no change in expression.

"You—you can't do that." She pulled up the sleeve on her shirt and held up her wrist so the gold bracelet caught the light.

"Don't be ridiculous," he said. "Of course I can do it. I can do anything I want, child. Without me, there is no future. No one, especially Amelie, begrudges me the occasional tidbit. You're hardly large enough to qualify as a meal in any case, and besides, I'm making it well worth your while."

She took a step back from him. A big one. That crazy smile . . . She glanced toward the door of the other room, where Sam was waiting for her. No wonder Amelie had told him to stay.

Myrnin gave a sad, theatrical sigh. "Mortals simply aren't what they used to be," he said. "A thousand years ago, you would have bartered your immortal soul for a crust of stale bread. Now I can't even get you to gamble at all, even for your freedom. Really, people have become so . . . *boring*. So, no bet? Really?"

She shook her head. His expression fell into utter disappointment. "All right," he said. "Then you will write me an essay for tomorrow on the history of alchemy. I can't expect it to be scholarly, but I do expect you to understand the basis of what it is that I am trying to teach you."

"You're teaching me *alchemy*?"

He seemed surprised, and looked around his laboratory. "Can you not see what I'm doing here?"

"But alchemy—it's crap. I mean, it's like magic, not science."

"Alchemy's accomplishments are sadly forgotten, and yes, magic is an excellent description for things for which you have no basis to understand. As for science . . ." Myrnin made a rude noise. His eyes had taken on that hectic shine again. "Science is a method, not a religion, yet it can be just as close-minded. Open minds here, Claire. Always open minds. Question everything; accept nothing as fact until you prove it for yourself. Yes?"

She nodded hesitantly, more afraid to disagree with him than convinced. Myrnin grinned at her and slapped her back with stinging force.

"That's my girl," he said. "Now. What do you know of this theory of Schrödinger's? The one about the cat?"

Myrnin didn't go weird until the very end of Claire's time with him, when he was—she thought—getting tired. She had to admit, there was something fun about working in his lab; he had so much passion, so much enthusiasm for everything. Even for scaring her silly. He was like a little kid, all nervous energy and fiddling hands, quick to laugh, quick to cut her down if she made a mistake. He liked to mock, not correct. He thought if she had to figure it out for herself, she'd learn it properly.

She checked her watch and found it was almost eight o'clock—late. She was supposed to be home by now. Myrnin was ignoring her, temporarily, as she copied out tables of incomprehensible symbols from a book he said was so rare his was the only copy left. She yawned, stretched, and said, "I need to be going."

He had his eye fixed to what looked like a clunky, ancient microscope. "Already?"

"It's late. I should go home."

Myrnin straightened, stared at her, and she saw the storm forming in his expression. "You are dictating to me now?" he snapped. "Who is the master? Who is the student?"

"I—sorry, but I can't stay here all night!"

Myrnin walked toward her, and she couldn't even recognize him. No more manic energy, no more humor, no more sharp, brilliant anger. He looked troubled and clouded.

"Home," he repeated. "Home is where the heart is. Why don't you leave yours here? I'll take very good care of it."

"M-my—heart?" She dropped the pen and backed up, putting a big lab table full of chemical equipment between them. Myrnin bared his teeth and put down his fangs. *Discovery Channel. King cobra. Oh God, can he spit venom or something?* His eyes flared bright, fueled with something that looked to her like . . . fear.

"Don't run," he said, and sounded annoyed. "I hate it when they run. Now, tell me what you're doing here!" he demanded. "Why do you keep following me? *Who are you?*"

"It's Claire, Myrnin. I'm your apprentice. I'm supposed to be here, remember?"

That was the wrong thing to say, and she had no idea why. Myrnin stopped, and the light in his eyes intensified to insanity. Ugly, and very scary. When he moved, it was a smooth, sinuous glide. "My apprentice," he said. "So I own you, then. I can do as I wish."

King cobra.

"Sam!" Claire yelled, and bolted for the stairs.

She didn't get more than two steps. Myrnin came *over* the table, scattering glass instruments to shatter in glittering sprays on the floor, and she felt his cold, impossibly strong hands close on her ankles and jerk backward. She flailed for something to grab on to, but it was only a tower of books, and it collapsed as she fell.

She hit the floor hard enough to put the world on a sparkling, unsteady hold for a few seconds, and when she blinked away the stars, Myrnin had taken hold of her shoulders and was staring down at her, inches away.

"Don't," she said. "Myrnin, don't. I'm your friend! I won't hurt you!"

She didn't know why she said it, but it must have been the right thing to do. His eyes widened, white showing all around, and then the glitter of crazy was replaced by a flood of tears. He patted her cheek, soft and confused, and the fangs folded up in his mouth. "Dear child," he said. "What are you doing here? Is Amelie making you come here? She shouldn't. You're far too young and kind. You should tell her you won't come back. I don't want to hurt you, but I will." He tapped his forehead. "*This* is betraying me. This stupid, stupid flesh." The tapping became violent slaps to his forehead, and tears broke free to run down his cheeks. "I need to teach someone, but not you. Not you, Claire. Too young. Too small. You bring out the beast."

He stood up and wandered away, *tsk*ing over the broken glass, righting the fallen books. As if she'd ceased to exist. Claire sat up and rolled to her feet, shaky and scared.

Sam was standing just a few feet away. She hadn't seen or heard him approach, and he hadn't acted to save her. His face was tense, his eyes uneasy.

"He's sick," Claire said.

"Sick, sick, sick, yes, I am," Myrnin said. He had his head in his hands now, as if it hurt him. "We're all sick. All doomed."

"What's he talking about?" Claire turned to Sam.

"Nothing." He shook his head. "Don't listen to him."

Myrnin looked up and bared his teeth. His eyes were fierce, but they were sane. Mostly sane, anyway.

"They won't tell you the truth, little morsel, but I will. We're dying. Seventy years ago—"

Sam moved Claire out of his way, and for the first time since she'd met him, Sam actually looked threatening. "Myrnin, *shut up*!"

"No," Myrnin sighed. "It's time for talking. I've been shut up enough." He looked up, and his eyes were red-rimmed and full of tears. "Oh, little girl, do you understand? My race is dying. My race is dying and I don't know how to stop it."

Claire's mouth opened and closed, but she couldn't find anything to say. Sam turned toward her, fury still radiating off him like heat. "Ignore him," he said. "He doesn't know what he's saying. We should go, before he remembers what he was about to do. Or forgets what he shouldn't."

Claire cast a look back over her shoulder at Myrnin, who was holding a broken glass pipe in his hands, trying to fit the two pieces back together. When it wouldn't go, he dropped it and covered his face with both hands. She could see his shoulders shaking. "Can't—shouldn't somebody help him?"

"There's no help," Sam said in a voice flat with anger. "There's no cure. And you're not coming back here again if I can do anything about it."

6

Claire kept her silence for about half the ride home, and Sam didn't offer anything, either. The pressure of questions finally was too much for her. "He was telling the truth, wasn't he?" she asked. "There's some kind of disease. Amelie tried to make me think that not making more vampires was her choice, but that's not really true, is it? You *can't*. She's the only one who isn't sick."

Sam's face went tight and still in the glow of the dashboard lights. Sitting in the car was like traveling through space; the dark-tinted windows refused even starlight, so it was just the two of them in their own pocket universe. He had the radio on, and it was playing classical music, something light and sweet.

"No use telling you to shut up, is there?"

She said regretfully, "Probably not. And I wouldn't stop trying to find out."

Sam shook his head. "Do you even *have* a sense of self-preservation?"

"Shane asks me that all the time."

That made Sam smile, despite his obvious unease. "All right," he said. "Amelie's sick, too. It's getting harder and harder for her to create new vampires—she was barely able to bring Michael over; I was terrified it would kill her this time. The truth is, we're all sick. Myrnin's been searching for the cause—and the cure—for seventy years now, but it's too late now. He's too far gone, and the chance that anyone else could help him through it is too small. I can't let her sacrifice you like this, Claire. I told you that he's had five assistants. I don't want you to become another statistic."

Oh God. *The vampires were all dying.* Claire felt a rush of pure adrenaline, enough to make her hands tremble with the force of it. She felt a fierce surge of something like . . . satisfaction. And then another one, right on top of it, of guilt. *What about Sam? What about Michael?* Yeah, and what about Oliver and all those scary vamps like him? Wouldn't it be great to see them go?

"What if he doesn't find the cure?" Claire asked. She tried not to give away any of what she was feeling, but she was sure Sam could hear her elevated heartbeat. "How long—?"

"Claire, you need to forget you ever heard any of this. I mean it. There are a lot of secrets in Morganville, but this one could kill you. Say *nothing*, understand? Not to your friends, and not to Amelie. *Do you understand?*"

His intensity was even more terrifying than Myrnin's, because it was so controlled. She nodded.

It didn't stop the questions from swirling in her brain, or the possibilities.

Sam let her out at the curb and watched her until she was inside the house—it was full dark, and there were plenty of hunting vampires out on a clear, cool night like this. Nobody would hurt her—probably—but Sam wasn't in the mood to take chances.

Claire shut the door and locked it, leaned against the wood for a long few seconds, and tried to get her head together. She knew her friends would bombard her with questions—where had she been, was she crazy being out alone in the dark—but she couldn't answer them, not without violating some order from either Amelie or Sam.

They're dying. It seemed impossible; the vampires seemed so strong, so frightening. But she'd seen it. She'd seen the way Myrnin was decaying, and how afraid Sam was. Even Amelie, perfect icy Amelie, was doomed. Wasn't that a good thing? And if it was, why did she feel so sick when she thought about Amelie going slowly mad, like Myrnin?

Claire took a few more deep breaths, willed her mind to shut up for a while, and pushed off to walk down the hall.

She didn't get far. There was stuff piled everywhere. It took her a second, but she recognized it with a shock of horror. "Oh no," she whispered. "Shane's stuff." It was blocking the hallway. Claire shoved a path through the boxes and suitcases piled there. *Oh crap.* There was the PlayStation, unplugged and looking mournful, in a heap with its game controllers.

"Hey? Hey guys? What's going on?" Claire called, edging around the barricades. "Anybody here?"

"Claire?" Michael's shadow appeared at the end of the hall. "Where the *hell* have you been?"

"I—got held up late at the lab," she said. Which wasn't a lie. "What's happening?"

"Shane says he's moving out," Michael said. He looked deeply angry, but it was covering up hurt, too. "Glad you're here. I was about to come looking for you."

Claire heard the indistinct buzz of voices upstairs. Eve's voice, high and strident. Shane's rumbling low. There was about a sixty second delay, and then Shane came down the stairs carrying a box. His face was pale but determined, and although he hesitated for a second when he saw Claire was back, he kept coming down.

"Seriously, dumbass, what the *hell* are you doing?" Eve demanded from the top of the stairs. She darted around and got into his path, forcing him to back up and try to get around her. "Yo, village idiot! Talking to you!"

"You want to live here with him, fine," Shane said tightly. "I'm going. I've had enough."

"You're moving *at night*? Do you have a head wound?"

He faked Eve to the right and moved past her to the left.

And ran into Claire, who didn't move. She didn't say anything, and after a few seconds of silence he said, "I'm sorry. Got to do it. I told you."

"Is this about your dad?" she asked. "About this prejudice you've got against Michael now?"

"Prejudice? Jesus, Claire, you act like he's still really Michael. Well, he's not. He's one of them. I'm done with this crap. If I need to I'll go break some laws and get my ass thrown in jail. Better that than living here, looking at him—" Shane stopped dead and shut his eyes for a second. "You don't understand. You just don't understand, Claire. You didn't grow up here."

"But I did," Eve said, stepping up closer. "And I don't get your paranoid bullshit, either. Michael hasn't hurt *anybody*! Especially you, you jerk. So lay off."

"I am," Shane said. "I'm leaving."

Claire didn't move out of his way. "What about us?"

"You want to go with me?"

She slowly shook her head, and saw the pain in his face for a split second before it turned hard again.

"Then we've got nothing to talk about. And sorry to break it to you, but there's no *us*. Get it straight, Claire, it's been fun, but you're not really my type—"

Michael *moved*. He smacked the box out of Shane's hands, and it flew halfway across the room, skidded across the wood floor the rest of the way, and slammed into the baseboard, where it tipped over and spilled things all over the place.

"Don't," he said, and grabbed Shane by the shoulders and flattened him against the nearest convenient wall. "Don't you disrespect her. Be an asshole to me, fine. Be an asshole to Eve if you want to; she can give it right back. But don't you take it out on Claire. I've had enough of your crap, Shane." He stopped and took a breath, but the anger wasn't burning out of him, not yet. "You want to go, get the hell out, but you'd better take a good hard look at yourself, my man. Yeah, your sister died. Your mom died. Your dad's a violent, prejudiced asshole. Your life has *sucked*. But you don't get to be the victim anymore. We keep cutting you breaks, and you keep screwing up, and it's *enough*. I'm not letting you whine anymore about how your life sucks worse than ours."

Shane's face went dead white, then red.

And he socked Michael in the face. It was a solid, painful punch, and Claire winced and covered her mouth in sympathy, moving back.

Michael didn't move. Didn't even react. He just stared into Shane's eyes.

"You're just like your dad," he said. "You want to stake me now? Cut my head off? Bury me out back? That work for you, *friend*?"

"Yes!" Shane screamed, right in his face, and there was something so frightening in his eyes that Claire couldn't move. Couldn't breathe.

Michael let him go, walked over, and picked up a couple of things from the pile that had spilled from the box Shane had been carrying out.

A pointed stake.

A wickedly sharp hunting knife.

"You came prepared," he said, and tossed them to Shane, who caught them out of the air. "Go for it."

Eve screamed and threw herself in front of Michael, who gently but firmly moved her out of the way.

"Go on," he said. "We do this now, or we end up doing it later. You want to move out so you can kill me with a clear conscience. Why wait? Come on, man, do it. I won't fight."

Shane turned the knife in his hand, the edge slashing the light with every agitated move. Claire felt frozen, winter-cold, unable to think of anything to say or do. What had happened? How did things get this bad? What—

Shane took a step toward Michael, a sudden long lunge, and Michael didn't move. His eyes—they weren't cold at all, and they weren't vampire-scary, either. They were human, and they were afraid.

For a long breath, nobody moved, and then Michael said, "I know you feel like I betrayed you, but I didn't. This wasn't about you. It was for me; it was so I didn't have to be trapped here anymore. I was dying here. I was buried alive."

Shane's face twisted, as if that hunting knife had slid into his own guts. "Maybe you should have stayed dead." He raised the stake in his right hand.

"Shane, *no!*" Eve was screaming, trying to get between them, but Michael was holding her off. She turned on him in a fury. "Dammit, stop it! You don't really want to die!"

"No," Michael said. "I don't. He knows I don't."

Shane paused, trembling. Claire watched his face, his eyes, but she couldn't tell what he was thinking. What he was feeling. It was just a face, and she didn't know him at all

"You were my friend," Shane said. He sounded lost. "You were my best friend. How screwed up is this?"

Michael didn't say anything. He took a step forward, took the knife and stake out of Shane's hands, and pulled him into a hug.

And this time, Shane didn't resist.

"Asshole," Michael sighed, and slapped his back.

"Yeah," Shane muttered, stepped back, and scrubbed at his eyes with the heel of his hand. "Whatever. You started it." He looked around and focused on Claire. "You. You were supposed to be home already."

Crap. She'd hoped they'd forget all about her late arrival, in the explosion of Shane's freak-out. But of course, he'd try to find a way to shift attention away, and there she was, a sitting duck.

"Right," Eve said. "Guess you forgot the number to call and tell us you weren't dead in a ditch."

"I'm fine," Claire said.

"Amy wasn't. She was murdered and stuffed in our

trash can, so excuse me if I got a little bit worried that you might be *dead*." Eve crossed her arms, her dark stare getting even more fierce. "I already checked out there for you, before Shane decided to pull this crap."

Oh man. Somehow, in all of the stress of her afternoon with Myrnin, Claire had forgotten about Amy's death. Of *course* Eve was angry; not so much angry, really, as plain terrified.

Claire didn't dare meet Shane's gaze. She looked at Michael instead, helplessly. "I'm sorry," she said. "I got—I was at the lab, and—I should have called, I guess."

"And you walked home? In the dark?" Another question she had to avoid. She just shrugged. "You know what we call pedestrians in Morganville? Mobile blood banks." Michael sounded cold, too. Cold and angry. "You scared the shit out of us. That's not like you, Claire. What happened?"

Shane moved to her side, and she felt a moment of relief that at least *he* wasn't angry at her. But then he yanked her shirt away from her neck on the left, then on the right, an efficient rough search that surprised her too much to fight him. He skinned up her right sleeve all the way to the elbow and turned her arm to inspect it.

As he reached for the left, she felt an electric bolt of alarm. *The bracelet. Oh God.*

She yanked free and shoved him back. "Hey!" she said. "I'm fine, okay? I'm fine! Fang-free!"

"Then show me," Shane said. His eyes were steady and scared, and that broke her heart. "C'mon, Claire. Prove it."

"Why do I have to prove anything to you?" She knew she was wrong, and it made her stupidly angry that he cared so much. "You don't own me, like some vampire! I just *said* I'm fine! Why can't you just trust me?"

She would have done anything to take it back, but

it was too late, and it hit him like a punch in the face. *He's been hurt so much. Why did I do that? Why . . .*

Michael stepped in between them. He threw a glance over his shoulder at Shane. "I'll do it." He was blocking Eve and Shane's view. Before Claire could do anything to stop him—as if she *could* do anything—he grabbed her left hand and pulled the sleeve up to her elbow.

He stared at the gold bracelet for a paralyzing second before turning her arm first one way, then the other. Then pulling her sleeve back down over the telltale jewelry evidence.

"She's fine," he said, and met her eyes. "She's telling the truth. I'd know if a vampire had bitten her. I'd feel it."

Shane's mouth opened, then closed. He took another step back, stared at her for a second, then walked away. Eve called, "Hey, how about taking some of your crap back upstairs, if you're planning on staying?"

"Later," Shane snapped, and went upstairs without looking back.

"I'd better go talk to him," Claire said. Michael kept hold of her arm.

"No," he said. "First, you'd better talk to me."

He hustled her toward the kitchen. Behind them, Eve said, "Just another great family dinner. Whatever! I'm taking the last hot dog!"

Even with the kitchen door shut, Michael wasn't taking any chances. He pulled Claire along with him to the pantry, opened the door, and turned on the light. "Inside," he ordered. She stepped in, and he shut the door after her. It was cramped with two people, and it smelled like old spices and vinegar, from where Shane had dropped the bottle a few weeks back. Michael's voice dropped to a fierce hiss. "What the *hell* do you think you're doing?"

"What I had to," she said. She was shaking all over, but she wouldn't let Michael intimidate her. She was tired, and besides, *everybody* seemed to be trying to intimidate her these days. She was small; she wasn't weak. "It was the only way. Amelie—"

"You should have talked to me. Talked to *us*."

"Like *you* came clean with us, when you were a ghost? And did you have a house meeting before you decided to go all the way to vampire?" Claire shot back. "Right. Well, you're not the only one who can make choices, Michael. This was mine; I made it; I'll live with it. And it'll keep all of you safe."

"Who says?" Michael asked bluntly. "Amelie? You're trusting vampires now?"

She didn't look away from his big blue eyes. "I trust you."

He suppressed a smile. "Dumbass."

"Dork." She shoved him, just a little, and he let her do it. He even pretended to stagger, although she didn't imagine vampires got knocked off balance very often, except by other vampires. "Michael, she didn't give me any choice. Shane's dad—even though he left, he did damage. Shane wasn't going to be trusted here, and you know what happens if—"

"If they don't trust him," Michael said somberly. "Yeah. I know. Look, don't worry about Shane. I'll protect him. I told you—"

"You may not be able to. Look, no offense, but you've only been a vampire for a couple of weeks. I have library books that have been out longer. You can't promise—"

Michael reached out and put one cool finger across her lips, stilling them instantly. His blue eyes were intense, narrow, and very focused.

"Shhhh," he whispered, and turned out the light.

Claire heard the kitchen door thump, and then the hard-heeled clonk of Eve's shoes crossing the wood floor. "Hello? Hellllooooooooo? Great. Why do all my housemates sulk like little girls or vanish when the dishes are dirty? If you can hear me, Michael Glass, I'm talking to *you*!"

Claire snorted, almost laughed. Michael's hand closed

over her mouth, stifling her. He tugged on her arm, and she followed him, moving carefully so as not to knock anything off the shelf. She heard the scrape of the door opening at the rear of the pantry, the tiny little bolt-hole, and bent down to go through it. The other side was pitch-black, with not even the tiny crack of light that the pantry had enjoyed, and Claire felt a flutter of panic. Michael's hand pushed her onward, and she stepped hesitantly into the close, thick dark. Behind her, she heard him close the door with a very soft *click,* and bright electric light flooded over the floor.

"Here," Michael said, and handed her the flashlight. "She might come looking for us here, but not for a while."

It was a secret hidey-hole, one that Claire had been shoved into on her very first morning in the Glass House; no exits, only the one entrance. She'd thought from the beginning it looked like someplace a vampire might stash a couple of handy coffins, but it was empty. And as far as she knew, Michael slept on a Serta.

"I meant to ask you. What is this?"

"Root cellar," he said. "This house was built before refrigerators, and ice deliveries were only so-so. This was where they kept most of their vegetables."

"So . . . not a vampire hideout?"

Michael stretched his long legs out with a sigh and leaned against the wall. God, he was pretty. No wonder Eve was willing to overlook the lack of pulse. "Not so far as I've ever known, but the vampires in Morganville never really had to hide. Only the humans did."

Which wasn't what they were here to talk about, she supposed. She crossed her arms and felt the bracelet bite into the skin of her wrist under the shirt. "Whatever lecture you were going to give me, it's too late. I signed, it's done, I've got the souvenir bracelet." Which made her suddenly, strangely want to cry. "Michael—"

"What's she asking you to do?" Which was so right-on that she felt the pressure of tears behind her eyes and in her nose get even higher.

"Um . . ." She couldn't tell him; Amelie and Sam had both made it clear. "It's just extra schoolwork. She wants me to study some things."

"What things?" Michael's voice got sharp and worried. "Claire—"

"It's nothing. Science stuff. I would have probably been doing it anyway, but it's just—it's a lot more time, and I don't know how I'm going to—" *Keep it from Shane.* Because she had to, right? Bad enough he hated Michael for being a vampire, but what was he going to think about *her,* selling herself to Amelie? "I just don't know how I'm going to do all this."

And suddenly, she was crying. She didn't mean to, but there it was, boiling out of her. She expected Michael to do the Shane thing, come and comfort her, but he didn't. He sat right where he was and watched her. When her sobs died down, and she swiped her hands across her wet cheeks, he said, "Finished?"

She gulped and nodded.

"You made the choice; now you want to have it both ways—the benefits, but not the consequences. You can't, Claire. It's coming home to roost, and you'd better handle it now rather than later." Michael's tone softened, just a little. "Look, I'm not an asshole; I know how scared you are. But you're a player in this town now. You're not the fragile little thing we took in for protection. You're trying to protect *us.* That means you may not be as well liked anymore, and you're going to have to sack up about that."

"What?" She felt dazed. Somehow, this wasn't how she'd expected all this to go. Especially Michael's cool, challenging look, and the lack of hugging.

"Signing the contract isn't the last choice you're going to have to make," he said. "It's the choices you make from now on that show whether you did the right thing or not." He stood up, pale and strong and as gorgeous as an angel in the glow of Claire's flashlight. "And stop lying to me. You ought to get off to a better start."

"I—what?"

"You said what Amelie has you doing is just more studying," he said grimly. "And I can tell when you're lying. No, I'm not going to ask, because I can tell it scares you, but just remember, vampires know, all right?"

He swung the door open and ducked out. Claire stared after him, openmouthed, but by the time she'd scrambled through and switched off the flashlight, Michael was already gone, out of the pantry. In fact, by the time Claire followed, Michael was already sitting on the couch, Eve curled next to him with her head on his chest. They were watching something on TV, and Eve's gaze followed Claire as she hurried past them, mumbling an apology.

She stopped on the stairs and looked back at them. Two people she cared about, wrapped in a moment of warmth and happiness.

Michael was a vampire, and that meant that Michael was *dying*. Like Myrnin. He was going to suffer and lose his mind and hurt people.

He could even hurt Eve, no matter how much he cared about her.

Tears pricked at her eyes, and she felt suddenly short of breath. When it had been just an abstract problem, just Morganville minus vampires equals safety, then that had been one thing, but it wasn't abstract. It was people she knew, liked, even loved. She wouldn't shed any tears over Oliver, but how could she not care about Michael? Or Sam? Or even Amelie?

Claire picked up her book bag and went upstairs.

Shane's door was shut. She knocked. He didn't answer for a long moment, and then said, "If I ignore you, will you go away?"

"No," she said.

"Might as well come in, then."

He was flopped on the bed, staring at the ceiling, hands under his head, and he didn't look at her as she entered and closed the door behind her.

"So is this how it's going to go?" she asked. "I do something dumb like stay out late; you get mad and run away; I come and apologize and make everything better?"

Shane, surprised, looked at her, then said, "Well, that kinda works for me, yeah."

Claire thought about Michael, about the suddenly grown-up way he'd treated her. She sat down on the bed next to Shane, staring down at the floor for a few seconds to gather her courage, and then she pulled back her sleeve to expose the bracelet.

Shane didn't make a sound. He slowly sat up, staring at the shiny gold band with its Founder's Symbol.

"We need to talk," she said. She felt sick and terrified, but she knew it was the right choice. The only other thing to do was lie, but she couldn't keep on lying. Michael was right about that.

Shane could have done anything—he could have run away, he could have thrown her out of his room. He could even have hit her.

Instead, he took her hand in his, bent his head, and said, "Tell me."

Eve wasn't so understanding. "Are you *out of your mind*?" She picked up the handiest thing to throw—it happened to be the PlayStation controller—and Shane quickly, carefully de-gamed her. Claire thought he probably wouldn't have moved that fast if Eve had grabbed, oh, say, a book.

"Let's be adults about this," Michael said. They were downstairs again, together, although Shane and Michael were still clearly standing at opposite poles. It was getting late—eleven already—and Claire was feeling the strain of a very long, hard day. In fact, she yawned, which only made Eve shoot her a look of absolute exasperation.

"Oh, I'm sorry, are we *keeping you awake*? Michael, how the hell do we be adults about this when one of us *isn't an adult*?" Eve leveled a shaking finger at her. "You're a *kid*, Claire. As in, you're still a wet-behind-the-ears dumbass who hasn't even been in this town a couple of months. You have no idea what you're doing!"

"Maybe I don't," Claire agreed. Her voice was almost steady, which pleased and surprised her. She didn't like having Eve angry at her. She didn't like having *anyone* angry at her. "The thing is, it's done. I made the choice; that discussion was over before we had it. I wanted you to know, though. I didn't want to"—her eyes met Michael's briefly—"lie to you."

"Why the hell not? Everybody around here lies. Michael lied about being a ghost. Shane lies about shit all the time. Why not you, too?"

Shane groaned. "Yo, Drama Princess, want to tone it down a little? Somewhere, Sandra Bernhard wants her tantrum back."

"Oh, like *you* don't throw a hissy every time somebody trips your angst switch!"

Claire looked helplessly at Michael, who was having a hard time not smiling. He shrugged and took a step forward. That meant, of course, that Shane backed up. "Eve," Michael said, ignoring Shane for the moment. "Give the girl some credit. At least she told you, instead of letting you figure it out on your own."

"Yeah, and she told me *last*!" Eve glared at the two boys, hands on her hips.

"Boyfriend," Shane said, holding up his hand.

"Landlord," Michael chimed in.

"Crap," Eve sighed. "Right, next time you sell your soul to the devil, *I get first contact*! Girl solidarity, right?"

"Um—okay?"

"Dumbass," Eve sighed, defeated. "I can't believe you did that. I worked so hard to get away from that Protection crap, and here you are, all . . . Protected. I just wanted you to be—safe. And I'm not sure this is."

"Yeah," Claire said. "Me neither. But I swear, it was the best thing I could think of. And at least it's Amelie. She's okay, right?"

They all looked at each other. Shane said, "But you won't tell us what she's got you doing that keeps you out late."

"No. I—I can't do that."

"Then she's not okay," Shane said. "And neither are you."

But none of them had any good suggestions for how to fix it, and Claire fell asleep on the couch with her head in Shane's lap as he and Michael and Eve kept talking, and talking, and talking. It was three a.m. when she woke up. Shane hadn't moved, but she was covered with a blanket, and he was sound asleep, sitting straight up.

Claire yawned, groaned at sore muscles, and rolled to her feet. "Shane. Up. You need to go to bed."

He woke up cute, softened by sleep. "Come with?" He was only half joking. She remembered being curled up with him in her bed the night she'd been so scared; he'd been careful then, but she wasn't sure she could count on that kind of self-restraint at three a.m., when he was half-awake.

"I can't," she said reluctantly. "Not that I don't want to. . . ."

He smiled and stretched out on his side on the couch, leaving a narrow space between his warm, solid body and the cushions. "Stay," he said. "I promise, no clothes will come off. Well, maybe shoes. Do shoes count as clothes?"

She kicked hers off and climbed over him to slip into that small pocket, and sighed in relief as his body pressed against hers. She didn't even need the blanket, but he put it over the two of them, anyway, and then combed her hair back from her neck and kissed her on the soft, vulnerable skin.

"You were leaving," she whispered. He stopped moving. As far as she could tell, he stopped breathing. "You were leaving, and you didn't even know if I was okay."

"No. I was going to go look for you."

"After you packed."

"Claire, I didn't even know you hadn't come home until Eve came upstairs to yell at me. *I was going to look for you.*"

She looked back at him, over her shoulder, and saw the desperation hiding in his eyes.

"Please," he said. "Please believe me."

Against her will, even against her better judgment, she did believe him. She felt safe, anchored against the troubled world by the heat of his body against hers.

His arm went around her waist, and she felt absolutely protected.

"I won't let anything happen to you," he said. It was a promise he probably couldn't keep, but in the night, in the dark, it meant everything to her. "Hey."

"What?"

"Wanna fool around?"

She did.

She must have drifted off to sleep, because she woke up with her heart pounding, and feeling like there was something really, really wrong. For a second, as she came awake, she thought she smelled smoke, and that propelled her upright in a surge of panic. The house had almost burned once already. . . .

No, not fire, but something was definitely wrong. There was something in the whole atmosphere of the house. The smoke had been some kind of signal, from it to her. A *get your butt out of bed* signal.

Shane was still lying next to her on the couch, but he was already awake, too, and in the next second he rolled off to his feet as if he'd also felt it.

"What's happening?" Claire felt a jolt go through her like electricity. "Shane?"

"Something's wrong."

They both froze as they heard the sudden loud blare of a siren. It sounded as though it was right in front of the house.

Claire heard feet on the stairs and saw Eve hurrying down in a satin nightgown and fluffy black robe. Eve's face was bare of any Goth makeup, and she looked flushed and anxious and scared.

"What is it?" Eve called. "What's going on?"

"I don't know," Shane said. "Something bad. Can't you feel it?"

This was an event; they were all up and it was barely six a.m.

Eve plunged down the steps and yanked up the cord to raise the blinds on the window that faced the front yard. They all looked out. A police car was in the middle of the street, siren still wailing, and its headlights cast a hot circle of light on a maroon sedan stopped on the street, its driver's-side door open. Its lights were still on, and there was a body slumped on the road next to it.

The windows were dark-tinted.

It was a vampire's car.

Eve screamed, spun, and looked at them with wide, terrified eyes. "Where's Michael?" she asked, and Claire stupidly looked behind her, as if she were going to find him standing there.

They all looked back at the street, the car, the body.

"It can't be," Claire whispered. Shane was already moving for the door at a flat run, but Eve just stood there staring, frozen. Claire put her arm around her and felt her shaking.

She saw Shane blow through the gate at the fence and run toward the body; the cop who'd just emerged from the patrol car grabbed him, slung him around, and slammed him face-first onto the hood. Shane was yelling something.

"I need to go out there," Claire said. "Stay here."

Eve nodded numbly. Claire hated leaving her there, but Shane was going to get himself arrested if he kept it up, and who knew what could happen to him in jail?

She was only to the porch when another police car turned the corner, lights flashing, siren adding its howl to the chaos. It braked beside the first one, and another policeman got out and moved to where Shane was being restrained.

Claire didn't recognize the cop who had Michael facedown on the hood, but she knew the new arrival. It was Richard Morrell, Monica's big brother. He wasn't a bad guy, although he was definitely from the same icky gene pool. He took over for the other cop, who backed away.

"Shane! Dammit, Shane, calm the hell down. This is a crime scene; I can't let you run out there, do you understand? Calm down!"

Richard was occupied with keeping Shane under control, so the other policeman went to crouch next to the body on the street. *The body.* Claire took a step closer, and the policeman produced a flashlight and focused it on the face of the man lying in the street. Red hair flared in the light.

Not Michael.

Sam.

There was a stake in his chest, and he was still and white and *not moving.*

"Richard!" the cop yelled. "It's Sam Glass! Looks dead to me!"

"Sam," Claire whispered. "No."

Sam had been kind to her, and somebody had dragged him out of his car and put a stake through his chest.

"Shit!" Richard spat. "Shane, sit your ass down. Down, right now. Don't make me handcuff you." He yanked Shane by the collar of his T-shirt and sat him down on the curb, glared at him for a second, then came over to look at the body. "Holy Mother of— grab his feet."

"What?" The other cop—his name tag said FENTON—looked at him with a frown. "It's a crime scene; we can't—"

"He's still alive, you idiot. Grab his damn feet, Fenton! If he burns, he's dead."

The first rays of sun crept over the horizon and fell on Sam's still form.

And Claire saw him start to smoke.

"What are you waiting for?" Richard shouted. "Pick him up!" The other cop, after a blank hesitation, grabbed Sam by the feet. Richard took him under the arms, and together they bodily threw him into the maroon sedan, the one with tinted windows and slammed the door shut. Fenton started for the driver's side, but Richard got there first. "I'll drive," Richard said. "The wound's still fresh. He's got a chance if I can get him to Amelie."

Fenton backed off. Richard gunned the engine and slammed the door even as he was peeling rubber toward the end of the street.

Officer Fenton glared at Shane. "You going to give me trouble, boy?" he demanded. Claire sure hoped not. This man was twice the size of Richard Morrell, twice as old, and he looked like a human pit bull.

Shane held up his hands. "No trouble from me, Officer. Sir."

"You two see what happened here?"

"No," Claire said. "I was asleep. We all were."

"All in the same room?" the cop grunted, and looked her over, from her bed-head to the wrinkled clothes. "Didn't take you for the type."

She couldn't figure out what he meant for a few seconds, and then felt a wave of hot embarrassment sweep over her. "No, I mean—Eve was in her own room. We were asleep on the couch."

Shane said, "Yeah, we were all asleep. Woke up when we heard the siren." Which wasn't quite true, was it? They'd woken up, and *then* heard the siren. But Claire wasn't sure why that would be important.

The cop tapped on a handheld device, still frowning. "Ought to be four of you in the house. Where're the other two?"

"Eve's still inside. And Michael—" Where the hell was Michael? "I don't know where he is."

"I'll go see if he's in his room," Shane volunteered, but the cop froze him in place with another thunderous scowl.

"You'll sit your ass down on that curb and be quiet. You, what's your name?"

"Claire Danvers."

"Claire, get in there, find out if Michael Glass is inside. If he's not, find out if his car is missing."

Claire stared at him, wide-eyed. "You don't think . . . ?"

"I don't think anything until I have facts. I need to know who's here, who isn't, and work from there." The cop transferred his dark stare to Shane, who was starting to get up. "I already told you, sit your ass down, Collins."

"I didn't have anything to do with this!"

"If I had to put together a list of prime suspects out to stake some vampires, you'd be right at the top, so yeah, you do. *Sit down.*"

Shane sat, looking furious. Claire silently begged him not to do anything stupid, and hurried back into the house. Eve was upstairs dressing—black baby-doll T with a bling-enhanced cartoon Elmer Fudd on the front, and black jeans with clunky Doc Martens.

"It wasn't—"

"I know. I saw," Eve said. Her voice sounded stuffy, as though she'd been crying, or was about to. "It was Sam, right? Is he alive? Or—whatever?"

"I don't know. Richard said something like he could still be okay." Claire gripped the doorknob tightly, and glanced down the hall. Michael's door was closed. It was always closed. "Did you look—?"

"No." Eve took a deep breath and stood up. "I'll go with you."

Michael's door was unlocked, and it was completely dark inside. Claire flipped on the lights. Michael's bed was empty, neatly made, and the room looked absolutely normal. Eve checked the closets, under the bed, even the master bathroom.

"No sign of him," she said breathlessly. "Let's check the garage."

The garage was a shed in the back, not attached to the house; the two of them went out the back kitchen door and crossed the rutted driveway. The shed's doors were closed.

Eve opened one side, Claire the other.

Michael's car was gone.

"What about work? Could he be at work?"

"TJ's doesn't open until ten," Eve said. "Why would he be in there at six?"

"Inventory?"

"You think they're going to call a vampire in at six a.m. to do *inventory*?" Eve slammed the shed door and kicked it for good measure. "Where the hell is he? And why the *hell* don't I have a working cell phone? Why don't you?"

Hers had been lost, Eve's had been smashed; both of them miserably looked at each other for a few seconds, then, without a word, walked to the front yard where Shane was still sitting on the curb. If anybody could sit rebelliously, he was doing it.

"Give me your phone," Eve demanded and held out her hand. Shane looked at her with a frown. "Now, dumbass. Michael's not inside, and his car's gone."

"Michael's got a car? Since when?"

"Since the vampires issued him one. He didn't tell you?"

Shane just shook his head. A muscle jumped in his jaw. "He doesn't tell me shit, Eve. Not since—"

"Not since you started treating him like the Evil Dead? Yeah. Imagine that."

He silently handed over his cell phone and looked away, staring at the street where Sam's body had been tossed. Claire wondered if he was thinking about his dad's crusade, about how *the only good vampire is a dead vampire.*

Claire wondered if he really, deep down, still agreed.

Eve dialed and put the phone to her ear. For a tense few seconds nothing happened, and then Claire saw relief melt the tension out of Eve's face and body. "Michael! Where the hell are you?" Pause. *"Where?"* Pause. "Oh. Okay. I need to tell you—" Pause. "You know." Pause. "Yeah, we'll . . . talk later."

Eve closed the phone and handed it back. Shane slipped it in his pocket again, eyebrows up and signaling questions.

"He's okay," she said. Her eyes had gone dark and narrow.

"And?"

"And nothing. He's fine. End of story."

"Bullshit," Shane said, and tugged her down to sit next to him on the curb. "Spill it, Eve. Now."

Claire sat, too, on Eve's other side. The curb felt cold and hard, but the good thing was that the patrol car blocked Fenton's view of them. He was talking to the occupants of another car, vampire-tinted, who had pulled up behind the cruiser.

"He was downtown," Eve said. "At the Elders' Council. They pulled him in there early this morning."

"Who did?"

"The Big Three." Oliver, Amelie and the mayor, Richard and Monica's dad. "Amelie just got word about Sam. But Michael's not hurt or anything." An unspoken *for now* was at the end of that. Eve was worried. She bent her head closer to Shane's, lowered her voice even further, and said, "You didn't have anything to do with what happened to Sam, right?"

"Jesus, Eve!"

"I'm only asking because—"

"I know why you're asking," he whispered back fiercely. "Hell no. If I were going to go after some vampire, it wouldn't have been *Sam*. I'd be staking somebody like Oliver, make it worth my time. Speaking of Oliver, he'd be my number one suspect."

"Vampires don't kill their own."

"He arranged for Brandon to die," Claire offered. "I think Oliver's capable of anything. And he'd love to see Amelie even more isolated." She swallowed hard. "She told me once that Sam was safer if she didn't keep him close. I guess she was right."

"Doesn't matter. Oliver keeps his hands clean, no matter what. Some broke-ass human is going to burn for this, and you know it," Shane said. "And it happened in front of our house, and nobody's forgotten what happened with my dad. You don't think we're being set up?"

Crap. Shane was right. The fact that Michael was safe was good, but it was also a double-edged sword; it meant that Michael had been gone when Sam had been attacked.

And Michael was the only one of them whose word might be worth anything to the vampires.

Sure enough, Fenton came back around the cruiser and stared at the three of them for a few seconds, then said, "You're being taken in for questioning. All three of you. Get in the backseat."

Shane didn't move. "I'm not going anywhere."

The policeman sighed and leaned against the quarter panel. "Son, you've got a lot of attitude, and I respect that. But get it straight: either you get in my car, or you get in *their* car." He pointed toward the silent dark sedan, the one with vampires inside. "And I promise you, that won't end so well. You get me?"

Shane nodded, stood, and gave Eve a hand up.

Claire stayed seated. She pulled up the sleeve on her left arm. The bracelet glittered and glimmered in the morning light, and she held it up for Fenton's clear view.

His eyes widened. "Is that . . . ?"

"I want to see my Patron," Claire said. "Please."

He went off to talk on his radio, then came back and jerked his head at Shane and Eve. "In the backseat," he said. "You're going to the station. You, kid . . ." He nodded toward the other sedan. "They'll take you to Amelie."

Claire swallowed hard and exchanged a look with Shane, then Eve. That hadn't been her plan. She wanted them all to stay together. How could she keep them safe if they got separated?

"Don't," Shane said. "Come with us."

Truthfully, that was starting to sound like a better idea. The vampires weren't going to be happy, and her shiny gold bracelet didn't exempt her from suspicion. Amelie could still order her hurt, or killed.

"Okay," Claire said. Shane looked massively relieved as he ducked his head and entered the backseat of the cruiser. Eve followed him in.

The cop slammed the door after Eve, before Claire could get in the patrol car.

"Hey!" Shane yelled, and hit the car window. He and Eve were both trying to get out, but the doors weren't opening.

Fenton grabbed her by the arm and hustled her over to the other sedan, opened the door, and put her in the backseat before she could protest. Claire heard the faint click of locks engaging, and sat very still, trying to see through the gloom.

One of the vampires flicked on the overhead light. *Oh crap.* It was two of her not-favorite people. The woman was pale as snow, with white-blond hair and eyes of palest silver. Gretchen. Her partner, Hans, was a hard man made of angles, with graying short hair, and a stony expression.

"I wish we'd gotten the boy instead," Gretchen said, clearly disappointed. Her voice was low-pitched, throaty, with a heavy foreign accent. Not quite German, but not quite anything else, either. An old accent, Claire thought. "He was so rude to us when last we spoke. And surely his father deserves a lesson, even if the boy does not."

"Amelie says just bring this one," Hans said, and put the car in gear. He looked at Claire in the rearview mirror. "Seat belt, please."

She had trouble wrapping her head around that— why did he care?—but she clicked the safety restraint shut and sat back. Like the ride in Sam's car the day before, she couldn't see a thing outside the windows except a faint gray dot where the sun was rising.

"Where are you taking me?" she asked. Gretchen laughed. Claire caught the flash of fangs, but Gretchen didn't really need them to be scary. Not at all.

"To the Elders' Council," she said. "You remember it, Claire. You had such a good time there when last we visited."

7

There was Morganville—the dry, dusty, run-down town that was all most people ever saw—and then there was Founder's Square, a lush little piece of Europe where people with a pulse weren't welcome. Claire had been inside once, and it wasn't a fond memory; no matter how cute the little cafés were, or how nice the shops, she could see only the center of the square in the park, with the cage where they'd locked up Shane.

Where they'd been meaning to burn him alive as punishment for something he hadn't even done.

For some reason, Claire had expected to be parked in the same place as last time—outside of the square, at the police checkpoint—but of course that wasn't possible, was it? A few of the older vampires might be able to stand the sun, but they wouldn't willingly stroll around in it. Morganville was built for the convenience of vampires, not humans, and when Claire's door opened, and Gretchen impatiently gestured for her to get out, they were in an underground parking garage. It was full of cars, all nice ones, with darkened windows. Like a Beverly Hills mall or something.

There were armed guards. One of them started toward them as Gretchen pulled Claire out of the car, but Hans flashed him a badge, and the other guy—vampire, presumably—backed off.

"Let's go," Hans said. "Your Patron is waiting."

Gretchen chuckled. Not a happy sound. Claire stumbled over her own feet trying to keep up as the two vampires set off at a brisk walk, Gretchen's iron-hard grip on her upper arm setting in with bruising force. Claire was short of breath by the time they got to a long double flight of stairs, which the vampires took at a jog. At the top of the stairs was some kind of fire door, with a code panel. Claire didn't dare try to sneak a look at what Hans entered; knowing the vampires' paranoia, it wouldn't do her any good. The machines were probably calibrated to exclude anybody with a heartbeat.

Which made her wonder: was Myrnin behind the town's security, too? Was that something else she was supposed to learn? It could really come in handy if she could persuade him to show her. . . .

She was obsessing on technicalities to avoid feeling the terror, but as soon as the door lock released, she had nothing else to focus on except fear, and it washed over her in a sticky, cold wave. Gretchen seemed to sense it. She looked down at Claire with those cool, mirror gray eyes, and smiled. "Worried, little one?" she asked sweetly. "Worried for yourself, or for your friends?"

"Worried for Sam," Claire said. Gretchen lost her smile, and for just an instant, she seemed honestly off balance and surprised. "Is he alive?"

"Alive?" Gretchen's armor slid firmly back in place, and she raised a slender arched eyebrow. "He may yet be saved, if that is what you mean. I suppose your friend Shane will have to try again."

"Shane didn't do anything!"

This time, Gretchen's smile got positively cruel. "Perhaps not," she said. "Perhaps not *yet*. But be patient. He will. It's in his nature, as much as killing is in ours."

Claire had to save her breath, because they were walking again, big strides across thick maroon carpet. Claire's first impression of the Elders' Council building had been that it was a funeral home; it still felt like that to her, all hushed and quiet and elegant.

They'd had roses in the last time, when the vampire they'd thought Shane killed had been lying in state. She didn't see any flowers this time.

Gretchen led her down a hallway and through thick double doors, into the round entry hall. There were four armed vampire guards in the room, and Gretchen and Hans had to stop and show ID, and surrender their weapons. Claire got searched—quick, competent pats from cold hands that made her shiver.

And then the doors opened, and she was pulled into a big round room with a high ceiling, chandeliers like falls of ice, and dim, expensive paintings on the walls. She hadn't imagined the smell of roses. In the center of the room stood a massive round conference table, surrounded by chairs, and in the center was a vase filled with red, red blooms.

Nobody was at the table. Instead, a group of at least ten was standing at the other side of the room, looking down.

Some of them turned, and Claire's gaze fixed irresistibly on Oliver. She hadn't seen him since he'd threatened her life, trying to lure Shane out of hiding, and as he stood up, now she had a flash of that again, how icy and hard his hands had been around her throat. How scared she'd been.

Oliver snarled, low in his throat but loud enough to be heard, and his eyes were like a wolf's. Not human at all.

"I see you brought us a criminal for punishment," he said, and moved toward them.

Gretchen looked at Hans, and then shoved Claire behind her. "Stop," she said. Oliver did, mostly in surprise. "The girl asked to come, to see her Patron. We have no proof she is guilty."

"If she lives in that house, then she's guilty," Oliver said. "You surprise me, Gretchen. When did you begin taking the side of the breathers?"

She laughed, but it had a bright, false sound to it. She said something in a language that Claire didn't recognize; Oliver spat something back, and Hans put a big hand on Claire's shoulder.

"She's our responsibility," he said. "And she's Amelie's property. Nothing to do with you, Oliver. Move."

Oliver, smiling, raised his hands and backed away. Hans moved Claire forward, past him, and she felt his stare on the back of her neck, as sharp as knives.

The circle of people parted as Hans approached. It was mostly (Claire guessed) vampires; they didn't wear tags or anything, but most of them had the same cool, pale skin, the same whip-snake quickness when they moved. In fact, the only two humans—breathers?—she saw were Mayor Morrell, looking miserably uncomfortable as he stood near the edge of the group, and his son Richard. Richard's uniform was damp in places, and it took Claire a few seconds to realize that it was wet with blood.

Sam's blood,

Sam was lying on his back on the carpet, with his head cradled in Amelie's lap. The elder vampire was kneeling, and her hands were stroking gently through Sam's bright copper hair. He looked pale and dead, and the stake was still in his chest.

Amelie's eyes were closed, but opened as Hans pushed Claire toward her. For a long second the older vampire didn't seem to recognize Claire at all, and then weariness flashed through her expression; she looked down at Sam, her fingers trailing across his cheek.

"Claire, assist me," she said, as if they were continuing a conversation Claire hadn't even been in on. "Give her room, please."

Hans let go, and Claire felt a wild urge to run, run out of this room, get Shane and just *go*, anywhere but here. There was something too big to understand in Amelie's eyes, something she didn't want to know. She started to take a step back, but Amelie's hand flashed out and grabbed her wrist and pulled, and

Claire fell to her knees on the other side of Sam's body.

He looked dead.

Really, really dead.

"When I tell you, take hold of the wood and pull," Amelie said, her voice low and steady. "Not until I tell you."

"But—I'm not very strong. . . ." Why wasn't she asking Richard? Asking one of the vampires? Oliver, even?

"You are strong enough. When I tell you, Claire." Amelie closed her eyes again, and Claire scrubbed her damp palms nervously over her blue jeans. The wooden stake in Sam's chest was round, polished wood, like a spike, and she couldn't tell how deep it was in his body. Was it in his heart? Wouldn't that kill him, once and for all? She remembered they'd talked about other vampires who'd gotten staked, and they'd died. . . .

Amelie's expression suddenly twisted in pain, and she said, "Now, Claire!"

Claire didn't even think. She fastened her hands around the stake and pulled, one massive yank, and for a terrifying second she thought it wouldn't work, but then she felt it sliding free, scraping against bone as it went.

Sam's whole body arched, as though he'd been shocked with one of those heart machines, and the circle of vampires moved back. Amelie kept hold of him, her fingers white as bone where they pressed on the sides of his head. Her eyes flew open, and they were pure blazing silver.

Claire scrambled backward, clutching the stake in both hands. Someone plucked it out of her grip— Richard Morrell, looking grim and tired. He put it into a plastic bag and zipped it shut.

Evidence.

Sam went limp again. The wound in his chest was bleeding a steady, slow trickle, and Amelie took off her jacket—white silk—and folded it into a pad to press it against the flow. Nobody spoke, not even Amelie. Claire sat there feeling helpless, watching Sam. He wasn't moving, not at all.

He still looked dead.

"Samuel," Amelie said, and her voice was low and quiet and warm. She bent closer to him. "Samuel. Come back to me."

His eyes opened, and they were all pupil. Scary owl eyes. Claire bit her lip and thought again about running, but Hans and Gretchen were at her back and she knew she didn't have a chance, anyway.

Sam blinked, and his pupils began to shrink slowly to a more normal size. His lips moved, but no sound came out.

"Breathe in," Amelie said, in that same quiet, warm one. "I'm here, Samuel. I won't leave you." She stroked fingers gently over his forehead, and he blinked again and slowly focused on her.

It was as though there was nobody else in all the world, just the two of them. *Amelie was wrong,* Claire thought. *It isn't just that Sam loves her. She loves him just as much.*

Sam looked from Amelie to the circle of people, searching it for someone. When he didn't find the right one, he looked at Amelie again. His lips formed a name. *Michael.*

"Michael is safe," Amelie said. "Hans. Fetch him here."

Hans nodded and left, walking quickly. *Michael.* Claire realized with a jolt that she'd forgotten he'd be here, forgotten all about him in the shock of all that had happened. Sam was, at least, looking better with every passing second, but Amelie continued to press the makeshift bandage to the wound in his chest.

Sam's hand crept up, clumsy and slow, to cover hers, and for a long few seconds they looked at each other silently, and then Amelie nodded and let go.

Sam held the bandage in place and, with Amelie's help, pulled himself to a sitting position. She helped him lean against the wall.

"Can you tell us what happened?" she asked him. Sam nodded, and Claire looked up to see Richard Morrell crouching down, notebook and pen at the ready.

Sam's voice, when it finally came, was soft and thin, and it was clearly an effort for him to speak at all. "Went to see Michael," he said.

"But Michael was here, with us," Amelie said. "We summoned him during the night."

Sam's hand—the one not occupied holding the jacket to his chest—rose and fell helplessly. "Sensed he wasn't home, so I backed out of the drive. Someone pulled open the car door—Taser, couldn't fight back. Staked me while I was down."

"Who?" Richard asked. Sam's eyes closed briefly, then opened.

"Didn't see. Human. Heard the heartbeat." He swallowed. "Thirsty."

"You must heal first," Amelie said. "A few more moments. Is there anything at all you can tell us about this human who attacked you?"

Sam's eyes opened again, with an effort. "He called me Michael."

Michael arrived just in time to hear that last part. He looked at Claire, wide-eyed, then crouched down beside Sam. "Who did? The one who did this?"

Sam shook his head. "I don't know who. Male, that's all I know. He used your name. I think he thought I was you." Sam's lips curled in the pale ghost of a smile. "Guess he didn't see the hair before he staked me."

The article in the newspaper. *Captain Obvious*. Somebody had decided to take out the newest vampire in town, and it was sheer luck that they'd gotten Sam instead. It could have been Michael lying in the street.

And from the look on Michael's face, he was thinking the exact same thing.

Amelie was agitated. It wasn't really obvious, but Claire had seen her enough to know the difference. She moved more swiftly, and there was something less calm than usual in her eyes. Claire shivered a little when Amelie summoned her into a side room. It was small and empty, probably some kind of meeting room. Amelie didn't come alone; a tall blond vampire guy followed along and stood with his back to the door, a flesh-and-blood deadbolt. No getting out quickly, or at all, really.

"What happened?" Amelie demanded.

"I don't know," Claire said. "I was asleep. I woke up when—" *When I heard the sirens,* she'd been about to say, but again, that wasn't really true. She'd felt something, a flash of alarm that had come out of nowhere. And Shane and Eve had felt it, too. It normally would take a nuclear explosion to blast Shane out of sleep in the predawn hours, but he'd been wide-awake. "It was like some alarm went off in the house."

Amelie's face went very still and smooth. "Indeed."

"Why? Is that important?"

"Maybe. What else?"

"Nothing—we went downstairs. The sirens were going outside, and by the time we got down there it was all over, I guess. Sam was down on the road, and the cop was already there."

"You saw no one else?"

Claire shook her head.

"And your friends?" Amelie asked. "Where were they?"

It wasn't a casual question. Claire felt her pulse speed up, and tried to stay calm. If Amelie didn't believe her . . . "Asleep," she said firmly. "Shane was with me, and I saw Eve come out of her own room. They couldn't have done it."

Amelie shot her a look. Not one that made her feel any too secure. "I know how much you value their lives. But understand, Claire, if you lie for them, I will not forgive it."

"I'm not lying. They were in their rooms when I came out. The only one missing was Michael, and he was here with you."

Amelie turned away from her and paced the length of the room in slow, graceful steps. She looked so perfect, so . . . *together.* Unable to help it, Claire blurted out, "Aren't you worried about Sam?"

"I am more concerned about whoever attacked him not receiving another chance to do such harm," Amelie said. "Sam was old enough to survive such a thing—but only barely. If the stake had remained in his chest much longer, or the sun had burned him, he could not have survived. Had the assassin succeeded in attacking Michael, he would have died almost instantly. It would take decades for him to build up an immunity."

Claire's mouth opened, shut, and opened again when she found the words. "You mean—vampires *don't* die from stakes in the heart?"

"I mean that it takes quite a lot to kill one of us," Amelie said. "More every year we survive. You could put a stake through *my* heart, and I would simply pull it out and be very annoyed with you for ruining my wardrobe. If I failed to remove it within a few hours, it would damage me, perhaps seriously, but it would not destroy me in the way you're thinking. We are not so fragile, little Claire." Her teeth gleamed for a second like pearls as she smiled. "You would do well to tell your friends. Especially Shane."

"But—Brandon—"

Amelie's smile faded. "He was tortured," she said. "Burned with sunlight to reduce his resistance. By the time he was murdered, he had no more strength than a newborn. Shane's father understands us too well, you see."

And now, so did Claire. Which probably wasn't good. "The cops took Shane and Eve to the police station. I don't want anything to happen to them."

"I'm sure you don't. As I did not want anything to happen to my dear Samuel, who would willingly die for the rights of breathers in this town." Amelie's tone had gone cold and dark, and it gave Claire a deep-down trembling in her stomach. "I wonder if I have been too lenient. Allowed too much freedom."

"You don't own us," Claire whispered, and it seemed like the bracelet around her wrist tightened all of a sudden, pinching. She grabbed at it, wincing.

"Do I not?" Amelie asked coolly. She exchanged a glance with the vampire at the door. "Let her leave. I am done with her."

He bowed slightly and stepped out of the way. Claire resisted the urge to lunge for the exit. Being in the same room with Amelie, never mind her guard, was scary and intense, but she needed to at least try. "About Shane and Eve—"

"I don't interfere in human justice," Amelie said. "If they are innocent, then they will be released. Go now. I shall expect you to attend to Myrnin today, and I have arranged for some additional classes at university for you to attend. A list has been provided to you at your home this morning."

Claire hesitated.

"Sam was supposed to take me to Myrnin—who's going to—"

Amelie spun on her, and there was something wild and terrible in her eyes. "Little fool, don't bother me with trivia! Go *now*!"

Claire ran.

The house was empty when she arrived. No Shane, no Eve, and she hadn't seen Michael again at the Elders' Council building before Hans and Gretchen had bundled her off. Claire felt very alone, and she locked all the doors and made sure of all the windows.

The house felt . . . warm, somehow. Not in the hot-air sense, but cozy. Welcoming. Claire put her hand flat on the wall in the living room. "Can you hear me?" she asked, and then felt stupid. It was just a house, right? Just wood and bricks and concrete and wiring and pipes. How could it hear her?

But she couldn't shake the feeling that the *house*

had jabbed her awake this morning, her and Shane
and Eve. That it had been trying to warn them. The
house had saved Michael, after all, when he'd been
killed by Oliver; it had given him what life it could,
as a ghost. It *wanted* to help.

"I wish you could talk," she said. "I wish you could
tell me who tried to kill Sam."

But it couldn't, and she was talking to a dumbass
wall. Claire sighed, turned away, and caught a glimpse
of a piece of paper stirring in a breeze.

A breeze that wasn't there.

The paper was lying on the table, on top of Michael's guitar case. Claire grabbed it and read it,
barely daring to believe—

What was she thinking? That the house was going
to provide her with the name of Sam's would-be Van
Helsing? Of course not. It wasn't an answer to her
question.

It was a class schedule printout, stamped AMENDED
in big red letters. Her core classes were mostly gone;
the notation next to them showed that she'd tested
out.

What caught her attention, though, was what had
been scheduled in their place. *Advanced Biochem.
Philosophical Studies. Quantum Mechanics. Honors
Myth and Legend.*

Wow. Was it wrong that she felt her heart skip a
beat over that? Claire checked the times, then her
watch. She barely had an hour until the first new class,
but she couldn't go yet. Not until she'd heard from
Shane and Eve.

Thirty minutes later she was on the phone, trying
to get somebody to answer her questions at the police
station, when she heard the locks rattle on the door
and Eve's voice saying, "—dumbass," and the knot of
fear in Claire's chest began to loosen. "Yo, Claire!
You here?"

"Here," she said, and hung up to come down the
hall toward them.

Eve had her arm around Shane, half supporting him.

Claire blinked and focused on his face. At the swelling and bruises. "Oh God," she said, and hurried to his side to help Eve. "What happened?"

"Well, Big Man here decided to get a little shirty with Officer Fenton. You ever see *Bambi Versus Godzilla*? It was like that, only with more punches," Eve said. She sounded false and bright, like tinsel. "I tried to take him to the hospital and get checked out, but—"

"I'm fine," Shane gritted out. "I've had worse."

Probably true, but Claire still felt painfully helpless. She wanted to *do* something. Anything. She and Eve got Shane to the couch, where he collapsed against the cushions and closed his eyes. He looked pale, under the bruises. Claire stroked his matted hair anxiously, silently asking Eve what to do; Eve shrugged and mouthed, *Just let him rest.* She looked scared, though.

"Shane," Eve said aloud. "Seriously, I don't want to leave you here alone. You need to go to the hospital."

"Thanks, *Mom*," he said. "It's bruises. I think I'll live. Go on, get out of here." He reached up and captured Claire's hand, and his dark eyes opened. Well, one of them. The other was swelling shut. "What happened to you? You okay?"

"Nothing happened, I'm fine. I talked to Amelie." Claire pulled in a deep breath. "Sam's going to be okay, I think."

"And Michael? Michael was all right?" Eve asked.

"Yeah, he was all right. I'm sorry I couldn't get you out any earlier. Amelie—" Probably best not to get into how not-bothered Amelie had been by the idea of Eve and Shane behind bars. "She was busy with Sam."

Eve shrugged and shot Shane an exasperated look. "We probably would've been out of there in ten minutes if he'd behaved himself," she said. "Look, Shane, I know you're a hard-ass, but do you have to pick a fight with *every* jerk in the world? Can't you just choose half or something?"

"The scary thing? I *do* only pick fights with half of

them. That's how many there are." He groaned and adjusted himself to a more comfortable position on the couch. "Crap. Officer Asshole can really hit."

"Shane," Claire said, "really. Are you okay? I can take you to the hospital if you're not."

"They'd just give me an ice pack and send me home, minus a hundred bucks I don't have." He caught her hand in his. His knuckles were scraped. "What about you? Nothing bitten or broken, right?"

"No," she said softly. "Nothing bitten or broken. They're angry, and they're worried, but nobody tried to hurt me." She checked her watch, and her heart skipped and hammered faster. "Um . . . I have to go. I have class. You're sure you're—"

"If you ask me if I'm okay again, I'm going to smack myself in the face just to punish you," he said. "Go on. Eve, make sure she doesn't go wandering off by herself, okay?"

Eve already had her keys in her hand, and she was jingling them impatiently. "I'll do my best," Eve said. "Hey. This came special delivery for you." She tossed Claire a package with her name neatly lettered on it. Same handwriting, Claire thought, as the package that had held her bracelet.

This one held a sleek new cell phone, complete with MP3 player and a tiny little flip-open keypad for texting. It was on, and it was fully charged.

The note said, simply, *For safety.* The signature, of course, was Amelie's. Eve saw it, and raised her eyebrows. Claire quickly crumpled it up.

"Do I even want to know what that is?" Shane asked.

"Probably not," Eve said. "Claire, little girls who take candy from strangers in Morganville get hurt. Or worse."

"She's not a stranger," Claire said. "And I really need a phone."

The classes were nothing like Claire had experienced before. It was as if she'd finally come to school.

From the first moment of the first class, the professors seemed bright, engaged; they seemed to *see* her. Even better, they *challenged* her. She fumbled her way nervously through Advanced Biochem, made notes of the books she needed, and did the same in Philosophy. There was a lot of talking in Philosophy, and she didn't understand half of it, but it sounded a lot more interesting than the droning voices of her core class instructors.

She felt exhilarated by the time her late lunch break rolled around . . . she felt, in fact, *alive.* She was happy as she hunted for used copies of the textbooks she needed, and even happier when she discovered that, mysteriously, she had a scholarship account set up to cover the costs. It even came with its own cash card.

She bought a new long-sleeve T-shirt, too. And some disposable razors. And some shampoo.

Scary, how good it felt having money in her pocket.

By the time three p.m rolled around, she was starting to wonder if she was expected to head out for Myrnin's house on her own, but she decided to wait. Nobody had told her of a change of plan, so she headed over to the UC to get in some study time while she waited. The big main study room was packed, and somebody was playing guitar in the corner of the room—quite a big crowd over there, clapping between songs. Whoever it was played well—something complicated and classical, then a pop song right after. Claire was spreading out her books on the table when she heard a song that sounded familiar, and stood up on her chair to get a better look over the heads of the people gathered in the corner.

As she'd suspected, it was Michael. He was sitting down to play, but she could see his head and shoulders. He looked up and met her eyes, nodded, then went back to focus on the music. Claire jumped down, wiped her dusty footprints off the wooden chair, and sat. Her brain was racing. *Michael* was here. Why? Was it just a coincidence? Or was it something else?

She sat down and tried to concentrate on the properties of low frequency wave modes in magnetized plasma, which was frankly pretty cool. The physics of stars. She couldn't wait for the lab demonstrations . . . the reading was slow going, but interesting. It linked to another thing about plasma physics that had caught her attention: confinement and transport. It might have been coincidence, but somehow she felt there was something there she ought to understand. Something that related to what Myrnin had been telling her about recomposition, which was a key element in alchemy. Was it possible there really was a link between the two?

Plasma is charged particles. It can be controlled and influenced by shaped magnetic fields. Plasma was the raw state between matter and energy . . . between one form and another.

Reconstitution.

It hit her, suddenly, what Myrnin had discovered. *The doorways.* They were shaped magnetic fields, holding a tiny, pliable field of plasma held in a steady state. But how did he make them into portable wormholes? Because that was what they had to be, to bend space like that . . . and the plasma couldn't be regular plasma, could it? Low-heat plasma? Was that even possible?

Claire was so absorbed that she didn't even hear the chair scrape back across from her, didn't know someone had sat down, until a hand grabbed the book propped in front of her and pushed it down.

"Hey, Claire," said Jason, Eve's nutty brother. He looked weaselly and pale—not Goth-pale, sick-pale. Anemic. There were crusty sores on his neck, and his eyes were wide and red-veined, and he looked high. Really, crazy high. He also hadn't had a bath or been near a Laundromat in a few days or weeks; he smelled filthy and rotten. Ugh. "How you doing?"

She couldn't quite think what the right move would be. Scream? She closed the book and held on to it—it was pretty heavy, and would make a decent blunt object—and darted a look around. The UC was filled with people. Granted, Michael's playing was the center of attention at the moment, but there were plenty of others walking around, talking, studying. From where she sat, Claire could see Eve at the coffee bar, smiling and pulling espresso shots.

It was as though Jason were invisible or something. Nobody was paying him the slightest bit of attention.

"Hi," she said. "What do you want?"

"World peace," he said. "You're pretty."

You're really not. She didn't, and couldn't, say it. She just waited. *I'm perfectly safe here. There are a lot of people, Michael's right over there, and Eve . . .*

"Did you hear me?" Jason asked. "I said, you're pretty."

"Thank you." Her mouth felt dry. She was scared, and she couldn't even think why, really, except what Eve had told her about Jason. He did look dangerous. Those scabs on his throat—had he been bitten? "I have to go."

"I'll walk you to class," Jason said. Somehow, he made that sound filthy, like some porn movie come-on. "I always wanted to carry some hot college girl's books."

"No," she said. "I can't. I mean—I'm not going to class. But I have to go." And why couldn't she just tell him to leave her alone? *Why?*

Jason blew her a kiss. "Go on. But don't blame me when the next dead girl shows up in the trash because you wouldn't do me a simple favor."

She was in the act of standing up when he said it, and she just . . . stopped. Stopped moving, and stared. "What?" she asked, stupidly. Her brain, which had been moving at light speed while skipping from one physics problem to the next, felt sluggish now. "What did you say?"

"Not that I did anything. But if I had, I'd be planning another one. Unless somebody talked to me and convinced me to stop, for instance. Or I made a deal."

Claire felt cold. Worse, she felt *alone.* Jason wasn't doing anything—he was just sitting there, talking. But she felt violated, and horribly exposed. *Michael's right over there. You can hear him playing. He's right there. You're safe.*

"All right," she said, and swallowed a mouthful of what felt like dust and tacks. She sank slowly back into her chair. "I'm listening."

Jason leaned forward, rested his arms on the table, and lowered his voice. "See, it's like this, Claire. I want my big sister to understand what she did to me when she sent me to that place. You know what a jail is like in Morganville? It's as though some third-world country threw it out for prisoner abuse. *Eve put me there.* And she didn't even try to save me."

Claire's fingers felt numb, she was holding her book so tightly. She forced herself to relax. "I'm sorry," she said. "That must have been bad."

"Bad? Bitch, are you even *listening*?" He kept on staring at her, and, as though he were dead, he never blinked. "I was supposed to be his, you know. Brandon's. He was going to make me a vampire someday, but now he's dead, and I'm screwed. Now I'm just waiting around for somebody to put me back in jail, and guess what, Claire? I'm not going. Not without a little fun first."

He grabbed her wrist, and she opened her mouth to scream. . . .

All of a sudden he had a knife, and he was pressing it to her wrist. "Hold still," he said. "I'm not done talking. You move, you bleed."

She was going to yell anyway, but when it made it to her lips it died into a weak little yelp. Jason smiled, and he tossed a filthy-looking handkerchief on top of her wrist and the knife, covering it up. "There," he said. "Now nobody's going to notice, not that they'd care. Not in Morganville. But just in case there are any dumbass heroes, let's keep this between just us."

She was shaking now. "Let me go." Somehow, her voice stayed low and steady. "I won't say anything."

"Oh, come *on.* You'll run to your friends, and then you'll run to the cops. Probably those two dicks Hess and Lowe. They've been out to get me since I was a kid, did you know that? Sons of bitches." He was sweating. A milky drop ran down the side of his pale face and splashed on his camouflage jacket. "I hear you're in good with the vamps. That true?"

"What?" The knife pressed harder against her wrist, hot and painful, and she thought about how easy it would be for him to cut right through her veins. Her whole arm was shaking, but somehow, she managed to hold still against an overwhelming urge to try to yank her wrist away. It would only do the job for him. "I'm—yes. I'm Protected. You'll get in trouble for this, Jason."

He had a truly creepy smile, a rubbery snarl that didn't affect his hot, strange eyes at all. "I was born in trouble," he said. "Bring it on. You tell whatever vamp put the mark on you that I know something. Something that could blow this town in half. And I'll sell it for two things: rights to do whatever I want to my sister, and a ticket out of Morganville."

Oh God oh God oh God. He wants to bargain. For Eve's life.

"I'm not making any deals," she said, and knew it was probably a death sentence. "I'm not going to let you hurt Eve."

He actually blinked. It made him look almost human, for a second, and Claire remembered that he wasn't much older than she. "How you going to stop me, cupcake? Hit me with your book bag?"

"If I have to."

He sat back, staring at her, and then he laughed. Loudly. It was a harsh, metallic clatter of a laugh, and she thought, *Oh God, he's going to kill me,* but then he lifted up the handkerchief covering her wrist and like a magic trick, the knife was gone. There was a trickle of blood dripping from the shallow cut in her skin, and she was starting to feel the burn.

"You know what, Claire?" Jason asked. He got up, stuck his hands in his jacket pockets, and smiled at her again. "I'm going to like you a lot. You're a scream."

He strolled off, and Claire tried to get up and see where he was going, but she couldn't. Her knees wouldn't cooperate. He was out of sight in seconds.

Claire looked at the coffee bar. Eve was standing there, motionless, staring right at her with huge dark eyes, and even without the Goth rice powder she'd have been pale as death.

Eve mouthed, *You okay?*

Claire nodded.

She really wasn't, though, and the cut on her wrist wouldn't stop bleeding. She dug in her backpack and found an adhesive bandage—she always kept them, just in case she got blisters on her feet from all the walking. That seemed to do the trick.

She was smoothing it in place when she felt someone standing over her, and jumped, expecting the return of Jason, complete with psycho stabbing attack.

But it was Michael. He had his guitar case in his hand, and he looked—great. Relaxed, somehow, in a way that she'd never really seen him. There was even a slight flush of color in his face, and his eyes were shining.

But that quickly faded, and he frowned. "You're bleeding," he said. "What happened?"

Claire sighed and held up her wrist to show him the bandage. "Man, you would be so embarrassed if I said it was something else." Michael looked blank. "I'm a girl, Michael, it could have been all natural, you know. Tampons?"

Vampire or not, he was *such* a guy, and his expression was priceless—a combination of embarrassment and nausea. "Oh crap, I hadn't really thought that through. Sorry. Not really used to this yet. So—what happened?"

"Paper cut," she said.

"Claire."

She sighed. "Don't freak, okay? It was Eve's brother, Jason. I think he just wanted to scare me."

Michael's eyes widened, and his head turned fast, searching the coffee bar for Eve. When he saw her, the relief that spread over his face was painful—and it didn't last long before it curdled into something grim. "I can't believe he'd come here. Why can't they catch this jerk?"

"Maybe somebody doesn't want to," she said. "He's only killing human girls. *If* he's the one doing it." Although he'd pretty much confessed, hadn't he? And the knife was a big clue. "We can talk about it later. I need to get—" She remembered, just in time, that she couldn't talk to Michael about Myrnin. "Get to class," she said. She hadn't really thought Amelie would make her go alone, and she wasn't sure she could do it. Myrnin was fascinating, most of the time, but then when he turned . . . no, she couldn't go alone. What if something happened? Sam wouldn't be there to help get him off her.

Michael didn't move. "I know where you're going," he said. "I'm your ride."

She blinked. "You're my —what?"

He lowered his voice, even though nobody was paying attention. "I'll take you where you're supposed to go. And I'll wait for you."

Amelie had told him, Claire found out on the way to Michael's new car. She'd needed to, apparently; she hadn't trusted any vampire but Sam with the information and access to Myrnin, but Michael had an investment in Claire's well-being, and Sam was going to be out of action for a couple of days at least. "But he's okay?" Claire asked.

Michael opened the door to the parking garage for her, an automatic gesture that he'd probably learned from his grandfather, once upon a time. He had some of Sam's mannerisms, and they had the same walk. "Yeah," Michael said. "He nearly died, though. People—vampires—are pretty wired right now. They want the one who staked him, and they don't really care how it happens. I made Shane promise to keep his ass inside, and not to go out alone."

"You really think he'll keep his word?"

Michael shrugged and opened the door of a standard-issue, dark vampire-tinted sedan, exactly the same as the one Sam had driven. A Ford, as it happened. Nice to know the vamps were buying American. "I tried," he said. "Shane doesn't listen to much of anything I have to say. Not anymore."

Claire got into the car and buckled in. As Michael climbed in the driver's side, she said, "It's not your fault. He's just not dealing with it very well. I don't know what we can do about that."

"Nothing," Michael said, and started the car. "We can't do anything about it at all."

It was a short drive, of course, and as far as Claire could tell from the dimly seen streets outside, Michael took the same route Sam had to the alley, and Myrnin's cave. Michael parked the car at the curb. When she got out, though, Claire realized something, and bent to look into the dim interior of the car, then ducked back inside.

"Crap," she said. "You can't come inside, can you? You can't go out in the sun!"

Michael shook his head. "I'm supposed to wait out here for you until the sun goes down; then I'll come in. Amelie said she'd make sure you were safe until then."

"But—" Claire bit her lip. It wasn't Michael's fault. There were about three hours of sun left, so she was just going to have to watch her own back for a while. "Okay. See you after dark."

She closed the car door. When she straightened she saw that Gramma Katherine Day was on the porch of her big Founder House, rocking and sipping what looked like iced tea. Claire waved. Gramma Day nodded.

"You bein' careful?" she called.

"Yes ma'am!"

"I told the queen, I don't like her putting you down there with that thing. I told her," Gramma Day said, with a fierce stab of her finger for emphasis. "You come on up here and have some iced tea with me, girl. That thing down there, he'll wait. He don't know where he is half the time, anyway."

Claire smiled and shook her head. "I can't, ma'am. I'm supposed to be there on time. Thank you, though." She turned toward the alley, then had a thought. "Oh—who's the queen?"

Gramma made an impatient fly-waving gesture. "*Her,* of course. The White Queen. You're just like Alice, you know. Down the rabbit hole with the Mad Hatter."

Claire didn't dare think about that too much, because the phrase *Off with her head!* loomed way too close. She gave Gramma Day another polite smile and wave, hitched her backpack higher on her shoulder, and went to night school.

8

Amelie had made sure she was safe, all right. She'd done it by locking Myrnin up.

Claire dropped her backpack at the bottom of the stairs—where it was easy to grab in midrun—and spotted a new addition to the lab: a cage. And Myrnin was inside it.

"Oh my God—" She took a few steps toward him, navigating around the usual haphazard stacks of books, and bit her lip. It was, as far as she could tell, the same cage that the vampires had used to lock up Shane in Founder's Square—heavy black bars, and the whole thing was on wheels. Vampire-proof, hopefully. Whoever had locked Myrnin in had been nice enough to give him a whole pile of books, and a comfy (if threadbare) tangle of blankets and faded pillows. He was lounging in the corner on the cushions, with a pair of old-fashioned, Benjamin Franklin–style glasses perched on the end of his hooked nose. He was reading.

"You're late," he said, as he turned a page. Claire's mouth opened and closed, but she couldn't think of a thing to say. "Oh, don't fret about the cage. It's for your precaution, of course. Since Samuel isn't here to watch over you." He turned another page, but his eyes weren't moving to follow text. He was pretending to read, and somehow that was worse than heartbreaking. "Amelie's idea. I can't say that I really approve."

She finally was able to say, "I'm sorry."

Myrnin shrugged and closed the book, which he dropped with a bang on the pile next to him. "I've been in cages before this," he said. "And no doubt I will be let out once your appointed guardian is here to chaperone. In the meantime, let's continue with our instruction. Pull a chair close. You'll excuse me if I don't get up, but I'm a bit taller than—" He reached up and rapped the bars overhead. "Amelie tells me you have enrolled in advanced placement classes."

Claire gratefully took that as an opportunity not to think about how disturbingly reassuring this was, seeing him locked up like an animal in a cage, because of *her.* She read off her class schedule, and answered his questions, which were sharply worded and a strange mix of expert knowledge and complete ignorance. He understood philosophy and biochem; he didn't know anything at all about quantum mechanics, until she explained the basics, and then he nodded.

"Myth and Legend?" he echoed, baffled, when she read off the class title. "Why would Amelie feel it necessary . . . ah, no matter. I'm sure she has reason. Your essay?" He held out his hand. Claire dug the stapled computer printout from her bag and handed it over. Six pages, single spaced. The best she could do on the history of a subject she was only just now starting to understand. "I'll read it later. And the books I gave you?"

Claire went to her backpack and pulled them out, then came back to her chair. "I read through *Aureus* and *The Golden Chain of Homer.*"

"Did you understand them?"

"Not—really."

"That's because alchemy is a very secretive field of study. Rather like being a Mason—are there still Masons?" When she nodded, Myrnin looked oddly relieved. "Well, that's good. The consequences would be quite terrible, you know, if there weren't. As to alchemy, I can teach you how to translate the codes that were spoken and written, but I'm more concerned that you learn the mechanics than the philosophy. You do understand the methods outlined in the texts for constructing a calcining furnace, yes?"

"I think so. But why can't we just order what we need? Or buy it?"

Myrnin flicked the silver ring on his right hand into the bars of his cell, setting up a metallic ringing. "None of that. Modern children are fools, slaves to the work of others, dependent for everything. Not you. You will learn how to build your tools as well as use them."

"You want me to be an *engineer*?"

"Is it not a useful thing for one who studies physics to understand such practical applications?"

She stared at him doubtfully. "You're not going to make me get an anvil and make my own screwdrivers or anything, are you?"

Myrnin smiled slowly. "What a good idea! I'll consider it. Now. I have an experiment I'd like to try. Are you ready?"

Probably not. "Yes sir."

"Move that bookcase—" He pointed to a leaning monstrosity of shelves that looked ready to collapse. It was groaning with volumes, of course. "Push it out of the way."

Claire wasn't at all sure the thing would hold together to *be* pushed, but she did as he said. It was better built than it looked, and to her surprise, when she'd pushed it aside, she found a small arched doorway. It was secured with a big heart-shaped iron lock.

"Open it," he said, and picked up the book he'd dropped upon her entrance, leafing randomly through the pages.

"Where's the key?"

"No idea." He flipped faster, frowning at the words. "Look around."

Claire looked around the lab in complete frustration. "In *here*?" Where was she supposed to start? It was all piles and stacks and half-open drawers, nothing in any order at all that she'd been able to determine so far. "Can you give me a hint, at least?"

"If I remembered, I would." Myrnin's voice was dry, but just a little sad, too. She shot him a glance out of the corner of her eye. He folded the book closed again and stared out of the cage—not at her, or at anything, really. There was a careful blankness to his face. "Claire?"

"Yeah?" She pulled open the first drawer near the door. It was full of bottles of what looked like dust, none of them labeled. A spider scuttled frantically out of sight into the darker recesses, and she made a face and slammed it shut.

"Can you tell me why I'm in this cage?" He sounded odd now, strangely calm with something underneath. Claire pulled in a deep breath and kept looking in the drawers. She didn't look directly at him. "I don't like cages. Bad things have happened to me in cages."

"Amelie says you have to stay in there for a while," she said. "Remember? It's to help us."

"I don't remember." His voice was warm and soft and regretful. "I'd like to get out of here. Could you open it, please?"

"No," she said. "I don't have the—"

Keys, except that she did. There was a ring of them sitting right there in front of her, half-hidden by a leaning tower of loose, yellowing pages. Three keys. One was a great big iron skeleton key, and she was instantly almost sure that it fit the big heart-shaped lock on the door behind the bookcase. The other one was newer, still big and clunky, and it had to be the key to Myrnin's cage.

The third was a tiny, delicate silver key, like the kind that opened diaries and suitcases.

Claire reached out for the key ring and pulled it toward her, trying to do it silently. He heard, of course. He got up from the corner of the cage and came to the front, where he held on to the bars. "Ah, excellent," he said. "Claire, please open the door. I can't show you what you need to do if I'm locked in this cage."

God, she couldn't look at him, she just couldn't. "I'm not supposed to do that," she said, and sorted out the big iron skeleton key. It felt cold and rough to her fingers, and old. Really old. "You wanted me to open this door, right?"

"Claire. Look at me." He sounded so *sad*. She heard the soft ringing chime of his ring on the bars when he gripped them again. "Claire, *please*."

She turned away from him and put the key into the heart-shaped lock.

"Claire, *don't open that*!"

"You told me to!"

"*Don't!*" Myrnin rattled the bars of his cage, and even though they were solid iron, she heard them rattle. "It's *my* door! *My* escape! Come here and release me! *Now*!"

She checked her watch. Not enough time, not nearly enough; it was still at least an hour to sunset, maybe more. Michael was still stuck in the car. "I can't," she said. "I'm sorry."

The sound Myrnin made then was enough to make her glad that she was across the room. She'd never heard a lion roar, not in person, but somehow she imagined that it would sound like that, all wild animal rage. It shredded her confidence. She closed her eyes and tried not to listen, but he was talking; she couldn't understand what he was saying now, but it was a constant, vicious stream in a language she didn't know. The tone, though—you couldn't *not* get the evil undercurrents.

He'd kill her if he got hold of her now. Thank God, the cage was strong enough to . . .

He snarled something low and guttural, and she heard something metal snap with a high, vibrating sound.

The cage wasn't strong enough.

Myrnin was bending the bars away from the lock.

Claire spun, key still in her hand, and saw him rip at a weak point in the cage as though it were wet paper. How could he do that? How could he be that strong? Wasn't he hurting himself?

He was. She could see blood on his hands.

It came to her with a jolt that if he got out of that cage, he could do the same thing to *her*.

She needed to get out.

Claire moved around the lab table, squeezed past two towering stacks of volumes, and tripped over a broken three-legged stool. She hit the floor painfully, on top of a pile of assorted junk—pieces of old leather, some bricks, a couple of withered old plants she guessed Myrnin was saving for botanical salvage. Man, that hurt. She rolled over on her side, gasping, and climbed to her feet.

She heard a long, slow creak of metal, and stopped for a fatal second to look over her shoulder.

The cage door was open, and Myrnin was out. He was still wearing his little Ben Franklin glasses, but what was in his eyes looked like something that had crawled straight out of hell.

"Oh crap," she whispered, and looked desperately toward the stairs.

Too far. *Way* too far, too many obstacles between her and safety, and he could move like a snake. He'd get there first.

She was closer to the door with the lock on it than the stairs, and the key was still clutched tightly in her hand. She'd have to abandon her book bag; no way to get to it now.

She didn't have time to think about it. The cut Jason had put on her wrist was still fresh; Myrnin could still smell it, and it was ringing the dinner bell loud and clear.

She kicked stacks of books out of the way, jumped over the pile of junk, and, with the key outstretched, raced for the locked door. Her hands were shaking, and it took two tries to get the oversized key into the hole; when she started to turn it there was a terrible moment of utter panic because *it wouldn't turn. . . .*

And then it did, a smooth metallic slide of levers and pins, and the door swung open.

On the other side was her own living room, and Shane was sitting on the couch with his back to her, playing a video game.

Claire paused, utterly off balance. That couldn't be real, could it? She couldn't be seeing him, right there, but she could hear all of the computerized grunts and punches and wet bloody sounds from whatever fight game he had on. She could *smell* the house. Chili. He'd made chili. He still hadn't taken some of his boxes back upstairs. They were piled in the corner.

"Shane," she whispered, and reached out, through the doorway. She could feel something there, like a slight pressure, and the hair on her arm shivered and prickled.

Shane put the game on pause, and slowly stood up. "Claire?" He was looking in the wrong place; he was looking up, at the staircase.

But he'd heard her. And that meant she could just step right through and she'd be safe.

She never got the chance.

Myrnin's hand landed on her shoulder, dragged her back, and as Shane started to turn toward them, Myrnin slammed the door and turned the key in the lock.

She didn't dare move. He was crazy; she could see it. There was nothing in him that recognized her at all. Amelie's warnings screamed through her head, and Sam's. She'd underestimated Myrnin, and that was what had gotten all the other would-be apprentices killed.

Myrnin was shaking, and his broken hands were crunched into fists. His blood was dripping on an open copy of an old chemistry textbook that lay by his feet.

"Who are you?" he whispered. The accent she'd noted the first time she'd met him was back, and strong. Really strong. "Child, what brings you here?

Do you not understand your danger? Who is your Patron? Were you sent as a gift?"

She closed her eyes for a second, then opened them and looked right into his eyes and said, "You're Myrnin, and I'm Claire; I'm your friend. I'm your friend, okay? You should let me help you. You hurt yourself."

She pointed to his injured fingers. Myrnin looked down, and he seemed surprised, as if he hadn't felt it at all. Which maybe he hadn't.

He took two steps backward, ran into a lab table, and knocked over a stand that held empty glass test tubes. They fell and shattered on the dirty stone floor.

Myrnin staggered, then sank down to sit against the wall, his face covered by bloody hands, and began to rock back and forth. "It's wrong," he moaned. "There was something important, something I had to do. I can't remember what it was."

Claire watched him, still scared to death, and then sank down to a crouch across from him. "Myrnin," she said. "The door. The one I opened. Where does it go?"

"Door? Doorways. Moments in time, just moments, none of it stays; it flows like blood, you know, just like blood. I tried to bottle it, but it doesn't stay fresh. Time, I mean. Blood turns, and so does time. What's your name?"

"Claire, sir. My name's Claire."

He let his head fall back against the wall, and there were bloody tears running down his cheeks. "Don't trust me, Claire. Don't ever trust me." He bounced the back of his head off the wall with enough force to make Claire wince.

"I—no, sir. I won't."

"How long have I been your friend?"

"Not that long."

"I don't have friends," he said hollowly. "You don't, you know, when you're as old as I am. You have competitors, and you have allies, but not friends, never. You're too young, far too young to understand that." He closed his eyes for a moment, and when he opened them, he looked mostly sane. Mostly. "Amelie wants you to learn from me, yes? So you are my student?"

This time, Claire just nodded. Whatever the fit was, it was leaving him, and he was empty and tired and sad again. He took off his glasses, folded them, and put them in the pocket of his coat.

"You won't be able to do it," he said. "You can't possiby learn quickly enough. I nearly killed you tonight, and next time I won't be able to stop. The others—" He stopped, looked briefly sick, and cleared his throat. "I'm not—I wasn't always like this, Claire. Please understand. Unlike many of my kind, I never wanted to be a monster. I only wanted to learn, and this was a way to learn forever."

Claire bit her lip. "I can understand that," she said. "I—Amelie wants me to help you, and learn from you. Do you think I'm smart enough?"

"Oh, you're smart enough. Could you master the skills, given enough time? Perhaps. And you'll have no choice in the matter; she'll keep you coming until you learn, or I destroy you." Myrnin slowly lifted his head and looked at her. Rational again, and very steady. "Did I remind you not to trust me?"

"Yes, sir."

"It's good advice, but just this once, ignore it and allow me to help you."

"Help . . . ?"

Myrnin stood up, in that eerie boneless way that he seemed to have, and rummaged around through the glass jars and beakers and test tubes until he found something that looked like red salt. He shook the container—it was about the size of a spice jar—and opened it to extract one red crystal. He touched it to his tongue, shut his eyes for a second, and smiled.

"Yes," he said. "I thought so." He recapped it and held it out to her. "Take it."

She did. It felt surprisingly heavy. "What is it?"

"I have no idea what to call it," he said. "But it'll work."

"What do I do with it?"

"Shake a small amount into your palm, like so." He reached out for her hand. She pulled away, curling her fingers closed, and Myrnin looked briefly wounded. "No, you're right. You do it. I apologize." He handed her the shaker and made an encouraging gesture. She hesitantly turned the shaker upside down over her palm. A few red chunky crystals poured out. He wanted her to keep going, so she did, making quick jerks with the container until there was maybe half a teaspoon of the stuff piled up.

Myrnin took the shaker from her, set it back where he'd found it, and nodded at her. "Go on," he said. "Take it."

"Excuse me?"

He mimed popping it into his mouth.

"I—um—what is it, again?"

This time, Myrnin rolled his eyes in frustration. "Take it, Claire! We don't have much time. My periods of lucidity are shorter now. I can't guarantee I won't slip again. Soon. This will help."

"I don't understand. How is this stuff supposed to help?"

He didn't tell her again; he just pleaded silently with her, his whole expression open and hopeful, and she finally put her hand to her mouth and tentatively tasted one of the crystals.

It tasted like strawberry salt, with a bitter after-flavor. She felt an instant, tiny burst of ice-cold clarity, like a strobe light going off in a darkened room full of beautiful, glittering things.

"Yes," Myrnin breathed. "Now you see."

This time, she licked up more of the crystals. Four or five of them. The bitterness was stronger, barely offset by the strawberries, and the reaction was even faster. It was as though she'd been asleep, and all of a sudden she was awake. Gloriously, dizzyingly awake.

The world was so sharp she felt as though even the dull battered wood of the table could cut her.

Myrnin picked up a book at random and opened it. He held it up in front of her, and it was like another burst of light in the darkness, brilliant and beautiful, *oh, so pretty,* the way the words curved themselves around each other and cut into her brain. It was painful and perfect, and she read as fast as she could.

> *The essence of gold is the essence of Sun, and the essence of silver is the essence of Moon. You must work with each of these according to its properties, gold in the daylight, silver in the night . . .*

It all made sense to her. Total sense. Alchemy was nothing but a poet's explanation of the way matter and energy interacted, the way different surfaces vibrated at different speeds; it was physics, nothing but physics, and she could understand how to use it now.

And then . . . then it was as though the bulbs all dimmed again.

"Go on, take it," Myrnin said. "The dose in your hand will last for an hour or so. In that time, I can teach you a great deal. Enough, perhaps, for us to understand where we should be going."

This time, Claire didn't hesitate licking up every last bit of the red crystals.

Myrnin was right; the crystals lasted for a little more than an hour. He took some as well, one at a time, carefully measuring them out and making them last until finally even a red crystal couldn't drive the growing confusion out of his eyes. He was getting anxious by the end. Claire started closing the books and stacking them up on the table—the two of them were sitting cross-legged on the floor, practically buried in volumes. Myrnin had jumped her from one book to another, pulling out a paragraph here, a chapter there, a chart from physics, and a page from something so old he had to teach her the language before she could understand.

I learned languages. I learned . . . I learned so much. He'd shown her a diagram, and it hadn't been just a diagram—it had been three dimensional and as intricate as a snowflake. Morganville hadn't just happened; it had been planned. Planned around the vampires. Planned *by* the vampires, carried out by Myrnin and Amelie. The Founder Houses, they were part of it—thirteen bright, hard nodes of power in the web, holding together a complex pattern of energy. It could move people from one place to another, via the doorways, although Claire didn't yet understand how to control them. But the web could do more. It could change memories. It could even keep people away, if Amelie wanted it to do that.

Myrnin had shown her the journals, too, with all his research conducted over the last seventy years into the vampire's sickness. It was chilling, the way his notes degenerated from meticulous to scrawls at the end, and sometimes into nonsense.

Some part of her still wondered if she shouldn't just stand by and let it happen, but Myrnin . . . what he knew, what he'd accomplished—and she'd never learned so much, never, not from anyone.

Maybe just a little. *Maybe I could help him just a little.*

The influence of the crystals was dimming now, and Claire felt horribly tired. There was a steady ache in her muscles, a feverish throb that told her this stuff wasn't exactly kind to the human body. She could feel every heartbeat pounding through her head, and everything looked so *dark.* So . . . so confusing.

She felt a breath of air stir against her cheek, and she turned toward the stairs. Michael was descending, moving faster than she'd ever seen him, and he came to a fast halt when he saw her sitting beside Myrnin.

"He's supposed to be—"

"Locked up in a cage? Yeah, I know." Claire knew she sounded bitter. She didn't care. "He's sick, Michael. He's not an animal. And anyway, even if you lock him up, he'll get out."

Michael looked young to her, all of a sudden, although he was older than she was. And a vampire, on top of that. "Claire, get up and come to me. Please."

"Why? He's not going to hurt me."

"He can't help what he does. Look, Sam told me how many people he's killed—"

"He's a *vamp,* Michael. Of course he's—"

"How many he's killed *in the last two years.* It's more than all the other vampires in Morganville combined. *You're not safe.* Now, get up and walk over here."

"He's right," Myrnin said. He was losing it, Claire could see that, but he was desperately hanging on to being the man who'd been with her for the last hour. The gentle, funny, sweet one, ablaze with excitement and passion for showing her his world. "It's time for you to go." He smiled, showing teeth—not vampire teeth. It was a very human kind of expression. "I do all right on my own, Claire, or at least there's rarely anyone for me to harm. Amelie will send someone to look after me. And I usually can't leave here, once I—forget things. It's too difficult for me to find the keys, and I can't remember how to use them once I have them. But I never forget how to kill. Your friend is right. You should go, please. Now. Continue your studies."

It was stupid, but she hated leaving him like this, with all the light going out in his eyes and the clouds of fear and confusion rolling in.

She didn't mean to do it; it just happened.

She hugged him.

It was like hugging a tree; he was so surprised, he was as stiff as a block of wood. She wasn't actually sure how long it had been since anybody had touched him like this. For a second he resisted her, and then his arms went around her, and she felt him heave a great sigh. Still not a hug, not really, but it was as close as he was likely to get.

"Go away, little bird," he whispered. "Hurry."

She backed away. His eyes were strange again, and she knew they were out of time. *Someday, he won't come back. He'll just be the beast.*

Michael was beside her. She hadn't heard him cross the room, but his hand closed around hers, and there was real compassion in his face. Not for Myrnin, though. For her.

"You heard him," Michael said. "Hurry."

She bumped into the table, and the small jar of red crystals shuddered a little, nearly tipping over. She grabbed it to put it back upright, and then thought, *What if he loses this? He loses stuff all the time.*

She would only be keeping it safe, that was all. It helped him, right? So she ought to make sure he didn't knock it over or throw it away or something.

She slipped it into her pocket. She didn't think Myrnin saw, and she knew Michael didn't. Claire felt a hot burst of something—shame? Embarrassment? Excitement? *I should put it back.* But really, she'd never find it again if he moved it around. Myrnin wouldn't remember. He wouldn't even know it was gone.

She kept looking back, all the way up the stairs. By the time they were halfway out, Myrnin had already forgotten them, and he was restlessly flipping through a pile of books, muttering anxiously to himself.

Gone already.

He looked up at them and snarled, and she saw the hard glint of fangs.

She hurried to the door at the top of the stairs.

9

Michael wasn't talking to her, and that was bad. He wasn't sullen, like Shane got from time to time; he was just thoughtful. That made the drive uneasily quiet. It was fully dark out, not that she could see through the window tinting, anyway.

The world didn't seem real to her anymore, and her head ached.

"This is the deal you made with Amelie," Michael said. "To work for him."

"No. I made the deal with Amelie; *then* she told me to work for him. Or learn from him."

"Is there a difference?"

Claire smiled. "Yeah. I don't get paid."

"Brilliant plan, genius. Is *anybody* paying you?"

Actually, she had no idea. The thought hadn't occurred to her, to ask Amelie for money. Was that normal, to get paid for a thing like this? She supposed it was, if she was supposed to risk her life with Myrnin on a regular basis. "I'll ask," she offered.

"No," Michael said grimly. "*I'll* ask. I want to talk to Amelie about this whole thing, anyway."

"Don't get all older-brother on me, Michael. It's not safe. You may be one of them now, but you're not—"

"One of them? Yeah, I know that. But you're way too young for this, Claire, and you don't know what you're doing. You didn't grow up in this town; you don't understand the risks."

"What, death? I understand that one pretty well already." She was feeling tired and achy, but also strangely annoyed with Michael's protectiveness. "Look, I'm fine, okay? Besides, I learned a lot today. She'll be happy, trust me."

"Amelie's mood isn't what bothers me," Michael said. "It's you. You're changing, Claire."

She looked straight at him. "Like you haven't?"

"Cheap shot. Look, I'm sick of having to tiptoe around Shane. Don't make me do it with you, too." Ah, now Michael was annoyed, too. Great.

"Tell you what? I'll stop nagging you about your life if you'll stay out of mine. You're not my brother, you're not my dad—"

"No," he interrupted. "I'm the guy who says if you get to stay in the house."

He wouldn't. He *wouldn't*. "Michael—"

"You made a deal with Amelie without talking to anyone, and then you covered it up. Look, the only reason you even came clean was because I saw the bracelet. If I hadn't, you'd still be lying to us. That doesn't exactly make you the ideal housemate." Michael paused for a second. "And then there's Shane."

"How am I to blame for *Shane*?"

"You're not. But I can't deal with both of you, not now. So just straighten up, Claire. No more lying, and no more risk-taking, all right? I'll convince Amelie to let you out of these sessions with Myrnin. You're too young to be doing this; she ought to know that."

No more lying. No more risk-taking. Claire shifted and felt the bottle in her pocket, and had a flash of that perfect clarity again. She wondered what Michael would have to say about her letting Myrnin give her the crystals. Probably nothing. He was talking about throwing her out of the house, right? So he probably didn't care at all.

The car slowed and turned, then bumped down a rutted drive. Home.

Claire bolted before Michael could say anything else to her.

Shane was in the kitchen, pouring himself a beer. He toasted her silently, took a sip, and nodded toward a pot on the stove. "Chili," he said. "Extra garlic."

Michael was closing the kitchen door, and he sighed. "When is this going to stop?"

"When you quit sucking blood?"

"Shane—"

"Don't get pissy. I made yours garlic-free." Shane looked at her again, and frowned a little. "You okay?"

"Sure. Why wouldn't I be?"

"Just—I don't know. Whatever." He slung an arm over her shoulders and kissed her on the forehead. "Bad day, probably."

Let's see, she'd been threatened by Eve's brother, had her wrist cut, and then played keep-away with Myrnin for hours. Did that qualify as a bad day in Morganville? Probably not. No body count.

Not yet, anyway.

Michael pushed past them and through the door into the living room. Claire pulled free of Shane's arm and went to the stove to ladle herself a bowl of chili. It smelled hot and delicious. But mostly hot. She tasted a drop and nearly choked; was it usually this molten-lava wicked spicy? Everything felt raw to her right now. She supposed that was a side effect of the crystals.

"I thought I heard you," Shane said. "Weirdest thing, I heard your voice today. Right out of the air. I thought you—I kept thinking about Michael, how he used to be during the daytime. . . ."

When he was a ghost. "You thought I was—?"

"I thought maybe something happened," he said. "I called your cell number, the new one."

She'd left it in her backpack. Claire reached down and unzipped the pocket, then checked the phone. Three calls, all from Shane. With voice mails. "Sorry," she said. "I didn't hear it. Guess I need to turn the ringer up."

He looked at her very steadily, and she felt the cold spot in her center, the place that had chilled while she'd been with Myrnin, slowly warm. "You worry me," he said, and put his hand on her cheek. "You know that, right?"

She nodded, and hugged him. Unlike Myrnin, he was warm and solid, and his body just molded right into hers, perfect and sweet. When he kissed her she tasted beer and chili, but only for a second. After that, it was pure Shane, and she forgot all about Myrnin, and any kind of physics except friction. Shane backed her up against the stove. She felt the low heat of the burner at her back, but she was too preoccupied to worry much about bursting into flames from outside sources. Shane just had that effect on her.

"I missed you," he whispered, brushing her damp lips with his. "Want to go upstairs?"

"What about my chili?"

"Get it to go."

There were good things about the way she felt tonight, she decided; her nerves might be raw, but that only made his touch all the sweeter. She would have felt awkward, usually, and uncertain, and scared, but it seemed like the afternoon that had started with Jason and ended with Myrnin's snarl had burned all that out of her.

"Not hungry," she said breathlessly. "Come on."

She felt as wild and free as a little kid, running up the steps with Shane in hot pursuit, and when he grabbed her around the waist, spun her around into his room, and kicked the door shut, she squealed in delight. And wiggled to fit herself against his warm, hard body as she kissed him again, breathless and flying.

He kissed as though their lives depended on it. As though it were an Olympic event and he intended to earn a medal. Somewhere in the back of her head she was chattering to herself, warning that this was going to go too far, that she was just making things worse for both of them, but she couldn't help it. Before long they were stretched out together on Shane's bed, and his big, warm hands were teasing under the hem of her shirt, stroking the fluttering skin of her stomach and stealing her breath. She lost it all when he spread his fingers out, pressing his palm flat against her, and she felt an almost irresistible impulse to feel those hands all over. Everywhere. Her heart was hammering hard enough to make her dizzy, and it was all just so . . .

Perfect.

She reached down and pulled up her shirt. Slowly, feeling the cool air slip over tender skin.

Up, to the bottom line of her bra. Then up.

Shane stopped.

"I want to," she whispered against his mouth. "Please, Shane. I want to." She sat up and reached for the clasp on her bra, and unhooked it. "Please."

He pulled back from her and sat up, head down. When he looked up he licked his lips, and his eyes were wide and dark, and she could fall into them, fall forever.

"I know," he said. "Me too. But I made promises, and I'm going to keep them. Especially the one to your parents, because your dad said he'd hunt me down like a dog." Shane gave her a wild, bitter smile. "Sucks to be me."

"But—" She felt her bra slipping, and quickly grabbed to hold it in place. She felt ridiculous now, and wounded.

He sighed. "Don't, Claire. It's not like I'm a saint or anything; I'm not, and trust me, for you, a saint would buy a condom and go to confession. But it's not about that. It's about keeping my word, and around here, my word is all I've got."

She wanted him with a red fury that was all out of character for her, but somehow, the way he said it, the way he looked her straight in the eyes, she felt all that fall away and the fury turn into something pure, hot, and silver.

"Besides," Shane said, "I'm all out of condoms, and I hate confession."

He put his arms around her and hooked her bra with an ease that showed he had plenty of practice.

She threw a pillow at him.

Somebody was rummaging around outside the house.

Claire woke up with a start, instantly tense, as she heard the distant rattle of metal. She rolled out of bed and peeked out of the blinds. Her bedroom window looked out on the back, a glorious corner vantage point, and she had a clear view of the fence, and the trash cans on the other side.

Somebody was definitely out there, a black shape in the moonlight. Claire could see him moving around but couldn't tell what he was doing. She reached for her cell phone and dialed 911, and told the operator she needed either Joe Hess or Travis Lowe. Detective Lowe picked up the call, sounding wide-awake even at three in the morning; Claire described what she was seeing in a whisper, as if whoever was across the yard might hear her.

"It's probably Jason," she said. She heard the scratch of pen on paper on the other end of the phone.

"Why Jason? Can you see his face?"

"No," she admitted, "but Jason told me—he practically admitted it. About the dead girl. I think it's Jason, honest."

"Did he threaten you, Claire?"

The cut on her wrist was still throbbing. "I guess you could say so," she said. "I was going to tell you about it, but I—I had things to do."

"More important than keeping us in the loop? Never mind. What happened?"

"Shouldn't I tell you when you get here?"

"Patrol car's already en route. Where did you see him today?"

"At the university," she said, and told the story. He didn't interrupt her, just let her talk, and she could hear him continuing to take notes.

When she paused for breath, Lowe said, "You know that was stupid, right? Look, next time you see him, you start screaming bloody murder. And put me and Hess on speed dial. Jason's nobody to play around with."

"But—we were in public. He wouldn't have—"

"Ask Eve about why he ended up in jail in the first place, Claire. Next time, don't hesitate. This isn't about you being strong; this about you living through the day, all right? Trust me."

She swallowed hard. "I do."

"Is he still there?"

"I don't know. I can't see him. He might've gone."

"The patrol car ought to be there in just a couple of seconds; they're doing a silent approach. You see them yet?"

"No, but my room faces the alley." Something moved in the yard, and she felt a lurch of pure adrenaline. "I think—I think he's in the yard now. Coming to the house. To the back."

"Go wake up Michael and Shane. Make sure Eve's okay. Go now, Claire."

She wasn't dressed, but she supposed it didn't really matter; the oversized T-shirt she was wearing came to her knees, anyway. She unlocked her door and swung it open, and yelled in shock.

Tried to, anyway. She couldn't quite get the sound out, because Oliver's hand clapped over her mouth, spun her around, and dragged her backward over the threshold. She screamed, but it was barely a buzz in her throat. Her bare heels scraped on the wood as she tried to get her feet under her, but he had her helpless and off balance. She dropped the phone.

She could hear Lowe's voice distantly whispering her name, but it was blotted out by Oliver's soft voice in her ear as he bent close and said, "I only want to talk. Don't make me hurt you, girl. You know I will if you force me."

She went still, breathing hard. Had *he* been out

there in the yard? How had he gotten up here so fast? Didn't the protections on the house keep him out?

No. They only work against uninvited humans now, because Michael's—Michael's a vampire. Oliver had some way in and out. Easy access. *God.*

"Good girl. Stay quiet," Oliver whispered. He looked up and down the hall, moved the painting next to the doorway, and pressed the hidden switch. The secret doorway across from Eve's room opened with a soft sigh, and he dragged her inside, then shut it. No knob on the inside. The release switch was up a flight of stairs, and he'd never let her get there if she tried to run. When he let her go, Claire stayed where she was.

He let his voice return to normal levels. Not afraid of being overheard, not here. "I thought it was time we had a talk. You signed an agreement with Amelie. That hurts me, Claire. I thought we had a special friendship, and after all, I did offer first." Oliver smiled at her, that cold and oddly kind smile that had suckered her in the first few times she'd met him. "You turned me down. So why, I wonder, did you decide that Amelie would be a better choice?"

He might know about Myrnin, but not what Myrnin did. Amelie had been pretty specific: he could *never* know that.

"She smells better," Claire said. "And she made me cookies." Somehow, after the day she'd had, Oliver just didn't seem all that terrifying anymore.

Until he bared his fangs, and his eyes went a strange, wide black. "No games," he said. "The room's soundproofed. Amelie used to play with her victims here, you know. It's a killing jar, and you're inside. So perhaps you should be more polite, if you intend to see morning."

Claire held up her left wrist. The golden bracelet glinted in the light. "Bite it, Oliver. You can't touch me. You can't touch anybody in this house. I don't know how you got in, but—"

He grabbed her right wrist and ripped away the bandage covering the cut Jason had made. It broke open, and a red trickle ran from it down the interior of her arm.

Oliver licked it off.

"Okay, that's just *gross*," Claire said faintly. "Let go. *Let go*!"

"You belong to Amelie," he said, and let her go. "I can taste it. Smell it on you. You're right, I can't touch you, not anymore. But the others, you're wrong about them. While they're in the house they're safe, but not out there, not in *my* town. Not for long."

"I made a deal!"

"Did you? Did you see in writing that your friends would be protected from all attacks? Because I very much doubt that, little Claire. We've been writing agreements for thousands of years, and you're only sixteen years old. You have no idea what kind of deal you've made." Oliver actually sounded a little sorry for her, and that *was* scary. He folded his arms and leaned against the door. He was in his usual good-guy disguise tonight: a tie-dyed T-shirt, battered cargo pants, his graying, curling hair pulled back in a ponytail. He'd probably just closed up Common Grounds, she figured. He smelled like coffee. She wondered what Oliver wore on his days off, if he wasn't trying to intimidate. Pajamas? Fuzzy slippers? One thing she'd figured out about the vampires in Morganville, they were never exactly what they seemed to be, even the bad ones.

"Fine," she said, and backed away from him until her heels hit the first step. She sat down. "You tell me what I've done."

"You've upset the balance of power in the town, and that's a terrible thing, little Claire. You see, Amelie intended to be queen of this little kingdom. She thought I was safely dead when she did so. When I came here a year ago, many people decided that they'd rather listen to me than to her. Not all, of course, and not even a majority. But she's won no real friends during her long existence, and it isn't only the humans who are trapped here, you know. It's the vampires as well."

This was a new idea to her. "What are you talking about?"

"We can't leave," he said. "Not without her permission. As I said, she fancies herself the cold White Queen, and most are content to let her. Not all. I was working to come to some . . . arrangements with her, to let a number of us leave Morganville and set up a community outside of her influence. Things had been static here for fifty years, you see, since she made the last vampire. Now Amelie feels the need to protect her position. She's blocked me. She won't allow me to make a move without her permission." He lowered his chin and stared at her, and it chilled her deep inside. "I don't like to be controlled. I tend to get . . . unhappy."

"Why are you talking to me? What can I do?"

"*You*, stupid little child, are her pet. When you want something, she indulges you. I want to know why."

Amelie hadn't exactly indulged her the last time they'd talked, although the cell phone sitting abandoned in her room might argue otherwise. "I don't *know*!"

"She thinks you have something she needs, or she'd hardly bother. She's seen whole cities die without shedding a tear or lifting a finger. It's not altruism."

Myrnin. It's about Myrnin. If I weren't learning from him . . . She couldn't say that, didn't even dare to really think it through. Oliver was unnerving, and sometimes he seemed downright psychic. "Maybe she's lonely."

He laughed, a harsh bark of sound with no amusement in it. "She certainly deserves to be." He took a step forward. "Tell me why she needs you, Claire. Tell me what she's hiding, and I'll make a deal, a perfectly straightforward one: I'll give your friends my direct Protection. No one will hurt them."

She didn't say anything this time; she just looked

back at him. She didn't dare *not* look at him; even when she was watching him she had the eerie feeling that somehow he was creeping up behind her, ready to do something awful to her when she least expected it.

Oliver made a sound of deep frustration. "You stupid, stupid girl." He shoved past her, going up the stairs so lightly the wood hardly even creaked. After a second, the hidden, knobless door sighed open. Claire got up, steadied herself for a second, and then stepped out into the hallway. Nobody else had heard a thing, apparently. It was quiet as the grave.

Oliver's hands closed around her shoulders, and he moved her out of his way by simply picking her up and putting her down, as if she weighed nothing. He didn't let go once he'd done it; he stepped up behind her, bent down, and whispered, "Not a sound, Claire. If you wake your friends and they come against me, I'll destroy you all. Understand?"

She nodded.

She felt the cold pressure of his hands go away, but not his presence, and she was surprised when she looked back and saw that he was gone.

As if he'd never been there at all.

She pressed the button behind the painting, and the hidden door sealed itself. Then she picked up her phone from the floor of her bedroom. The call had ended; Travis Lowe was probably on his way over, burning sirens all the way.

She sat down to wait for the panic to start.

There just had to be something out there in the alley, given the response. It wasn't only a couple of cops, some yellow tape, and a write-up in Captain Obvious's underground newspaper; it looked, from Claire's window, like a full-blown *CSI*-style investigation, with people in white jumpsuits collecting evidence and everything. There was a big blocky van with heavily tinted windows that she guessed housed vampire detectives or forensics people or something, with the emblem of the Morganville police on the side, and she guessed the majority of people roaming around in Michael's backyard this morning were, in fact, the undead.

Crime-solving undead. That was new.

She wasn't sure what she was feeling anymore. Light-headed, disconnected, looped. Last night had felt like a dream, and it had passed in a blur from the time she and Shane had come upstairs until she'd heard the rattle of trash cans in the alley.

Someone was ringing the doorbell downstairs. She didn't move away from the window—couldn't seem to convince herself to move at all, in fact. It was probably the cops. Travis Lowe had, as she'd thought, already come racing to the rescue, but on finding her unfanged and still alive, he'd called in the full-on police assault. So those were probably the detectives, Gretchen and Hans, or maybe Richard Morrell coming to take her statement.

Claire looked down at herself. *I should probably get dressed.* Her wrist was a mess, smeared with slow-leaking blood, and she pressed her T-shirt against it before she could think about what she was doing. Great, now she wasn't only undressed, she was undressed in bloody nightclothes.

It took ten minutes to shower, change, and bandage up her arm, and then she padded down the stairs in bare feet to face the music.

Her housemates were all standing in the living room, and they all looked at her with identical expressions, blank enough that she came to a stop on the steps. "What?" Claire asked. "What'd I do now?"

Michael stepped aside so Claire could see who was sitting cross-legged in the chair, flipping through a bubble-gum pink edition of *Teen People.*

Monica Morrell.

She was dressed in a tight-fitting pink top with diamonds that spelled out BITCH/PRINCESS, and white short-shorts that even Daisy Duke would have thrown out as too trashy. Her tan was deep and dark, and she was lazily dangling a pink flip-flop with a yellow flower on top from her perfectly manicured toes.

"Hey, Claire!" she said, and stood up. "I thought we could grab some breakfast."

"I—what?"

"Break . . . fast," Monica said, drawing out the word. "Most important meal of the day? Do you even *have* parents?"

Claire felt ridiculously off balance. "I don't understand. Why are you here?"

Shane leaned against the wall, glaring at Monica. He had a serious bed-head thing going on, and Claire wanted to run her hands through his thick, soft hair and return it to its usual shaggy mess. "What a good question. The second best one being, who let her inside? And we're going to have to throw out that chair. The smell's never coming out."

"I let her in," Michael said quietly, and that got him a stare from Shane. "Lay off the daggers. It was better to let her in than have her pitch a fit on the porch with all the cops around. We've already got enough trouble."

"What's this *we,* paleface? I mean that in the vampire sense, not—"

"Shut up, man."

Claire rubbed her forehead, feeling her headache blooming back to hot, throbbing life. She ignored Michael and Shane with an effort and focused on Monica, who had a malicious smile curving her lips. "You're enjoying this," Claire said. Monica shrugged.

"Of course. They're jackasses to me most of the time; it's nice to see them take it out on each other for a change. Not that I care." Monica arched one perfectly groomed eyebrow. "So? I know you like coffee. I've seen you drinking it."

Eve stepped in between them, and for a second Claire thought her friend honestly looked . . . dangerous. "You're not taking Claire anywhere. And you're *sure* not taking her anywhere near that son of a bitch," she said.

"Which son of a bitch would that be, exactly? Because hey, she lives *here.* It's not like she's choosy about who she hangs out with."

Eve bunched up a fist, and for a second Claire thought she was going to haul off and slug Monica right in her perfect, pouty mouth. But Eve checked herself. Barely.

"You *so* need to leave our house," Eve said. "Now. Before something bad happens that I won't really regret."

Monica gave her a look. "I'm sorry, were you talking? Because I think I dropped off. Claire? I'm not here to banter with the mentally challenged. I'm just trying to be friendly. If you don't want to go, just say so."

Claire felt ridiculously like laughing, it was so weird. Why was this happening to her?

"What do you really want?" she asked, and Monica's lovely, crazy eyes widened. Just a little.

"I want to talk to you without the Losers Club hanging over my shoulder. I figured we could have breakfast, but if you're allergic to caffeine and pastry . . ."

"Anything you can say to me, you can say in front of my friends," Claire said. That brought *both* of Monica's eyebrows up.

"Oooookay. Your funeral," she said, and glanced at Shane. "So where was your boyfriend last night after midnight?"

"Who? *Shane*?" What time had she left his room, anyway? Late. But . . . not after midnight.

"None of your damn business where I was," Shane said to Monica. "Eve told you to get out. The next step is I throw your skanky ass and see if you bounce when you hit the porch. I don't care whose pet you are; you don't come here and—"

"Shane," Monica interrupted with elaborate calm, "shut the hell up. I saw you, idiot."

Claire waited for Shane to give her a biting comeback, but he just sat there. Waiting. His eyes had gone very dark.

"They don't know, do they?" Monica continued, and tapped her rolled-up copy of *Teen People* against her hip. "Wow. Shocker. Bad boy keeps secrets. That *never* happens."

"Shut up, Monica."

"Or you'll *what*? Kill me?" She smiled. "There wouldn't even be DNA left when they got done with you, Shane. And the rest of you, too. *And* your families."

"What's she talking about?" Eve asked. "Shane?"

"Nothing."

"*Nothing,*" Monica mocked. "Deny everything. That's a brilliant plan. Then again, it's what I'd expect from someone like you."

Michael was frowning at Shane now, and Claire couldn't resist, either. Shane's dark eyes darted to each of them in turn, Claire last.

"The cops aren't going to find any bodies out there in the alley. And they're not going to find one anywhere else in your house," Monica said, "because Shane moved a body last night, out the back door."

Shane *still* wasn't saying anything. Claire covered her mouth with her hand. "No," she said. "You're lying."

Monica folded her arms. "Why exactly would I do that? Why would I admit to hanging around watching your house unless I had to? Embarrassing! Look, if I'm lying, all it takes is for him to deny it. Ask him. Go on." She was staring right at Shane.

Shane's eyes narrowed, but he didn't say anything. For a frozen second or two, nobody moved, and then Michael said, "*Christ,* Shane, what the hell?"

"Shut up!" Shane snapped. "I had to! I thought I heard something down in the basement last night, when I was getting some water in the kitchen. So I went to check it out. And—" He stopped, and Claire saw his Adam's apple bob as he swallowed, hard. "She was dead down there. At the bottom of the stairs, as if somebody had just . . . thrown her. For a second I thought it was"—he glanced at Eve, then away—"I thought it was you. I thought you'd tripped and fallen down the stairs or something. But when I got down there, it wasn't you. And she was dead, not just knocked out."

Eve sank down on the arm of the sofa, looking as stunned as Claire felt. "Who? Who was it?"

"I didn't recognize her. Some college girl, I guess. She didn't look local and she wasn't wearing a bracelet." Shane took in an audible deep breath. "Look, we've been in enough trouble as it is. I had to get rid of her. So I wrapped her up in one of the blankets out of the boxes down there and carried her out. I put her in the trunk of your car—"

"You *what*?" Michael snapped.

"And I drove her to the church. I left her there, inside. I didn't want to just—dump her. I thought"— Shane shook his head—"I thought it was the right thing to do."

Monica sighed. She was checking out her fingernails with exaggerated boredom. "Yeah, yeah, touching. The point is, when I saw you, you were hauling a dead chick into the trunk of *his* car. And I just can't *wait* to tell my brother. You know my brother, right? The cop?"

Unbelievable. "What do you *want*?" Claire practically yelled it at her.

"I told you. Breakfast." Monica gave her a sunny movie-star smile. "Please. If you say yes, I just could forget all about what I saw. Especially since I was, you know, out after curfew, and I don't want to get asked about why. Think of it as mutually assured destruction."

It sounded like a deal, but it wasn't, not really. Monica had all the cards, and they had none. None at all.

"There's no body in the alley," Claire said. "The police aren't going to find anything. You're sure?"

"Don't think so, but wouldn't that suck for you if they did?" Monica shrugged, puckered her lips, and blew Shane a mocking kiss. "You've got guts, Shane. No brains, but a whole lot of guts. You thought it out, right? Now that Michael's one of the chosen un-dead, humans can't get in this house without an invita-tion. So you have to either blame it on a vampire, or face up to the fact that one of you killed her. Either way, it's not going to be pretty, and somebody's going down." She held up her hand. "I vote for Shane. Any-body else?"

"Leave him alone!" Claire said sharply. "You want to go out, fine. We'll go. No, don't you even start!" Eve hadn't even had a chance to do more than open her mouth, and now she shut it, fast. "You guys work it out between the three of you. I won't be long. Be-lieve me, I probably won't be able to keep anything down, whatever I manage to eat."

Monica nodded, as if she'd known it would happen all along, and did a runway model's walk down the hall toward the front door. From the back, her shorts were barely legal.

And however much they hated her, Shane and Mi-chael were watching her go.

"Guys," Claire muttered, and grabbed her back-pack.

Claire hadn't been inside Common Grounds in a while, but it hadn't changed. It was bohemian, warm, packed to the gills with college types grabbing their morning venti-whatever, and if Claire hadn't known better—known very well—she'd never have believed that the nice, smiling hippie type behind the counter was a vampire.

Oliver locked gazes with her and nodded slightly. His face stayed pleasant. "Nice to see you back," he said. "What'll it be?"

Much as she hated to admit it, he made the best drinks in town. Better than Eve, actually. "White mocha," she said. "With whip." She managed to hold back from adding anything more, because she didn't like being nice to him. God, he'd been licking blood off her wrist two hours ago! The least she could do was not say *please* and *thank you*.

"No charge," he said, and waved away the five dollar bill she dug out of her jeans pocket. "A welcome-back present, Claire. Ah, Monica. Your usual?"

"Half-caf no foam double pump latte, with pink sugar," she said. "In a real cup, not that foam stuff."

"A simple yes would suffice," he said. As Monica started to turn away, he reached out and grabbed her wrist. He did it in such a way that nobody but Claire would notice, but it was unmistakably threatening. "She doesn't pay. You do, Monica. You may think of yourself as a princess, but trust me, I've met them, and you don't qualify." He grinned just a little, but there was no humor in his eyes. "Well, perhaps *met* isn't quite the right word."

"Eaten?" Claire supplied acidly. His smile turned darker.

"Oh, the charm and eloquence of the younger generation. It does warm my heart." Oliver let go of Monica's arm and stepped away to make the drinks. Monica backed away, looking flushed. She threw a dirty look at Claire—*Yeah, like it's my fault,* Claire thought—and stalked to the table in the corner. The one the deceased vampire Brandon had once staked out—pun intended—as his own. There were two young college girls sitting there, with books and papers piled up. Monica folded her arms and took up a belligerent pose.

"You're in my chair," she said. "Move."

The two girls—shorter and pudgier than Monica—stared up with saucer-huge eyes. One of them stammered, "Which one of us?"

"Both," Monica snapped. "I like my space. Get out."

They gathered up papers and books and hurried away, nearly dumping coffee all over Claire in their haste to go. "Did you have to do that?" Claire asked.

"No. It was just fun." Monica sat, crossed her smooth tanned legs, and patted the table. "Come on, Claire. Have a seat. We have so much to talk about."

She didn't want to, but it was stupid to stand there, looking obvious. So she sat, dumped her backpack on the floor next to her feet, and concentrated on the scarred wood of the tabletop. She could see Monica's flip-flop living up to its name as the other girl casually jiggled her foot. Ridiculously, it reminded her of Myrnin.

"That's better." Monica sounded way too pleased with herself. Not cool. "So. Tell me all about it."

"About what?"

"Whatever Amelie's got you doing," Monica said. "Your supersecret stuff. I mean, she picked you for a reason, and it's not for your charm and good looks, right? Obviously. It's for your brains. You don't have any family here; you've got nothing anybody wants other than that."

Monica was smarter than she looked. "Amelie's not asking me to do anything," Claire lied. "Maybe she will later, I don't know. But she hasn't yet." She nervously twisted the gold bracelet circling her left wrist. It was starting to remind her of those bands biologists put on endangered species.

And lab animals.

Monica's eyes were half-closed when Claire risked a glance upward. "Huh," she said. "Really. Well, that's disappointing. I really thought you'd have something good I could use. Oh well. Then let's talk about making a deal."

"A deal?" First Jason, now Monica. How had Claire stepped into the role of negotiator?

"I want to talk to Amelie about Protection. You can give me an introduction. And a recommendation."

Claire nearly laughed. "Ask her yourself!"

"I would, but she won't let me near her. She doesn't like me."

"I'm shocked," Claire muttered under her breath.

Monica gave her a long look, one strangely missing

the usual hip, ironic, contemptuous features. It looked almost . . . earnest. "Since Brandon died, Oliver took over his contracts. The thing is, he's not keeping most of them. He's trading them for favors with other vampires. If I don't make a better deal, there's no telling what could happen to me." Monica pointed at Claire's bracelet. "Might as well start at the top."

Claire drummed her short fingernails on the table, glaring at the bar where it seemed like Oliver was taking forever to deliver their drinks. It occurred to her to wonder if it was really safe to drink something prepared by a vampire who'd been threatening her just a couple of hours before, but honestly, if Oliver wanted to get her, it wasn't as though it would be hard for him.

And she really wanted the white mocha.

"Oliver's your Patron now?"

"For now. Until he finds something he wants more than holding on to my contract, anyway."

"Is he behind your asking about why Amelie signed me up?"

"Do I look like I run somebody else's errands?"

Claire glanced back again at the bar. "Maybe."

Monica went quiet. It wasn't the comfortable kind of silence, and Claire was glad when Oliver called out their orders. She jumped up to get hers, hesitated, and then picked up Monica's as well. She managed to do it without making eye contact with Oliver. He was just a dark shape at the corner of her eye, and she turned her back on him as soon as she could.

Monica had gotten up, and she looked honestly surprised when Claire handed her the drink. "What?" Claire asked. "It's called being polite; they probably didn't teach you that at home. Doesn't mean I like you or anything."

Monica seemed to have to think hard about what to say to that, and finally came up with a simple "Thanks." Which, Claire had to admit, might have been the nicest thing Monica had ever managed to say to her. Claire gave her a nod and sat down again.

Peace in our time, she thought wryly. And promptly blew it by asking again, "Did Oliver put you up to it?"

Monica didn't even glance in his direction. "No." But somehow, Claire didn't believe her.

"Do you have to do everything he says?" she asked, as if Monica hadn't just lied. And Monica lifted one shoulder in a half shrug. No other answer. "So you don't really want to talk to me, do you? You've just been told to do it."

"Not exactly. I thought it was a good chance to get my name in front of Amelie, too." Monica smiled slightly, and very bitterly. "Besides, check it out: you're a star. Everybody wants to know about you, vampires and humans. They're looking into your history, your family's history. If you farted in grade school, somebody in Morganville knows it now."

Claire almost choked on her first mouthful of white mocha. "*What?*"

"The Founder isn't what you might call accessible. And most of the vamps don't understand her any better than we do. They're always looking for clues about who she is, what she's doing here, with this town. This isn't normal, you know. The way they live here." Monica's gaze flicked to Oliver, then away. "*He's* old enough to know more than most, but he still needs inside information. And the word is, you could be the way to get it. If I can't get Protection from Amelie, at least I can get in good with him if I have something new and valuable to tell him."

Claire rolled her eyes. "I'm nobody. And if she cared about me at all—which she doesn't—she'd never let anybody know it. I mean, look how she treats—" She stopped herself cold, heart suddenly hammering fast. She'd almost said *Myrnin,* and that would have been bad. "Sam," she finished lamely. Which was also true, but Monica had to have noticed her stumble.

Which Monica emphasized by waiting for a full ten seconds of silence before she continued. "Whatever. The point is, you're sort of famous, and by hanging with you, I get seen by the right people doing the right thing, and I do what Oliver wants. Which is all I care about. You're right, I don't care if we're BFFs. We're not going to trade clothes and get matching tattoos. I've got friends. I need allies." She sipped her complicated drink, her eyes steady on Claire. "Oliver wants what you know, yeah. And this"— she tapped her own bracelet—"this says that I do what he says, or else."

"Or else what?"

Monica looked down. "You've met him. Best case, it means he hurts me. Bad. Worst case . . . he trades me down."

"That's *worse*?"

"Yeah. That means I get handed to the bottom-of-the-barrel vamps, the ones too lame to get the good earners and the pretty people. That means I'm a loser." She looked down and fidgeted with her ceramic coffee cup, frowning at it. "Sounds shallow, maybe, but around here, it's survival. If Oliver blackballs me, I can't get anything but the freaks and the skanks, the ones who get their fix the hard way. They'll kill me, if I'm lucky. If not, I end up some strung-out junkie fang-banger."

She said it with such dry, matter-of-fact intensity that Claire could tell she'd spent a lot of time thinking about it. It was a long way to fall, from the darling daughter of the mayor to some addict trying to please a kinky freak for protection.

"You could be neutral," Claire blurted. She felt oddly sympathetic, even after everything Monica had done. She *had* been born here, after all. Not like she'd ever had a real choice in what she was going to be, or do. "Some people are, right? They're left alone?"

Monica sneered, and the second or two of humanity Claire had imagined she'd seen in that pretty face vanished. "They're left alone until they're not. Look, officially, they're untouchable because they've done favors, big favors, and their Patrons let them out of contracts. By big favors, I mean the kind they were lucky to live through, get it? I'm not interested in that kind of hero crap."

Claire shrugged. "Then go without a contract."

"Yeah, *right.* That works. I'm really looking forward to a future as second assistant fry wrangler at the Dairy Queen, and decomposing in some ditch before I'm thirty." Monica rested her elbows on the table, coffee cup cradled in both hands. "I thought about leaving. I actually went to Austin for a semester, you know? But . . . it wasn't the same."

"Meaning you flunked out of school."

That earned Claire a filthy look. "Shut up, bitch. I'm here only because I need to be, and you're here only because you have to be. Let's not get too touchy-feely."

Claire swallowed a mouthful of sweet, rich mocha. If it was poisoned, she'd die happy, at least. "Fine by me. Look, I can't help you get to Amelie. I don't even know how to get to her myself. And even if I did, I don't think she'd take your contract."

"Then just shut up and smile. If I don't get anything else out of this wasted morning, at least Oliver can see that I tried."

"How long do I have to do this?"

Monica checked her watch. "Ten minutes. Suck it up that long, and I won't call my brother about your boyfriend's little indiscretion."

"How can I be sure?"

Monica slapped both hands to her cheeks and looked overdramatically horrified. "Oh no! You don't trust me! I'm crushed." She dropped the act. "I don't care if Shane has opened his own corpse taxi service; I care only about what I can get out of it."

"Maybe you want revenge," Claire said.

Monica smiled. "If I'd wanted that, I'd have already turned him in. Besides, I hear it's best served cold."

Claire pulled out a book. "All right. Ten minutes. I need to study, anyway." Monica sat back and began a running, acidly accurate monologue on the outfits of the girls standing in line for coffee, which Claire tried earnestly not to find funny. Which she was able to do, until Monica pointed out a girl wearing a truly horrible polka-dot-leggings-under-shorts ensemble. "And somewhere in heaven, Versace sheds a single, perfect tear."

Claire couldn't control a snort of laughter, and hated herself for it. Monica cocked an eyebrow.

"See?" she said. "I'm so good I can even charm a hard case like you. It's a waste of my talent, but I need to keep myself sharp." She finished her coffee and picked up her little pink purse with the *Teen People* magazine sticking out of it. "Gotta fly, loser. Tell your boyfriend as far as I'm concerned, we're even. Well, okay, I'm a little bit more than even, and that's the way I like it. Consider this his restraining order: if I see him within fifty feet of me, I'll not only tell my brother about Shane's midnight adventure, but I'll get some football types to pay his kneecaps a visit."

She walked out, hips swaying dangerously. People got out of her way, and they watched her go. Fear and attraction, in just about equal measure.

Claire sighed. She supposed people always did like that sort of girl, and always would. And secretly? She envied Monica's confidence. Maybe just a little, traitorous bit.

10

The dead girl that Shane had taken to the church was Jeanne Jackson, a sophomore who'd gone missing from a sorority party two nights before. The papers said that she'd been raped and strangled, but nothing about suspects, and no cops showed up to interrogate Shane, much to Claire's relief. He'd done a dumbass thing, but she could understand his paranoia. In Morganville, he was one suspicion away from taking up residence in Jason's old cell, whether he'd actually done anything or not.

That was if the vampires didn't decide to hold their own brand of frontier justice.

Captain Obvious's *Fang Report* had a much more detailed article on the killings, linking the other two that Claire knew about with this one, and speculating that instead of a vampire menace, they might be dealing with a human one this time. He didn't seem as enthusiastic about forming vigilante parties for someone with a pulse, Claire noticed. Not that it mattered to the dead girls which type of monster had killed them.

She got a note from Amelie giving her time off from working with Myrnin for the rest of the week, so she devoted herself to keeping up with classes. They were tougher than she was used to, which was kind of a relief. She loved a good challenge, and the professors seemed to actually care whether or not their students had a clue. Myth and Legend wasn't what she'd expected, not at all; it wasn't Greek gods, or even Native American Trickster stories. No, it was about . . . vampires. Comparative vampires, actually, examining the literature and folklore from earliest recorded history to the latest vampire-as-hero in pop culture. (Which, now that Claire thought about it, kind of was the modern-day version of myth and legend.) Oddly, for Morganville, the professor wasn't skipping the parts about vampire-killing methods, but Claire guessed that she was one of the few in the class who'd ever know the score about the town, anyway. The rest would bumble cluelessly through their one or two years, transfer out to bigger schools, and never know they'd rubbed elbows at parties with real monsters.

She kept her mouth shut about anything that might get her in trouble, because the professor had a bracelet, too. She was trying to match up glyphs with vampires, and she thought he probably belonged to a female vamp named Susan, who seemed to be into finance. Susan owned a lot of property, anyway, and was some kind of bigwig at the Morganville Bank and Trust.

Claire began keeping notes in a special book about glyphs, vampires, who owned what. Not because she had any agenda, but just because it was interesting, and could be useful someday. She supposed if she'd asked, Amelie would have told her all about it, but it was more challenging to figure it out herself—and this way, Amelie couldn't be really sure how much Claire knew, which couldn't be a bad thing. *She's nice when it suits her. That doesn't mean she's nice.*

And on Friday, Eve left a note stuck to the bathroom mirror for Claire to find when she got up.

CB—Don't forget tonight is the party. Objective: look hotter than Monica and make everybody totally forget who threw the party in the first place. Outfit on back of door. Pay me back.—E.

The outfit was nothing Claire would ever, ever, *ever* have bought for herself. For one thing, the black leather skirt was . . . short. Like, really short. There were some kind of patterned panty hose and a sheer red shirt with big red roses woven into the fabric in flocked material. And a black cami to go under it.

There was another sticky note attached to the skirt. *Shoes under the cabinet.* Claire looked. They were thick clunky platforms, in her size, in shiny patent leather.

She took it all back into her bedroom and put it down, backed off, and stared at it for a few seconds. *I can't wear that. It's not me.*

Eve would totally mock her if she wore her blue jeans to the party. And she'd gone to a lot of trouble, because all of this stuff was Claire's size, not Eve's. Even the shoes.

And . . . it really *would* burn Monica if Claire looked hot. (She'd never be hotter than Monica; that was a fantasy, but still.) Imagining the expression on Monica's face, Claire slowly stroked her fingers down the soft leather of the skirt. *No. I can't.*

And then she imagined Shane's face when he saw her.

Well. Maybe she could, after all.

She hadn't gotten his expression quite right in her imagination, because the stunned, vacant expression on Shane's face when she started down the stairs was even better than fantasy. His mouth actually *dropped open.* Next to him, Michael turned around, and although she hadn't counted on it, there was a warm fuzzy feeling to making a hot golden-angel vampire blink and give her a quick, involuntary once-over.

Claire stopped on the steps above them and did a tentative hip shimmy. "Okay?" she asked. Shane's mouth shut with a snap, and Michael actually cleared his throat.

"Fine," Michael said.

"Fine?" That was Eve, coming down the stairs behind Claire. She moved around the roadblock and

punched Michael in the arm. "She looks amazing. I'm not half-gay, and I think she's hot."

Shane wasn't saying *anything*. Claire felt warm and a little dizzy, the way he was looking at her. She resisted the urge to check to see if her skirt was straight—she'd done it a dozen times already—and forced herself to meet his gaze and smile.

"You sure this is smart?" Shane asked, which was not what she'd expected, not at all. "You look fantastic."

"Thanks—"

He interrupted her. "*Fantastic* in this town pops you to the top of the take-out menu."

She held up her left hand and pointed to her wrist. The gold bracelet was clearly visible. "I'll be okay," she said. "The vamps won't bother me."

"Not even talking about the vamps. You're going to be drawing every guy there who's looking to get off."

Eve rolled her eyes. "Oh, *God*, Shane, buzz kill? She looks great, and you don't have to get all jealous and overprotective about it! She'll be with us; we'll all look out for her. And you've got to admit, girlfriend looks good all cleaned up. I did her hair, too. Smokin', right?" The hair, Claire felt, was just almost over the top. It was mostly gel and sprays and stuff, but it did have that carefully tousled look that models always seemed to wear.

Eve wasn't exactly wallflower quality tonight, either; she was wearing a dramatic, floor-sweeping black dress that left her pale arms bare, plunged a neckline halfway to China, and had a slit in the side that went all the way to her hip. Fishnet hose, even. It was outrageously sexy, and if Michael had noticed Claire's transformation, he was completely focused on Eve now.

Eve winked at him and spun around to show him the back. Of which there wasn't any. It was just her skin, and a crimson rose tattoo at the small of her back.

"Man," Shane said. "That's just—yeah."

It wasn't until she'd gotten past their reactions—
which were pretty fun—that Claire realized that Eve
must have done a number on the boys, too . . . because
they looked amazingly fine. Michael was wearing black
pants and a black leather coat, and a dark blue silk
shirt. It made him just . . . blaze, like white gold
against velvet.

Shane looked good enough to drag back to her
room. Eve must have forced him to get the worst
of his shag evened up, which brought out his strong
cheekbones and chin. He was wearing black, too,
with a dark maroon knit shirt. Claire had never seen
him in a jacket. She decided he needed to never take
it off.

Michael shook his head and offered Eve his arm.
She took it, smiling with her red, red lips, and winked
at Claire. Claire winked back, suddenly feeling *very*
wicked, and slid her arm through Shane's.

"I can't believe we're doing this," Shane said.

This was going to be fun.

Claire hadn't forgotten the address, even though
she'd given away the invitation, and Michael knew
Morganville like the back of—Eve's back, the way he
kept looking at her exposed skin, especially the tattoo.
And besides, if you were within a couple of blocks of
the party, you couldn't possibly miss it. Between the
glow of the lights and the low-pitched rumble of the
music, there was no sleeping through it if you lived
nearby.

Michael cruised around the block, looking for parking, and finally located a narrow few feet of curb. As
he pulled in, he said, "Ground rules. We don't split
up. Eve and Claire, you two especially. It's not just
because of the vampires; it's because of Jason. Got
it?"

They nodded.

"Besides," Shane said, and playfully tugged at Claire's
overgelled hair, "I want to see Monica's face when she
catches sight of the two of you. Kodak moment."

Eve fumbled in her tiny little coffin-shaped purse and held up a brand new cell phone, with camera. "I'm ready."

"Me too," Claire said, and pulled out the fancy phone that Amelie had given her. She felt a blast of shame as Shane glanced at it, but controlled it. She couldn't be ashamed all the time, and besides, it wasn't so bad, right? What she was doing? It wasn't any worse than having a day job. Just . . . different.

"Be careful what you eat and drink," Michael continued. "Monica's party is probably roofie heaven. I can smell what they put in the drinks; you guys can't. And if you get into any trouble, step back; let me handle it. If you're going to have a freak vamp friend, you might as well get your money's worth out of it."

Shane didn't answer, but Claire could see there was some smart-ass remark burning a hole in his tongue. She was glad he didn't let it loose. It was nice to feel like four friends again, instead of four people all about to spin apart in different directions.

"Anything else, Dad?" Eve asked. Michael kissed her, very lightly, sparing her lipstick.

"Yeah," he said. "You look good enough to eat. Promise me you'll remember that."

Claire was caught between a smile and a shiver, and saw that Eve was, too.

The Morrell home looked like Tara from *Gone with the Wind*, post–Sherman's march. Claire watched, blinking, as a mob of drunken frat boys stumbled down the walk, roaring something she couldn't make out, and carrying a *couch*.

The couch they deposited in the giant European-style fountain in front of the house. Apparently they were relocating most of the living room out there. Some partyers were already sitting in chairs, soaking in the fountain's spray, and now three or four of them piled giggling onto the wet couch.

"Now this," Shane said with respect, "is out of bounds. I like it."

It was totally out of control. The four of them stood together by Michael's shiny vampire-tinted car, watching in admiration. The house was blazing with lights, there were lit tiki torches tilting drunkenly all over the lawn, and partyers were *everywhere*. Making out under the trees, in full glare of the security lights. Doing shots on the big, white-columned front steps. A girl ran by, dressed in half a bikini. The top half.

"Damn," Michael said. "Monica does know how to throw it."

No kidding. Claire watched as a big bobtail truck inched its way through a knot of people toward the back of the house. It had the logo of BOB'S FINE LI-QUORS. Apparently, Monica had called in liquid reinforcements already, and the night was young.

"Well?" Eve said. "Are we standing out here all night? Because I'm ready to knock somebody dead."

The four of them strolled up the walkway, keeping an eye out for frat boys and wandering furniture. They went as a group up the front steps, where about ten people were playing some complicated game that involved drinking shots, spray cans of fluorescent paint, and giggling hysterically. Even the drunkest turned to look at the four of them and whistle.

The frat boys, the drunks in the fountain, and the even drunker people on the porch were all wearing standard college casual dress, mostly shorts and T-shirts. "Um," Claire said, "Maybe we should have come a little less formal."

"No way," Eve replied. "If you're going, go big."

"Remind me to play poker with you later," Michael said. "I love a girl who'll go all in."

She hip-bumped him. "*That's* what you want to do with me later? Dude. Respect the dress, at least."

Michael trailed his pale fingers down her back, following the line of her spine, all the way to the red rose. Eve shivered, and her eyes went half-closed. Whatever Michael whispered in her ear, Claire thought it was probably way too personal to hear.

Not that she could have, because right then the

front door banged open and the noise flowed out in a syrup-thick wave of pounding techno and yelled conversations. Two people stumbled out of the door, arms around each other. Claire blinked and recognized two of the gamers whom she'd given Monica's invitation to that afternoon on campus.

"Freakin' awesome party!" one of them screamed, and fell flat on his face.

"Apparently." Eve stepped over him and swept into the party, with Michael right behind her. Claire started to follow, but Shane's grip on her arm had tightened, and he was holding her back.

"What?" she asked, and turned to face him. God, he looked amazing. He needed to let Eve dress him all the time.

"Before we go in," he said, and bent and kissed her. Claire distantly heard the whistles and catcalls of the shot drinkers—distantly, because the kiss was sweet and hot and wild, and there was something crazy in it that made her just quiver inside.

He pulled away way too soon. "Stay with me," he said, with his lips near her ear, and she nodded. *Like I'd let you out of my sight.*

And then they followed Michael and Eve into the party of the century.

It was the second big party of Claire's life—not counting birthday parties and ones where there were as many chaperones as kids. The first one, the Dead Girls' Dance thrown by the EEK fraternity, hadn't exactly come out well, what with Shane's dad going on a rampage through the place looking for vampires to stake. This one looked, if possible, even crazier.

She was grateful to be with her friends. She couldn't imagine how scary it would be if she'd stepped into this by herself. The main hall was wide and tall, but it was jam-packed with people talking, dancing, kissing, groping—it was like the hottest dance club with all the lights up full. Claire brushed up against a couple who were—what *were* they doing? She looked away before she could be sure, but the guy's hand was in places that she couldn't imagine a porn actress allowing in public.

Michael and Eve pushed through the crowd into the next room, and Claire and Shane followed, staying close. There were a few people in the big living area who were dressed fancy, but most had on standard-issue college wear, and somehow, Claire had the distinct impression the casual-dress crowd had *not* come invited.

Monica was standing at the top of the stairs, arms folded, looking right at them.

"Oooh, that *is* a Kodak moment," Eve said, and held up her cell phone to snap a photo of Monica's scowl. "Yep. We're good."

She high-fived Shane, who seemed to be expecting it. Monica cleared the annoyance out of her expression with an effort and started down the steps. She was dressed in a pink, clinging sheath dress with huge lime-outlined flowers climbing the fabric, and her shoes were prissy-perfect in matching pink. Very fancy.

"Claire, you brought strays," Monica said. "How nice." And then she looked strangely sorry. "Michael, I didn't mean you. You're always welcome."

He raised his pale eyebrows. "I am?"

"Of course."

Claire elbowed him. "Because you're a VIP. Vampire Important Person."

Two more of the gamers Claire had gifted with the invitation stumbled by; one grabbed Claire's arm and planted a sloppy, wet kiss on her cheek. "We passed out copies," he said, and giggled. "Hope that was okay. Great party!"

Shane sighed and moved him off with one hand on his shoulder. "Yeah, yeah, whatever. Naked Vulcan chick in the next room. Better hurry."

The gamers sobered up fast, and moved on. Monica's glossy, perfect lips were open, her eyes wide.

"You?" she said. "*You* did this? These idiots made flyers! They put them all over campus! *This was supposed to be the best people!*"

"Don't worry," Eve said sweetly. "We're here." She

smiled, which in that lipstick was Wicked-Witch-of-the-West evil. "Air kiss!" She *mwahed* the air somewhere near Monica's cheek. "Lovely party. Shame about the furniture. Ta!" She sashayed on, Michael on her arm, as if she were the Queen of Everything, never mind Morganville. Claire got out her camera and captured a picture of the murderous fury on Monica's face as she watched her go.

"You treacherous little *bitch*!" Monica snarled.

Claire lowered the phone and met her eyes for a long second. She wasn't scared, not anymore. "You got your friends to roofie me and told them I wanted it rough. All I did was recycle your invitation. Let's call it even."

"Let's call it *not*!"

Shane leaned forward, dropped his voice so that Monica had to work to hear it, and said, "Calm down. You get blotchy when you're angry. And if you call my girlfriend a bitch one more time, I won't be so nice about it."

Monica's eyes were fierce and fiery, but she didn't move, and after a second she turned and ran up the steps to the second floor, where her formally dressed friends were huddled together like the cast of *Survivor: Abercrombie & Fitch Island.*

"Score one for the little guys," Shane said. He stared at a bunch of guys wearing football shirts who rumbled past, carrying a bed. Claire blinked. Yes, that was a bed. "Okay, I don't really think I want to know. So. Drinks?"

In the kitchen, a group was making punch in a trash can. Claire hoped it was a new trash can, but as blitzed as the guys were who were pouring stuff in, she really couldn't be sure of that.

"I'd avoid that," Shane said, his mouth close to her ear. "See anybody you know?"

She wasn't sure. There was barely room to move in here, with people crowding up to the counters, and streaming in and out with red plastic cups in their hands. . . .

A shock zipped down her spine. "Yeah," she said. "I see somebody."

How the hell had Eve's brother gotten into the party? He was standing in a corner, slouching and sneering. Lank hair dripped toward his shoulders, and he wore the same filthy, dangerous-boy clothes that he'd had on when he'd threatened Claire at the UC. He had a drink, but he wasn't drunk; there was too much hot contempt in his eyes as he surveyed the crowd. Crazy eyes. *Oh God, that's how they look, those guys who shoot up rooms full of people.*

His eyes locked with Claire's, and he gave her a bent smile. Claire anxiously looked at Eve, but her back was to her brother and she was talking to Michael; she clearly hadn't seen the potential trouble at all.

"What?" Shane asked.

Claire turned back and pointed.

Jason was gone.

Shane shook his head when she told him, and moved away to talk to Michael. Michael nodded, then handed Eve off to Shane. Claire saw his lips move: *Watch her.*

And then Michael angled off through the crowd.

So much for staying together.

Shane draped his arms over both of their shoulders and said, "Now this is the life. Want to get a room, girls?"

Eve rolled her thickly mascaraed eyes. "Like you'd know what to do with one of us, never mind two. Where's he going?"

"Bathroom," Shane said blandly. "Even vamps gotta pee."

Which, for all Claire knew, might be true, but she was sure that wasn't why Michael had cut out on them. Shane steered them up to the counter and snagged a sealed bottled water for Claire and two sealed beers, which he opened himself. *Not taking any chances,* Claire thought, and cracked the top on the bottle to take several gulps of the cool, sweet water. She hadn't realized how hot it was until then, but she could feel sweat sticking her flocked mesh shirt to her exposed skin.

Somebody grabbed her ass. Claire yelped and jumped, then turned and saw a drunk-off-his-butt frat boy leaning in next to her. "Oh baby, me like!" he yelled in her ear. "You, me, outside, okay?" He did a drunken pantomime of what he was thinking of doing outside, and she felt a hot roll of embarrassed shame.

"Get lost," she said, and shoved him off. His buddies tossed him back toward her, and this time, he crashed into her off balance and pushed her up against the bar. He took advantage of it, too, hands all over her, hips grinding her right into the counter.

Shane grabbed him by the collar of his TPU golf shirt, spun him around, and punched him right in the face.

Great, Claire thought in shaken disgust. *That's always the answer around here. Punch somebody.* Then again, she didn't think reasoned discourse was going to be big tonight.

And of course, the guy's friends piled on. Eve grabbed Claire's hand and pulled her out of the way; a tight circle formed around the combat, with people whooping and clapping. "We have to stop him!" Claire yelled. Eve patted her on the shoulder.

"This is Shane's idea of a good time," she said. "Trust me. You do *not* want to try to stop him right now. Let him do his thing. He'll be fine."

Claire hated it. She hated seeing Shane get hit, and she didn't much like the way his eyes lit up when he was knee-deep in conflict, either. Stupid to be upset by it, she guessed, considering this was part of why she was so attracted to Shane in the first place—the way he would unhesitatingly throw himself into things, especially when it came to protecting others.

Eve was practically reading her mind. "Let him be who he is," she said. "I know it's hard, because in general, guys are clueless, and you just want to fix it, but just—let him be. You don't want him trying to change you, right?"

Right. She didn't, although he *was* changing her, whether he knew it or not. *Not in bad ways,* she thought. *Just . . . change.* A year ago she'd have been paralyzed with terror at the idea of coming to a party like this, and even more terrified to imagine being groped by a stranger like that.

Now, she was mostly just annoyed, and felt like she needed a shower.

Eve whirled. "Hey! I know my ass is fine, but look, don't touch!" An eruption of drunken laughter. She took Claire's hand. "We need a wall behind us. Less chance of getting the stealth feel-up."

"But—" She gave up as somebody else patted her rear. "Yeah. Okay."

That put them half a room away from Shane, who was now somehow at the center of a knot of maybe ten guys, all whaling away at each other (mostly without connecting; they were all too drunk to really do damage). Claire leaned gratefully against the wall and sipped water. Somehow, she'd ended up holding Shane's beer, and with a quick sideways glance at Eve, she took a sip of that, too. Ugh. Nasty.

"Acquired taste," Eve said, laughing at her expression. "Shane buys like a college boy. If it's cheap and the ad has a girl in a bikini, it must be great."

"That's disgusting," Claire said, and took another long drink of water to wash her tongue clean. Even the water tasted bitter, after that.

"Well, in fairness, beer is mostly about the buzz, not the taste," Eve said. "You want taste *and* buzz, you get something like rum and Coke, or White Russians." She seemed to remember, suddenly, how old Claire was. "Not that I'm going to let you have any of that, by the way. We promised your parents." She managed to look almost righteous when she said it, and she took Shane's beer out of Claire's hand. "I'll keep this." Eve raised her normally soft voice to a parade-ground bellow. "Yo, Shane! Quit screwing around or I'm drinking this!"

A ripple of laughter through the room. The fight was mostly over, anyway, and Shane shoved away the last stumbling frat boy who'd tried to take a swing at him, wiped blood from his mouth with the back of his hand, and left the field of battle. He looked rumpled and flushed and a little bit savage, and Claire felt something in her just *growl* in response.

She stared at him, wide-eyed. *I'm not ready for this.* Parts of her clearly were.

"Have a drink, Galahad," Eve said, and handed him his bottle. They clinked glass. "Our hero. Here. Fix your hair." She picked at it with her black-manicured nails, twitching it this way and that, until it had that glamour-boy, carefully careless look again. "God, you're hot. Get felt up yet?"

"Couple of times," he said, and smiled at Claire. "Don't hurt them. They just couldn't help themselves."

Eve snorted and looked around. "Where's Michael?"

"Probably in line at the bathroom." Shane shrugged. It was probably true, but Claire didn't think that was the reason. Shane did that thing where he looked at Eve too long and didn't blink. She thought she could tell when he was lying, and that definitely was a flashing neon sign. "Ladies? Let's wander."

It wasn't so much *wander* as *wriggle,* like salmon heading upstream. What Claire could see of the house was amazing—fine art on the walls, gorgeous old furniture (mostly being splashed with drinks or shoved against the walls to make room for dancing), big, expensive Turkish rugs (Claire hoped they were drycleanable), and huge plasma TVs that were all playing the same music channel, blasting at ear-piercing volume. Nine Inch Nails' "Closer" was on now, and despite her best intentions Claire found herself moving to the rhythm. Eve was dancing, too, and then they were dancing together, which should have seemed weird but didn't, really. Shane formed the third point on their triangle, but Claire could see that he wasn't really giving in to the festive atmosphere; he was scanning the crowd, looking for trouble. Or Michael.

Somebody tried to pass her something—a shot glass with a hit of something clear. She shook her head and passed it right back. Not that she wasn't tempted, but after what had almost happened to her at the last party, she wasn't going to be stupid.

Well, not any stupider than she already was to come here in the first place.

The drinks and drugs kept coming. Liquid E, poppers, shots, even something that she was almost sure was a crack pipe. Morganville liked its drugs, but she guessed that made sense. There was a hell of a lot to escape from around here.

She kept on dancing. Shane and Eve didn't take anything, either—not that Claire saw, anyway. Shane was looking less into the party and more worried all the time.

Michael didn't come back. Two songs later—two long songs—Eve finally got Shane to look for him, and the three of them moved out through the bottom floor, checking out the rooms (all packed) and not finding Michael anywhere. In the hall bathroom a line of people was waiting for the toilet, but no sign of a tall, blond vampire.

When they went up the big, sweeping steps toward the second floor, Claire couldn't help but think about *Gone With the Wind*, and Rhett Butler carrying Scarlett. Her mom loved that movie. She'd always thought it was boring, but that scene stayed with her, and she could almost see it in this house. But instead of Scarlett, Monica Morrell was still standing at the top of the steps, surrounded by her protective circle of toadies. Gina and Jennifer were back, each wearing a dress that was plainer than what Monica had on, but in complementary colors. Her very own backup group. There were a couple of other girls in the crowd, but mostly it was guys—good-looking, polished types. The entitled of Morganville, and every one of them was wearing a bracelet.

"Well," Monica said. "Look who's coming up in the world." Her crowd laughed. Monica's eyes were vicious. If she'd been sort of human when they'd been alone in the coffee shop, she'd gotten over it. "Scrubs stay downstairs. We're going to have to have the place gutted and rebuilt anyway, after this."

"Yeah, I'll bet Daddy's going to be furious when he gets home," Eve said. "I meant to ask, is that dress vintage? Because I could swear I saw it on my mother once." She swept up, heading straight for one of Monica's big strong linebacker types; he looked confused, and edged out of her way. Shane and Claire followed. Monica was dangerously silent, probably realizing that any comeback she could try would sound cheap.

"We're going to have trouble getting out of here," Shane said. It was quieter upstairs, although the continuing clamor downstairs throbbed through the floor and walls. The hallway was deserted, and all the doors were closed. It was lined with expensive portraits and framed formal photographs of the Morrell family. Not surprisingly, Monica took a lovely picture. Claire had never seen Mrs. Mayor, but there she was in the family photos—a wispy, half-ethereal woman always looking somewhere other than her family. Unhappy, somehow. Richard Morrell seemed grounded and adapted to this town, and of course, so did the mayor; Monica might not be stable, but she was definitely Morganville material.

Her mom, maybe not so much.

"Wonder where her parents are?" Claire said aloud.

"Out of town," Eve said. "So I heard, anyway. Bet they'll just love getting back to find somebody did an *Extreme Home Makeover: Crackhead Edition.*" She tested the doorknob of the first room on the left. Locked. Shane tried the one on the right, opened it, and leaned in. He leaned out again, eyebrows arched.

"Well, that's new," he said. Claire tried to look. He put his big hand over her eyes. "Trust me, you're not old enough. *I'm* not old enough." He carefully shut the door. "Moving on."

Claire opened the next room, and for a second she couldn't figure out what she was seeing. Once she did, she couldn't speak. She backed up and touched Shane wordlessly on the shoulder and pointed.

There were three guys in the room, and a girl on the bed, and she was passed out. They were taking off her panty hose.

"Shit," Shane said, and moved Claire back. "Eve, call the cops. Now. Time to shut this crap down before somebody gets really hurt."

Eve got out her cell phone and dialed, and Shane went into the room and closed the door. He came back after about a minute with the unconscious girl in his arms. "Anybody know who she is?"

Claire shook her head. "What about those guys?"

"They're sorry," Shane said. "Eve? You recognize her?"

"Um . . . maybe. I think I've seen her around the UC—couldn't swear to a name or anything. But she's definitely gown, not town. No bracelet."

"Yeah, I figured." Shane adjusted her to a more comfortable angle in his arms. The girl—petite, brunette, pretty—snuggled into his embrace with a sleepy moan. "Damn it. I can't just leave her."

"What about Michael? We need to find him!"

"Yeah, I know. Look, I'll carry her. Check the other rooms."

Claire was having trouble controlling her breathing. She'd almost been that girl, not so long ago. Only she'd been a little more alert, a little more able to take care of herself. . . .

Get it together, she told herself, and opened the next door. She gasped and covered her mouth with both hands, because there was a vampire in the room, and he was bending over a girl lying limp on the floor.

He looked up, and she saw the hard gleam of fangs

before his face came into focus and became shockingly familiar.

Michael.

There were two raw holes in the girl's neck, and her open, dry eyes had gone gray. Her skin was the color of old, wet paper, more blue than white.

"Oh," Claire whispered, and stumbled backward out of the room. "Oh no, no, no—"

Michael shot to his feet. "Claire, *wait*! I didn't—"

Eve was in the doorway now, and Shane. Eve took one look at the dead girl, one at Michael, and turned and ran. Shane just stood there, staring at him, then said quietly, "Claire. Go after her. Now. The two of you, stay together. I'll come find you."

Michael took a step toward them. "Shane, I know you're looking for reasons to hate me, but you know I wouldn't—"

Shane backed up, fast, keeping distance between them. His eyes had gone very dark, his face flushed and set with anger. "Claire," he said again. "Get the hell away from him. *Now.*"

"Shit!" Michael looked furious, but he also looked scared and hurt. "You *know me,* Shane. You know I wouldn't do this. Think!"

"You come near me or the girls, I will kill you," Shane said flatly, and then turned and yelled at Claire, full volume. *"Go!"*

She backed out of the room and ran after Eve. Her heavy platform shoes felt awkward, and her cool outfit was nothing but a cheap dress-up costume. She wasn't cool. She wasn't sexy. She was a stupid jerk to be here, and now Michael . . . God, he couldn't have, could he? But there was a flush to his skin, as though he'd fed. . . .

Eve was heading down a set of back stairs. Claire caught sight of the sweep of her long black dress around the spiral. She followed as fast as she dared, with the treacherous shoes. As she neared ground level, the volume of the party swelled and broke into a roar.

When she got to the bottom of the steps, there was no sign of Eve anywhere. It was a sea of moving, swaying bodies, a drunken orgy of dancing (and maybe, in the corners, just an orgy), but she didn't see anybody in formal wear.

"Eve!" She yelled, but even she couldn't hear it. She looked back up the stairs but she didn't see Shane, either.

She was alone.

When she craned her neck, she caught a flash of black velvet heading out of a door, and threw herself into the crowd to follow. If drunks groped on her way by, she barely noticed; she wanted out of here, badly, and she couldn't let anything happen to Eve. Her dignity was the least of her worries.

A hand slipped under her skirt. She turned, instinctively furious, and slapped the guy, hard. Didn't even register his face, or anything about him. He held up his hands in surrender, and she turned and plunged on.

The next room was nearly empty for some reason that Claire didn't understand, until she saw (and smelled) some guy throwing up in the corner. She hurried faster. *Was* that Eve she was following? She couldn't be sure. It looked like her, but the glimpses were too short, the angles all wrong. Claire had to move quicker.

She wasn't sure how it happened, but she ended up in the vast, gleaming kitchen. A bunch of burly guys were carrying in boxes of liquor. Claire pushed past two frat guys who were high-fiving each other. "Liquid panty remover's here!" one of them yelled, and there was a cheer in the other room.

Claire made it outside and gulped the cool, clear night air. She was shaking, sweating, and she felt utterly filthy, inside and out. That was *fun*? Yeah, she supposed if she were drinking and didn't care, it'd be fun, but then again, this was Morganville. Fun like that, you could end up passed out on a bed with strangers . . . or in a morgue drawer.

Eve was leaning against a tree in the glare of a

security light, gasping for breath. She looked glamorous, like some lost Hollywood starlet from the days of black and white, except for the red blaze of her lipstick.

"Oh God," she moaned, and as Claire came toward her she realized she was crying. "Oh God, he's done it; he's really done it—"

"We don't know that," Claire heard herself say. "Maybe he just found her. Was trying to help her."

Eve glared at her. "He's a *vampire*! There's a *dead girl with holes in her neck*! I'm not stupid!"

"I can't believe he'd do it," Claire said. "Come on, Eve, do you? Really? You know him. Is he a killer? Especially when he doesn't have to be?"

Eve shook her head, but that wasn't really an answer. She was shaking off the question.

Shane came out of the kitchen door with the brunette still held in his arms. "Let's go."

"We came in Michael's car," Eve said numbly. "He has the keys. I could—"

"No. Nobody goes up there, and you guys stay the hell away from Michael until we know what's going on." Shane thought for a second, then pulled in a breath. "We walk."

"Walk!" Claire and Eve both blurted. Eve improved it by squeaking, "Are you freaking *mental*?"

"Claire's got Protection, and I'm in the mood to beat the hell out of the first vamp to look at me sideways, and it's safer than getting the three"—he glanced down at the nameless girl in his arms—"four of us in the car with Michael right now. I want room to run if I have to. And fight."

"Shane—"

"We walk," he interrupted. "University first, we can drop this one off with the campus cops."

Claire cleared her throat. "Can't we wait for the police here?"

"Trust me, no," Eve said. "They're going to roust everybody that isn't tagged, and that includes me and Shane. And once they find a drained dead girl, it'll be a free-for-all. We can't take the chance. We need to go. Now."

Claire was half hoping that Michael would show up, but he didn't come out after them. She wondered why. She wondered where he'd been, while they'd been searching the house for him.

Shane started walking toward the street, with the drugged girl murmuring and giggling in his arms. He'd saved one victim, but lost another. And he was taking that second part very personally.

Claire looked at Eve, put her arm around her, and hurried the both of them after Shane.

It was a quiet walk to the university campus. They didn't see anybody. The few cars that passed didn't stop, and although they heard sirens converging on the party, none of the police cars cruised their way.

The night was just cool enough to be pleasant, and the air felt dry and crisp. No clouds. It would have been pretty and romantic, except for the general crappiness of the evening. Eve had stopped crying, but that was almost worse; she'd been so happy before, and now she'd sunk into a gloom so deep she really did seem like a true Goth.

Claire's feet hurt. She was glad when they turned the corner and caught sight of the big, well-lit campus behind the wrought-iron fencing. They'd have to go to one of the four entrances to get through. She'd never really thought about it before, but the place looked unnatural, like a wildlife park.

Or a zoo.

Shane was getting tired, and put the girl down on the first bench they came to once they were inside the fence, while Eve flagged down a passing campus cop car. The Q&A went pretty well, but then, the campus cops weren't especially sharp. It took about half an hour, and then the girl was whisked off to the clinic for detox and checkups, and the three of them looked at each other in the glow of the cop car's headlights as it backed up and pulled away.

"Right," Shane said. "Probably ought to get moving."
Eve got out her phone.

"What are you doing?" he asked.

"Calling a cab."

He snorted. "In Morganville? At night? Right. Eddie doesn't even like picking people up during the daytime. No way is he risking his ass out here for us at night. He probably took his phone off the hook, anyway. He hates frat parties."

"What about Detective Hess?" Claire offered. "I'm sure he'd give us a ride."

"Light it up."

Claire tried. The number rang, but nobody picked up. Same thing with Travis Lowe. She looked at Shane with a sinking feeling and shrugged helplessly. Eve stood up, shivered, and crossed her bare arms for warmth. Shane took his black jacket off and draped it around her shoulders.

"Guess we're on foot," he said, and took Claire's hand, then Eve's. "Don't slow down, and don't stop for anything. If I tell you guys run, you run. Got it?"

He didn't give them a chance to argue. They walked down the path to the exit from the university grounds. Outside, the streetlights were few and far between, and Claire could just feel eyes on her in the shadows. Whether that was real or not, she didn't know, but it made her shake all over with fear. *Come on, Claire, get it together. There are three of us, and Shane can kick enough ass for all of us.*

They crossed the street and headed over a couple of blocks, then down. It was the straightest shot to the house, and the best lit, but it also was going to take them right by Common Grounds. Somehow, Claire felt even more uncomfortable at the idea that Oliver was going to see them trailing by, in all their not-too-smart glory. They'd had a rough enough night without that.

Although, it was a cheering thought that Monica almost certainly was having a worse one, trying to explain to the cops about why there were more drugs in her house than the Rite Aid Pharmacy, not to mention the underage drunken orgies and the dead girl in the bedroom.

By contrast, walking home in darkness in Vampire U.S.A. seemed a little bit mild.

At least until Eve whispered, "Somebody's following."

Claire almost faltered, but kept walking when Shane's hand tightened around hers. "Who?" he asked. Eve didn't turn her head.

"Don't know; I just caught a glimpse. Somebody in dark clothes."

Since only Amelie seemed to like colors in the pale winter hues, Claire figured that didn't narrow it down much. She walked faster, tripped over a crack in the sidewalk and nearly went down, if it hadn't been for Shane's steadying grip. But it slowed them all down, and they couldn't afford for it to happen again.

"Crap," Shane breathed. They were still at least a block from the next burning streetlight, and now Claire could hear slow, steady footsteps behind them. Up ahead, a single open storefront spilled warm yellow light onto the street. Common Grounds. Neutral territory, at least theoretically. "Right. We're not going to make it all the way home. We go into Common Grounds, and—"

"No way, I'm not going in there!" Eve blurted. "I can't!"

"Yes you can; you have to. Neutral ground. Nobody will hurt you there. We can make some kind of deal with Oliver if we have to, temporary protection or something. Promise me—"

Shane didn't have time for anything else, because all hell broke loose. The footsteps behind them suddenly accelerated to a run, Shane swung around and pushed the two girls behind him, and there was a flash of movement Claire couldn't really see. Something hit Shane in the head. Hard. He stumbled and went down to one knee.

Claire screamed and reached for him, but Eve grabbed

her and hauled her by force toward the glow of Common Grounds.

"Get up!"

Claire twisted out of Eve's grip and whirled to see that the yell had come from the jerk from the party, the one who'd felt her up and then gotten his ass kicked by Shane. He'd followed them, and he had a baseball bat. He'd hit Shane in the head *with the baseball bat* and he was getting ready to do it again.

"No!" Claire cried, and lunged back toward them, but Eve grabbed her tightly and swung her around toward the coffee shop again.

"Get inside!" she screamed.

"Let go—"

They stopped fighting each other as a shadow stepped out of the alley, right in front of them, blocking the way.

A long silver line glinted in the starlight. A knife.

It was Eve's brother Jason, looking as greasy and starved and fevered as he had at the party.

"Hey, sis," he said, and the knife turned, and turned, and turned. "I knew you'd be coming this way. Soon as I heard you left the party without your blood-sucking bodyguard, I knew the time was right."

"Jason"—Eve let go of Claire and stepped in between the two of them—"this isn't her problem. Let her go."

Claire was torn—watch Jason, who was terrifying, or pay attention to what was happening behind her, because Shane was fighting now, fighting for his life, and he was already hurt. She risked a glance back and saw Shane grab the baseball bat from his attacker, hit a home run to the guy's shoulder, and send him spinning into the brick wall. The frat guy went down, screaming, but Shane was clearly not doing well, either—he lurched, off balance, and went down to his hands and knees. The bat rolled away.

"Oh God," Claire whispered. There was blood running down his face, dripping in a wet thread to the pavement. "*Shane!*"

Shane shook his head, and the blood flew in a spray, splattering the concrete around him. He looked up, saw her, and blinked.

Then he saw Eve, and behind her, with the knife, Jason.

Shane fumbled for the bat, found it, and climbed to his feet. He stumbled forward, grabbed Claire and pushed her behind him, then yanked Eve away from Jason, as well. He set his feet wide apart and took up a batting stance.

He looked pale and shaken and half-dead, but Claire knew he wasn't backing down.

"Leave them alone," he said. Not a yell, not a threat, just a low, quiet voice with absolute control. "Walk away, Jason."

Jason lost his smile. He put the knife in his pocket and held up his hands. "Sure. Sorry, man. Don't go all Sammy Sosa on me." He lowered his hands again and stuffed them in his coat pockets, looking casual, but there was an avid glitter to his eyes, and a cruel twist to his thin lips. "I heard you found a present in your basement. Something girl-shaped."

Eve groaned, and Claire reached out to steady her when she swayed. "Jason," Eve whispered, and she looked awful, as though she was going to throw up. "Oh God, *why?*"

Shane took a step forward, bat raised and ready, and Jason backed up again. "Doing it there, that was just fun," he said. "But it's not about the girls. I had to show them I was ready."

"Ready?" Eve echoed. "Oh *God,* Jase, is that what this is about? You're just some pathetic wannabe vampire making his bones?" Eve sounded so freaked it made Claire's guts knot up. "You're trying to *impress* them? By killing?"

"Sure." Jason shrugged. He looked thin and weedy, almost lost inside that black leather jacket. "How else do you get attention around here? And I'm going to get *lots* of attention. Starting with you, Claire."

Shane yelled—it wasn't even words, just a yell of

pure fury—and swung at him. Jason jumped back, faster than Claire would have expected, and the bat missed him. Then he lunged forward. Shane was off balance, not really steady on his feet, but that wouldn't matter; if Jason was crazy enough to want to go hand-to-hand with Shane, it was all over.

Wasn't it?

Jason punched Shane low in the stomach, and Shane made a surprised sound and took a step back from him.

Shane was *backing away.* . . .

And then Claire saw the knife in Jason's hand, glittering silver and red, and for a second she didn't understand, she didn't understand at all.

It wasn't until Shane's hand opened and the baseball bat hit the pavement with a noisy rattle, and Shane collapsed to his knees, that she realized that he'd been stabbed.

Shane didn't seem to understand it, either. He was panting, trying to say something, but he couldn't get the words out. His eyes were wide and confused. He tried to get up, but couldn't.

Jason pointed the knife at him, slung it in an arc that spattered them all with blood drops, and turned and walked away. He put the blade back in his pocket. People were coming out of Common Grounds, looking puzzled and alarmed, and at the forefront was Oliver. Oliver's head turned quickly to stare at Jason's departing form, and then he focused on them.

Claire dropped to her knees next to Shane. He looked desperately into her face, and slowly collapsed to his side.

His hands were clutching his stomach, and there was so much blood. . . .

Eve hadn't moved. She was just—standing there, in her lovely black dress, staring blindly after her brother.

Oliver grabbed her and shook her. Her black hair flew wildly, and when he let go, Eve sank down in a defeated slump against the building's brick wall. Oliver shook his head impatiently and turned to Claire, and Shane.

Claire looked up, mute with misery, and saw Oliver staring down at them.

For just a second, she thought she saw something in him. Maybe just a tiny glimmer of empathy.

"Someone is calling the ambulance," he said. "You should put pressure on the wound. He's losing a lot of blood. It's a waste." The blood, he meant. Not Shane.

"Help me," Claire said. Oliver shook his head. *"Help me!"*

"You'll find that vampires aren't particularly good with the wounded," he said. "I'm doing you a favor by staying away. And don't try to order me, little girl. That gold bracelet of yours means almost nothing to me, except that I shouldn't leave witnesses behind."

Shane coughed, wet and hard, and blood trickled out of his mouth. He looked as pale as Michael. Vampire pale.

Claire cradled him in her arms. Oliver glanced at Eve, frowned, and went away. People were coming closer, murmuring, asking questions, but Claire couldn't make any sense out of it. She pressed down on the wet bloody mess of Shane's shirt, felt him tense and try to squirm away, and didn't let him. *Pressure on the wound.* It seemed to take forever until she heard the distant sound of sirens approaching.

Shane was still breathing when they loaded him inside the ambulance, but he wasn't moving, and he wasn't talking.

Claire went to Eve, got her on her feet, and put an arm around her shoulders. "Come on," she said. "We should ride with Shane."

Oliver was staring at the wet, dark smears of blood on the concrete, and as Claire helped Eve up into the back of the ambulance, he looked at one of his coffee shop employees and nodded toward the mess.

"Clean it up," he said. "Use bleach. I don't want to smell it all night."

11

Shane survived the trip, and they rushed him right into surgery. Eve sat silent in her black velvet dress, looking more Goth than ever, and wildly out of place in the soothing neutral waiting room. Claire kept getting up and washing her hands, because she kept finding more of Shane's blood on her clothes and skin.

Eve was crying quietly, almost hopelessly. For some reason Claire didn't cry at all. Not at all. She wasn't even sure she could. Did that make her sick? Screwed up? She wasn't sure whom she could ask. She couldn't seem to feel anything right now except a vague sense of dread.

Richard Morrell came to take their statements. It was simple enough, and Claire had no hesitation in turning in Jason for the stabbing. "And he confessed," Claire added. "To killing those girls."

"Confessed how?" Richard asked. He sat down in the chair across from her in the lounge area, and Claire thought he looked tired. Older, too. She guessed it wasn't easy being the semisane one in the family. "What exactly did he tell you?"

"That he left one for us," she said, and glanced at Eve, who hadn't said a word. Hadn't, as far as Claire could tell, actually blinked. "He called them presents."

"Did he mention any of them by name?"

"No," she whispered. She felt very, very tired all of a sudden, as if she could sleep for a week. Cold, too. She was shivering. Richard noticed, got up, and came

back with a big gray fleece blanket that he tucked
around her. He'd brought a second one for Eve, who
was still wrapped in Shane's black coat.

"Is it possible that Jason just said that because he
knew about the bodies being found near your house?"
Richard asked. "Did he talk about anything more specific that wasn't in the papers?"

Claire almost said yes to that, but she stopped in
time. The police didn't know about the girl being
found in their basement. They thought she'd been
taken to the church by her killer.

She had no choice. She just shook her head.

"It's possible Jason's all talk, then," Richard said.
"We've been watching him. We haven't seen anything
to prove that he's got any involvement with these dead
girls." He hesitated, then said, very gently, "Look. I
don't want to make this about Shane, but he did have
a bat, right?"

Eve raised her head, very slowly. "What?"

"Shane had a bat."

"He took it from another guy," Claire said, nearly
tripping over the words in her hurry to get them out.
"A guy from Monica's party. Shane got jumped; he
was just defending himself! And he was trying to get
Jason to back off—"

"We have witnesses who say that Shane swung the
bat at Jason after Jason had put away his knife."

Claire couldn't find the words. She just sat there,
lips parted, staring into Richard's weary, hard eyes.

"So that's it," Eve said. Her voice started out soft,
but hardened quickly. "It's all going to be Shane's
fault, because he's Shane. Never mind that some frat
ass tried to knock his head off, or that Jason *stabbed
him*. It's still Shane's fault!" She stood up, stripped
away the blanket, and threw it at him. Richard
grabbed it before it hit his face, but just barely. "Here,
you'll need it for your cover-up!" She stalked away,
slender and pale as a lily in all that black.

"Eve—" Richard sighed. "Dammit. Look, Claire, I

have to have the facts, okay? And the facts are that during the confrontation, Jason put his knife away, Shane had a bat, and Shane threatened him. Then Jason stabbed him in self-defense Is that right?"

She didn't answer. She sat for a few seconds, just staring at him, and then stood up, stripped off the blanket, and handed it to him.

"You're going to need a bigger cover-up," she said. "See if there's a circus in town. Maybe you can borrow a tent."

She walked down the hall to see if Shane was out of surgery.

He wasn't.

Eve was pacing the hallway, stiff with rage, hands clenched into fists barely visible as knots in the too-long sleeves of the coat. "Those sons of bitches," she said. "Those *bastards*! They're going to put Shane down; I can feel it."

"Put him down?" Claire repeated. "What do you mean, put him down? Like, a dog?"

Eve glared at her. Her eyes were rimmed with red, and wet with tears. "I mean even if he makes it through the surgery, they're not going to let him get out of this. Richard practically told us; don't you get it? It's the perfect frame. Shane took the swing, Jason acted in self-defense, and nobody's even going to *look* at Jason for these murders. They'll just bury it, like they bury the bodies."

She stopped talking, and her eyes refocused over Claire's shoulder. Claire turned.

Michael was striding toward them, lean and powerful and tall, and he headed straight for Eve. No hesitation, as if nothing had happened. As if they hadn't seen him bending over a dead girl at the party.

He stopped just inches away from Eve, and held out his hands.

"I went looking for you guys. I finally tracked you to Common Grounds. How is he?" he asked. His voice was hoarse.

"Not so good," Eve whispered, and flowed into his arms like water through a broken dam. "Oh God. Oh God, Michael, it all went wrong, it's all wrong—"

He sighed and wrapped his arms around her, and rested his golden head next to her dark one. "I should have come with you. I should have made you get in the damn car. I was going to, but—things happened; I had to take care of it at the party. I never thought you'd try to walk home." He paused, and when he finally went on, his voice was thick with pain. "It's my fault."

"It's nobody's fault," Claire said. "You know you can't make Shane do something he doesn't want to do. Or Eve, for that matter. Or me." She put a hand hesitantly on Michael's arm. "You didn't kill that girl, did you?"

"No," he said. "I found her when I was searching for Jason. I was trying to find him and get him out of the party. He was probably already gone by then."

"Then who—"

Michael looked up, and his blue eyes were fiercely bright. "That's what I had to take care of. There were vampires there, hunting. I had to stop it."

One of the nurses passing by slowed, watching Michael and Eve. Her eyes narrowed, and she stopped to stare. She muttered something, then walked on.

Michael turned to the nurse, who was already halfway down the hall. "Excuse me," he said. "What did you say?"

The nurse stopped dead in her tracks and turned to face him. "I didn't say anything. *Sir.*" That last word sounded sharp enough to cut.

"I think you did," Michael said. "You called her a fang-banger."

The nurse smiled coldly. "If I muttered something under my breath, *sir,* that shouldn't concern you. You and your—*girlfriend*—ought to do your business in the waiting room. Or the blood bank."

Michael's hands curled into fists, and his face went tight with rage. "It's not like that."

The nurse—her name tag said her name was Christine Fenton, RN—outright sneered at him. "Yeah, it never is. It's always different, right? You're just *misunderstood.* You want to hurt me, go ahead and try. I'm not afraid of you. Any of you."

"Good," Michael said. "You shouldn't be afraid of me because I'm a vampire. You ought to be scared because you just trash-talked my girlfriend *to her face.*"

Nurse Fenton flipped him off and kept walking.

"Wow," Eve said. She almost sounded like herself again, as if having somebody diss her had helped, like a slap in the face. "And people treated me bad when I dated Bobby Fee. At least he was breathing. Mouth-breathing, yeah, but—"

Michael put his arm around her, still staring after the nurse. He had a frown on his face, but he forced it off to smile at Eve and plant a kiss on her forehead.

"You need some rest. Let's go back to the waiting room," he said. "I promise not to embarrass you anymore." He guided her in that direction, and threw a look back. "Claire? You coming?"

She nodded absently, but her mind was somewhere else, trying to sort through data. *Fenton.* She'd seen that name before, hadn't she? Not the nurse, though; she'd never met her before and now really didn't look forward to ever seeing her again.

Claire realized she was standing alone in the hallway, and shivered. While this was a modern building, not nearly as nasty as the old, falling-to-ruins abandoned hospital where she and Shane had been chased for their lives, it still gave her the creeps. She threw one last, aching glance at the frosted-glass doors that read SURGICAL AREA—ADMITTANCE TO AUTHORIZED PERSONNEL ONLY. She couldn't see anything beyond except vague moving shadows.

She followed Michael back to the waiting room. Richard Morrell was gone, which was good, and Claire sat in silence, rubbing her hands together, still feeling the phantom slickness of Shane's blood on her skin.

"Hey," Michael said. She didn't know how much time had passed, just that she was stiff and sore and tense. She looked up into his crystal blue eyes, and saw strength and kindness, but also just a little bit of a glitter that didn't seem . . . natural. "Rest. I can almost hear the gears grinding in your head." Eve was asleep in his lap, curled up like a cat. He was stroking her dark hair. "Here," he said. "Lean in." And he put his arm around Claire, and she leaned, and despite everything that had happened, she felt warm and safe.

It all fell in on her then, all the fear and the pain and the fact that Shane had gotten stabbed, right in front of her, and she didn't know how to deal with that, didn't know how to feel or what to say or do, and it was all just . . .

She turned her face into Michael's blue silk shirt and cried, silent heaving sobs that tore up out of her guts in painful jerks. Michael's hand cradled her head, and he let her cry.

She felt him press his cool lips to her temple when she finally relaxed against him, and then she just slid away, into the dark.

Claire fought her way, panicked, out of a nightmare, and into another one. *Hospital. Shane. Surgery.*

Eve was shaking her with both hands on her shoulders, babbling at her, and she couldn't follow the words, but the words didn't matter at first.

Eve was smiling.

"He's okay," Claire said in a whisper, then louder. "He's okay!"

"Yeah," Eve said, the words tumbling out in a confusing bright flood, way too fast. "He's out of surgery. It was touch and go. He had a lot of internal bleeding. He's going to be in ICU for a few days before they let him come home, and he'll have a temporary bracelet, you know, the plastic kind?"

Claire tried to literally shake the sleepy fog out of her head. "Plastic—wait, don't you always get one of those in the hospital? Like an ID tag?"

"Do you? Really? How weird. Oh. Well, in Morganville you leave it on when you leave, and it protects you for up to a month after surgery. Kind of like a temporary vampire restraining order." Eve actually bounced up and down. "He's going to be okay, oh my God, he's going to be okay!"

Claire scrambled out of her seat, grabbed Eve's arms, and the two of them bounced together up and down, then fell into a hug and squealed.

"I'll just—let you guys do that," Michael said. He was sitting in the chairs watching, but he was smiling. He looked tired.

"What time is it?" Claire asked.

"Late. Early." Eve checked her skull watch. "About six in the morning. Michael, you should get home; it'll be dawn soon. I'll stay here with Claire."

"We should all go home," Michael said. "He's not going to wake up for hours yet. You could change clothes."

Claire looked down at herself, and grimaced tiredly. "Yeah, I could," she admitted. Shane's blood had soaked into her patterned tights, and she thought Michael could probably smell it. *She* could even smell it, a musty, rotten odor that made her gag. "Eve? You want to go, too?"

Eve nodded. The three of them walked out of the waiting room and down the long, empty hallway toward the elevators. They passed the front desk, where Nurse Fenton glared at them. When Claire looked back, as they waited for the elevator, Nurse Fenton was dialing the phone.

"Why do I know that name?" she asked, and then realized, *duh,* she was with two Morganville natives. "Fenton? You guys know anything about her?"

The elevator arrived. Eve stepped in and pushed the button for the lobby, and she and Michael looked at each other for a second.

"The family's been here for generations," Michael said. "Nurse Charming out there's a new arrival. She came to TPU for school, married into the family."

"You met her husband," Eve said. "Officer Fenton. Brad Fenton. He's the one who—"

"The one who showed up when Sam was attacked," Claire blurted. "Of course! I forgot his name." Why did that still leave her vaguely uneasy? She couldn't remember anything that Officer Fenton had done that had made her think he was antivamp; he'd acted quickly enough when Sam was in trouble. Not like his wife, who clearly wasn't as open-minded.

She worried about it for a while, but couldn't see any real connection, and there were other things to think about. After all, Shane was okay, and that was all that mattered.

A shower helped, but it didn't banish the dull ache between Claire's eyes, or the strange gray cast the world had taken on. Exhaustion, she guessed, and stress. Nothing looked quite right. She changed clothes, grabbed her backpack, and went back to the hospital—this time, taking a cab, despite it being broad daylight—to wait for visiting hours to start in ICU. No sign of Jason, but then, she hadn't expected him to be that obvious. Or that stupid. He'd managed to get away with it this long.

But then again . . . He really hadn't struck her as all that far-thinking, either. More of a want-take-have kind of guy. So what did that mean? Was Eve right? Was this a giant official cover-up, and Jason had been given free rein to run around town raping and killing and stabbing as the mood moved him? She shuddered just thinking of it.

Nurse Fenton was, mercifully, off duty when Claire arrived. She checked in with the younger, nicer lady at the desk, whose name was Helen Porter, and went to find the least uncomfortable chair in the waiting area. The building wasn't completely lame; there were laptop connections and desks, and she set herself up there. The wireless was crap, but there was a LAN connection, and that worked fine.

Of course, the filters restricted where she could go

on the Internet, and she quickly grew frustrated trying to find out what was happening in the world outside of Morganville . . . more of the same, she guessed. War, crime, death, atrocity. Sometimes it hardly seemed that vampires were the bad guys, given the things people did to each other without the excuse of needing a pint of O neg to get through the day.

She wondered if the vampires had made any headway tracking down who could have staked Sam. Surely they'd found out something. Then again, they hadn't had a lot of luck cornering Shane's dad, either. . . .

Her laptop connection stopped working, right in the middle of an e-mail to her parents. She'd been avoiding making the call, because there was this dangerous temptation to start spilling out her hurt and fear and look for comfort—after all, wasn't that what parents were for?—but if she did, they'd either come running to town, which would be bad, or they'd try to pull her out of school again, which would definitely be worse. Worse in every way.

Still, she knew she was overdue to talk to her mom, and the longer she put it off, the more stress it was going to be for both of them.

Claire logged off the laptop, packed it, and opened up her new cool phone. It glowed with a pale blue light when she dialed the number, and she heard faint clicking. That probably meant the call was being recorded, or at least monitored. More reason to be careful about what she said . . .

Mom answered the phone on the third ring. "Hello?"

"Hi!" Claire winced at the artificial cheeriness of her tone. Why couldn't she sound natural? "Mom, it's Claire."

"Claire! Honey, I've been worried. You should have called days ago."

"I know, Mom, I'm sorry. I got busy. I got transferred into some advanced classes; they're really great, but there's been a lot of homework and reading. I just forgot."

"Well," her mother said, "I'm glad to hear those teachers are recognizing that you need special attention. I was a little worried when you told me the classes were so easy. You like challenges, I know that."

Oh, I'm challenged now, Claire thought. Between the classes and Myrnin, being stalked by Jason, and being terrified for Shane . . . "Yeah, I do," she said. "So I guess this is all good."

"What else? How are your friends? That nice Michael, is he still playing his guitar?" Mom asked it as if it was a silly little hobby that he'd give up eventually.

"Yes, Mom, he's a musician. He's still playing. In fact, he was playing in the University Center the other day. He got quite a crowd."

"Well, fine. I hope he's not playing in some of those clubs, though. That gets dangerous."

There was more of that, the danger talk, and Claire worried that her mother was, if not remembering exactly, at least remembering *something.* Why would she be so fixated on how dangerous things could be?

"Mom, you're overreacting," Claire finally said. "Honest, everything's fine here."

"Well, you started out this semester in the emergency room, Claire; you can't really blame me for worrying. You're very young to be out on your own, and not even in the dorm. . . ."

"I told you about the problems with the dorm," Claire said.

"Yes, I know; the girls weren't very nice—"

"Not very nice? Mom! They threw me down the stairs!"

"I'm sure that was an accident."

It hadn't been, but there was something about her mother that wasn't going to accept that, not really. For all her fluttering and worrying, she didn't want to believe that something really could be badly wrong.

"Yeah," Claire sighed. "Probably. Anyway, the house is great. I really like it there."

"And Michael has our numbers? In case there's any problem?"

"Yes, Mom, everybody's got the numbers. Oh, speaking of that, here's my new cell phone—" She rattled off the digits, twice, and made her mother read them back. "It's got better reception than the old one, so you can get me a lot more easily, okay?"

"Claire," her mother said, "are you sure you're all right?"

"Yes. I'm fine."

"I don't want to pry, but that boy, the one in the house—not Michael, but—"

"Shane."

"Yes, Shane. I think you should keep your distance from him, honey. He's old for you, and he seems pretty sure of himself."

She did *not* want to get into the subject of Shane. She'd nearly stumbled over saying his name, it hurt so bad. She wanted to talk to her mother the way she'd used to. They'd talked about everything, once, but there was no way she could really talk about Morganville with her family.

And that meant that there was no way she could talk about anything at all.

"I'll be careful," she managed to say, and her attention was caught by the young nurse standing in the doorway of the waiting area, waving for her attention. "Oh—Mom, I have to go. Sorry. Somebody's waiting for me."

"All right, honey. We love you."

"Love you, too." She hung up, slid the phone into her pocket, and grabbed her backpack.

The nurse led her through another set of glass double doors into an area labeled ICU. "He's awake," she said. "You can't stay long; we want him to rest as much as possible, and I can already tell he's going to be a difficult patient." She smiled at Claire, and winked. "See if you can sweeten him up a little for me. Make my life easier."

Claire nodded. She felt nervous and a little sick with the force of her need to see him, touch him . . . and at the same time, she dreaded it. She hated the thought of seeing him like this, and she didn't know what she was going to say. What did people say when they were this scared of losing someone?

He looked worse than she'd imagined, and she must have let it show. Shane grunted and closed his eyes for a few seconds. "Yeah, well, I'm not dead; that's something. One of those in the house is enough." He looked awful—pale as, well, Michael. The baseball bat had left him with Technicolor bruising, and he seemed fragile in ways Claire hadn't even thought about. There were so many tubes and things. She sat down in the chair next to his raised bed and reached over the railing to touch him lightly on his scraped, bruised hand.

He turned it to twine their fingers together. "You're all right?"

"Yeah," she said. "Jason ran away, after." Walked, really, but she wasn't going to say that. "Eve's okay, too. She was here while you were in surgery; she just went home to change clothes. She'll be back."

"Yeah, I guess the diva dress might have been a little much around here." He opened his eyes and looked at her directly. "Claire. Really. You're okay?"

"I'm fine," she said. "Except that I'm scared for you."

"I'm okay."

"Except for the stab wound and all the internal bleeding? Yeah, sure, tough guy." She heard her voice quiver, and knew she was about to cry. She didn't want to. He wanted to laugh it off, wanted to be tough, and she ought to let him, right?

He tried to shrug, but it must have hurt, from the spasm that went across his face. One of the machines near Claire beeped, and he let out a slow sigh. "That's better. Man, they give you the good stuff in ICU. Remind me to always get seriously wounded from now on. That minor injury stuff isn't as much fun."

It was wearing him out to talk. Claire got up and leaned over to stroke her fingertips lightly over his lips. "Shhhh," she said. "Rest, okay? Save it for somebody who isn't me. It's okay to be scared. It's okay to be hurt, Shane. With me, it's okay."

For a second his eyes glittered with tears, and then the tears spilled over, threading wet trails into his hair. "Damn," he whispered. "Sorry. I just—I felt it all going away, I felt you going away, I tried—I thought he was going to hurt you and there was nothing I could do about it—"

"I know." She leaned forward and kissed him very lightly, careful of the bruises. "I know."

He cried a little, and she stayed right where she was, his shield against the world, until it was over. Finally, he fell into a light sleep, and she felt a tap on her shoulder. The nurse motioned for her to step out, and Claire carefully pulled her hand free of Shane's and followed.

"Sorry," Helen said. "I'd like for him to sleep a while before we start with the poking and prodding. You can come back this afternoon, all right?"

"Sure. What time?"

Four o'clock. That left her the entire day to kill, and not the slightest idea what she ought to be doing with it. She didn't have to see Myrnin; Amelie hadn't given her any other instructions to follow. It was Saturday, so she wasn't cutting any classes, and she didn't want to go back to the Glass House and just . . . worry.

Claire was still trying to decide what to do when she spotted a familiar, well-groomed figure standing outside the hospital doors.

What was Jennifer, one of Monica's regular clique, doing hanging around here?

Waiting for Claire, apparently, because she hurried to catch up as Claire strode by, heading for the taxi stand. "Hey," she said, and tucked her glossy hair behind her ear. "So. How's Shane doing?"

"Like you care," Claire said.

"Well, yeah. I don't. But Monica wants to know."

"He's alive." That was no more than Monica could learn without her help, so it didn't really matter, and Claire didn't like having Jennifer this close. Monica was creepy, but at least she was Alpha Creepy. There was something pathetic and extra-weird about her two groupies.

Jennifer kept pace with her. Claire stopped and turned to face her. They were halfway down the sidewalk, in the full glare of early-fall sunlight, which at least meant it wasn't too likely some vampire would be sneaking up on her while Jennifer kept her distracted. "Look," Claire said, "I don't want anything to do with you, or Monica, okay? I don't want to be friends. I don't want you sucking up to me just because I'm . . . somebody, or something."

Jennifer didn't look like she wanted to be sucking up, either. In fact, she looked as bitter and resentful as a glossy, entitled rich girl could look—which was a lot. "Dream on, loser. I don't care who your Patron is; you're never going to be anything more than jumped-up trailer trash with delusions. Friends? I wouldn't be friends with you if you were the last person breathing in this town."

"Unless Monica said so," Claire said spitefully. "Fine, you don't want to exchange friendship rings. So why are you bothering me?"

Jennifer glared at her for a few seconds, stubborn and angry, and then looked away. "You're smart, right? Like, freak smart?"

"What does that have to do with anything?"

"You placed out of the two classes we were in together. You must have aced the tests."

Claire nearly laughed out loud. "You want *tutoring*?"

"No, idiot. I want test answers. Look, I can't bring home anything under a C; that's the rule, or my Patron cuts off my college. And I *want* my full four years, even if I never do anything with it in this lame-ass town." A muscle fluttered in Jennifer's jawline. "I don't get this economics crap. It's all math, Adam

Smith, blah blah blah. What am I ever going to use it for, anyway?"

She was asking for help. Not in so many words, maybe, but that was what it was, and Claire was off balance for a few heartbeats. First Monica, now Jennifer? What next, a cookie bouquet from Oliver?

"I can't give you test answers," she said. "I wouldn't even if I could." Claire took in a deep breath. "Look, I'm going to regret this, but if you really want help, I'll go over the notes with you. *Once.* And you pay me, too. Fifty dollars." Which was wildly out of line, but she didn't really care if Jennifer said no.

Which Jennifer clearly thought about, hard, before giving her a single, abrupt nod.

"Common Grounds," she said. "Tomorrow, two o'clock." Which was pretty much the safest time to be out and about, providing they didn't stay too long. Claire wasn't wild about visiting Oliver's shop again, but she didn't suppose there were too many places in town that Jennifer would agree to go. Besides, it wasn't far from Claire's house.

"Two o'clock," Claire echoed, and wondered if they were supposed to shake hands or something. Not, obviously, because Jennifer flipped her hair and walked away, clearly glad to have it over with. She jumped into a black convertible and pulled away from the curb with a screech of tires.

Leaving Claire to contemplate the afternoon sunlight and the odds of walking home through a Morganville where Jason was still on the loose.

She took out her cell phone and called the town's lone taxi driver, who told her he was off duty, and hung up on her.

So she called Travis Lowe.

Detective Lowe wasn't really happy to be the Claire Taxi Service. She could tell because he wasn't his usual self, not at all—he'd always been kind to her, and a little bit funny, but there wasn't any of that in the way he pulled his blue Ford to the curb and snapped, "Get in." He was accelerating away even before she got strapped in. "You do know I've got a real job, right?"

"Sorry, sir," she said. The *sir* was automatic, a habit she couldn't seem to break no matter how hard she tried. "I just didn't think I should be walking home, with Jason—"

"Right thought, just wrong timing," he said, and his tone softened some. He looked tired and sallow, and there were dark bags under his eyes as though he hadn't slept in days. He needed a shave and a shower. Probably the shower more than the shave. "How's Shane?"

"Better," she said. "The nurse told me he was going to be okay; it's just going to take some time."

"Good news. Could've gone the other way. Why'd you try to walk home like that?"

She fidgeted a little in the seat. In contrast to the vampire cars, with their dark tinting, the glare inside Lowe's car seemed way too bright. "Well, we tried getting a ride," she said. In retrospect, none of the explanations seemed all that good, really. She didn't mention that she'd tried both Lowe's phone and Joe Hess's. No point in making him feel guilty. Guiltier. "We thought with the three of us together . . ."

"Yeah, good plan, if it had been any other kids. You guys, you're just trouble to the power of three. And I'm no math whiz, but I'm betting that's a lot." His eyes were cold and distant, and she had the distinct feeling he wasn't really thinking about her at all. "Listen, I've got to make a stop. I'm running late as it is. You stay in the car, okay? Just stay in the car. Do *not* get out."

She nodded. He turned some corners, into a residential area of Morganville she didn't recognize. It was run-down and faded, with leaning fences that were marked with sun-bleached gang signs. The houses weren't much better. Most of them just had sheets tacked up in the windows instead of real curtains.

He parked in front of one, got out, and said, "Windows up. Lock the doors."

She followed his orders and watched him go up the narrow, cracked sidewalk to the front door. It opened on the second knock, but she couldn't see who was inside, and Lowe closed the door behind him.

Claire frowned and waited, wondering what he was doing—cop stuff, she guessed, but in Morganville that could be anything, from running errands for vampires to dog-catching.

He didn't come back. She checked her watch and found that more than ten minutes had passed. He'd ordered her to stay put, but for how long? She could have been home already if she'd been able to get the taxi, or even if she'd walked.

And it was getting hot in the car.

Ten more minutes, and she started to feel anxious. The neighborhood seemed deserted—no people on the street, even in the bright sunlight. Even for Morganville, that didn't seem . . . normal. She didn't know this area, hadn't been through it before, and she wondered what went on around here.

Before Claire could decide to do something really stupid, like investigating on her own, Detective Lowe came out of the house and, after rapping on the window for her to unlock the door, got back in the car. He looked, if possible, even more tired. Depressed, almost.

"What's wrong?" she asked. The sheets tacked up as curtains twitched in the window of the house, as if somebody was peering out at them. "Sir?"

"Quit calling me sir," Lowe snapped, and put the car in gear. "And it's none of your affair. Stay out of it."

There was blood on his hand. His knuckles were scraped. Claire pulled in a fast breath, her eyes widening as she noticed, and he sent her a narrow glance as the car accelerated away down the deserted street. "Were you in a fight?" she asked.

"What did I just tell you?" Detective Lowe had never been angry before, not with her, but she could tell he was being pushed pretty far. She nodded and turned face forward, trying too keep herself still. It wasn't easy. She wanted to ask questions, a dozen of them. She wanted to ask him where Detective Hess had gone. She wanted to find out who lived in that house, and why Lowe had gone there. And whom he'd hit, to scrape up his knuckles like that.

And why he was so desperately angry that he'd snap at her.

Lowe didn't enlighten her about any of it. He pulled the car to a stop with an abrupt jerk of brakes, and Claire blinked and realized that she was home. "You need another ride, call a taxi," Lowe said. "I'm on police business the rest of the day."

She climbed out and tried to thank him, but he wasn't listening. He was already flipping open his cell phone and dialing one-handed as he put the car in gear with the other. She barely got the door shut before he pulled away from the curb.

"Bye," she said softly, to the empty air, and then shrugged and went inside.

Michael was sitting in the living room, playing guitar. He looked up and nodded at her when she came in. "Eve went to the hospital," he said. "She must have just missed you."

Claire sighed and slumped down on the couch. "They won't let her in. Visiting hours are over." She yawned and curled up, tucking her feet under her. She ached all over, and everything seemed too bright, and not quite right. "Michael?"

"Yeah?" He was working out a chord progression and was focused on the music; his response didn't mean he was listening, really.

"Shouldn't you be asleep? I mean, don't vampires—?"

He was listening after all. "Sleep during the day? Yeah, mostly. But I—couldn't. I keep thinking . . ." The chord progression turned minor, then wrong, and he grimaced. "I keep thinking that I should have fixed this crap with Shane by now. I don't know if he's going to get over it, not really. Not in the ways that count. And I hate it. I can't stop thinking—I don't want him doing this stuff. Not without me watching his back."

Claire leaned her head against the battered black pillow on the corner of the couch. It smelled like spilled Coke, a little, but mostly it smelled like Shane, and she gladly turned her face into it and took a deep breath. It made it seem like he was here, at least for a second.

"He wouldn't hate you so bad if he didn't love you, at least a little bit," she said. "We'll be okay. We're going to stay together, right? The four of us?"

Michael looked up, and for a second she wasn't sure what he was going to say; but then he said, "Yeah. We'll stay together. No matter what."

It felt like a lie, and she wished he hadn't said it.

She fell asleep, listening to him compose a new song, and dreamed about vibrating strings and door ways that led nowhere, and everywhere. Someone was watching her; she could feel it, and it wasn't Michael. It wasn't warm and kind; it wasn't safe. She wasn't safe, and there was something wrong, wrong, *wrong*. . . .

She nearly fell off the couch, she jerked so hard. Michael wasn't there, and his guitar was in the case on the table. Claire squinted at the clock. It was nearly two o'clock, and she'd slept through lunch, but it wasn't hunger that had woken her up. She'd heard something.

It came again, a thumping knock on the front door. She yawned and pushed back the blanket that Michael had draped over her, and, still trying to rub the sleep out of her eyes, padded to the door.

She had to stand on tiptoes at the peephole to see out. Some guy, nobody that clicked any immediate recognition—not Jason, at least. That was good. Claire looked over her shoulder, but there was no sign Michael had heard. She had no idea where he'd gone.

She opened the door. The guy standing outside

looked up and held out a padded mailer with stickers on it; she took it and read her own name on it. "Oh," she said, preoccupied. "Thanks."

"No problem, Claire," he said. "Be seeing you."

There was something way too familiar about the way he said it. She jerked her head up, staring at him, but she still didn't know him. He was just . . . normal. Average height, average weight, average everything. There was a silver bracelet on his wrist, so he was human, not vampire.

"Do I know you?" she asked. He tilted his head a little, but didn't answer. He just turned and walked away down the sidewalk, toward the street. "Hey, wait! Who are you?"

He waved and kept walking. She went a couple of steps outside into the early-afternoon heat, frowning, but she'd left her shoes off, and the concrete was blazing hot. No way could she run after him in bare feet; she'd fry like bacon.

She retreated back into the cool darkness of the house and sighed in relief at the feeling of cool wood under her soles. She looked down at the envelope in her hand and suddenly wanted to drop it and step away. She didn't know who this guy was, and it was really strange that he wouldn't answer her. And strange, in Morganville, was rarely going to be a good thing.

She closed and locked the door, took a deep breath, and tore open the top of the envelope. No smell of blood or disgusting rotting things, which was a plus. She carefully squeezed the sides to open it up, and saw nothing in it but a note. She shook it out into her hand, and recognized the paper immediately—heavy, expensive paper, cream-colored, embossed with the same logo that was on her gold bracelet.

It was a note from Amelie. Which meant the guy who'd dropped it off had to be somebody she trusted, at least that far.

"Everything okay?" Michael's voice came from the

end of the hall. Claire gasped, stuffed the paper back into the envelope, and turned to face him.

"Sure," she said. "Just mail."

"Good stuff?"

"Don't know yet; I haven't read it. Probably junk."

"Enjoy the fact that you don't have electricity, water, cable, Internet, and garbage to pay for," he said. "Look, I'm going upstairs. Yell if you need anything. There's stuff in the fridge if you're hungry." A brief pause. "Don't open the pitcher in the back on the top shelf."

"Michael, *tell* me you're not putting blood in our refrigerator."

"I told you not to open it. So you'll never know."

"You *suck*!" Of course he did; he was a vampire. "I mean, not in a good way, either!"

"Eat something! I'm sleeping." And she heard his door shut, so she was effectively alone.

Claire fumbled out the letter and unfolded it. A smell of faint, dusty roses came from the paper, as though it had been stored in a trunk with dried flowers. She wondered how old it was.

It was a short, simple note, but it made her whole body turn cold.

It read:

> *I am displeased with your progress in your advanced studies. I suggest you spend additional time learning all you can. Time is growing short. I do not care how you arrange this, but you will be expected to demonstrate within the next two days at least a journeyman understanding of what you are being taught. You cannot involve Michael. He is not to be risked.*

Nothing else. Claire stared at the perfect handwriting for a few seconds, then folded the note up and put it back in the envelope. She still felt tired and hungry, but more than anything else, now she felt scared.

Amelie wasn't happy.

That wasn't good.

Two days. And Michael could go with her only in the evenings. . . .

She couldn't wait.

Claire checked in her backpack. The red crystal shaker was still inside, safely zipped into a pocket.

If she took Michael's car—no, she couldn't. She'd never be able to see through the tinting, even if she felt confident in her ability to drive it. And Detective Lowe wasn't going to give her a ride. She could try Detective Hess, but Lowe's attitude had made her gun-shy.

Still, she couldn't just go out alone.

With a sigh, she called Eddie, the taxi driver.

"What?" he snapped. "Don't I get a day off? What is it with you?"

"Eddie, I'm sorry, I'm really sorry. I need a favor." Claire hastily checked her wallet. "Um, it's a short trip, I'll pay you double, okay? Please?"

"Double? I don't take checks."

"I know that. Cash."

"I don't wait. I pick up, I drop off, I leave."

"Eddie! Double! Do you want it or not?"

"Keep your panties on. What's the address?"

"Michael Glass's house."

Eddie heaved a sigh so heavy it sounded like a temporary hurricane. "You again. Okay, I come. But I swear, last time. No more Saturdays, yes?"

"Yes! Yes, okay. Just this time."

Eddie hung up on her. Claire bit her lip, slipped the note from Amelie into her bag, and hoped Michael had been serious about going to bed. Because if he'd eavesdropped on her, even by accident, she was going to have a lot of explaining to do.

It took five minutes for Eddie to arrive. She waited on the sidewalk, and jumped in the back of the battered old cab—barely yellow, after so much sun exposure—and handed Eddie all the cash she had. He counted it. Twice.

Then he grunted and flipped the handle on the taxi meter. "Address?"

"Katherine Day's house." One thing Claire had learned about riding with Eddie—you didn't need numbers, only names. He knew everybody, and he knew where everybody lived. All the natives, anyway. The students, he just dropped on campus and forgot.

Eddie threw an arm over the back of his seat and frowned at her. He was a big guy, with a lot of wild dark hair, including a beard. She could barely see his eyes when he frowned, which was pretty much always. "The Day House. You're sure."

"I'm sure."

"Told you I'm not staying, right?"

"Eddie, *please*!"

"Your funeral," he said, and hit the gas hard enough to press her back into the cushions.

12

Myrnin's shack was easy enough to get into—the trick, after all, wasn't getting in. It was getting out. Light slashed in thin ribbons through the darkness where the boards didn't quite meet, but it wasn't exactly easy to see, and she didn't much like roaming around in Myrnin's lair in the dark. Or even half dark. She found a flashlight on the shelf near the door and thumbed it on. A pure white circle of light brushed across the dusty floor and showed her the narrow steps at the back that led down.

She went very slowly. Very carefully. "Myrnin?" She said it quietly, because he'd hear her; he'd told her that his ears were sensitive because of the silence and his lack of company.

He didn't answer.

"Myrnin?" Claire could see the hard edge of light at the bottom of the steps. He had everything on, it looked like—the light had a funny color, a mixture of fluorescent bulbs and oil lamps, candles and incandescents. "Myrnin, it's Claire. Where are you?"

She almost missed him, because he was so still. Myrnin was usually in motion of some kind—moving fast, like a hummingbird, from one bright attraction to the next. But what was standing in the center of the room looked like Myrnin—only completely still. Vampires did breathe, a little; the blood they took from humans needed oxygen, Claire had figured out, although a lot less than in a normal person. But his chest was still.

his eyes were open and staring, and he wasn't moving at all. Not even to look at her. His attention was focused somewhere off to the side.

"Myrnin?" She put her bag down slowly. "It's Claire. Can you hear me?"

His chest rose just a fraction, and he whispered, "Get out. Go."

And tears slid out of his wide, staring eyes to run down his pale cheeks.

"What is it? What's wrong?" She forgot about caution, and moved toward him. "Myrnin, please tell me what's wrong!"

"You," he said. "This is wrong."

And then he just—collapsed. Dropped like his knees had given out, and the rest of him followed. It wasn't a graceful fall, and it would have hurt a normal human, maybe badly. Myrnin's head hit the floor with a solid crack, and Claire crouched down next to him and put her hand on his chest—not sure what she was doing, what she was supposed to be feeling for. Not his pulse—vampires didn't have one, at least not that humans could detect. She knew that from leaning against Michael.

"I can't do this," Myrnin said. His cold hand flashed out and grabbed hold of her arm, hard enough to bruise. "Why are you here? You weren't supposed to come!"

"What are you talking about?" Claire tried to pull free, but she might as well have been pulling against a bridge cable. Myrnin could snap her bones, if he wanted. Or even if he got careless. "Myrnin, you're hurting me. Please—"

"Why?" He shook her, and she could see the panic in his eyes. That made her take a deep breath and forget the ache where he was holding her. "You weren't supposed to come back!"

"Amelie sent me a note. She said I had only two days to learn—"

Myrnin groaned and let her go. He covered his eyes with his hands, dry-scrubbed his face, and said, "Help me up." Claire put a hand under his arm and managed to get him upright, leaning against a solid lab cabinet that seemed like it was bolted to the floor. "Let me see the note."

She went back to the stairs, grabbed her backpack, and produced the note. Myrnin unfolded it in shaking hands and looked at it intently.

"What? Is it a fake?"

"No," he said slowly. "She sent you to me." He dropped the note in his lap, as if it had gotten unbearably heavy, and rested his head against the hard surface of the lab cabinet. "She's lost hope, then. She's acting out of fear and panic. That isn't like her."

"I don't understand!"

"That's exactly the problem," Myrnin said. "You don't. And you won't, child. I explained this to her before—even the brightest human can't learn this quickly. And you are so very young." He sounded tired and very sad. "Now we come to the last of it, Claire. Think it through: Amelie sent you to me, knowing that I do not believe you are the solution to my problems. *Why would she do that?* You know what I am, what I do, what I crave. Why would she put you in front of me if she didn't want me to—to—" He seemed to be begging her to understand, but he wasn't making any sense. "You don't know what she is capable of doing, child. *You don't know!*"

There was so much fear in his voice, and in his face, that she felt a real sense of dread. "If she didn't want you to teach me, why did she send me?"

"The question is, why—after being so careful to provide you with escorts—would she send you to me *alone*?"

"I—" She stopped, remembering. "Sam said to ask you about the others. The other apprentices. He said I wasn't the first—"

"Samuel is quite intelligent," Myrnin said, and squeezed his eyes tightly shut. "You glow, you glow like the finest lamp. So much possibility in you. Yes, there have been others Amelie sent to learn. Vampires and humans. I killed the first one almost by accident, you must understand, but the effect—you see, the more intelligent the mind, the longer my clarity lasts, or so we thought at first. The first bought me almost a year without attacks. The second . . . mere months, and so on, in ever-decreasing cycles as my disease grew worse."

"She sent me here to die," Claire said. "She wants you to kill me."

"Yes," Myrnin said. "Clever, isn't she? She understands my desperation so well. And you do glow so brightly, Claire. The temptation is almost—" He shook his head violently, as if trying to throw something out of his mind. "Listen to me. She seeks to fend off the inevitable, but I can't accept this trade. Your life is so fragile, just beginning; I can't steal it away for half a day, or an hour. It's no use."

"But—I thought you said I could learn—"

He sighed. "I wanted to believe, but it isn't possible. Yes, I could teach you—but you'd be nothing more than a gifted mimic, a mechanic, not an engineer. There are things you cannot do, Claire, not for years at best. I'm sorry."

Myrnin was saying that she was stupid, and Claire felt a hot, strange spark of anger. "Let go of my arm!" she snapped, and he was surprised enough that some of the blankness in his dark eyes went away, replaced with concern. He slowly relaxed his fingers. "Explain it to me. You're not all-knowing; maybe you forgot something."

Myrnin smiled, but it was a shadow of his usual manic grin. "I assure you, I probably have," he agreed. "But Claire, attend: already, my muscles disobey me. Soon I won't be able to walk, and then my voice will lock in my throat. And then blindness, and madness, and I will end my days locked in a black, dark place, screaming silently as I starve. If there were any shred of hope that I could avoid that fate, don't you think I would seize it?"

He said it so . . . calmly. As if it had already happened. "No," Claire said. She couldn't help it. "No, that isn't going to happen." She'd somehow thought that he'd just . . . fade away. Without pain. But this kind of torture—he didn't deserve it. Not even Oliver deserved to have this creeping up on him. "How— Do you know what causes it?"

Myrnin smiled, but the smile looked bitter. "I thought I did, once. Amelie knows much of what I've forgotten, but you may find your clues in the notebooks. I was cautious, of course, but if you look closely, you may find my theories. In any case, it no longer matters. I can feel myself slipping into the black. There's no return."

"How do you *know*?"

"I've seen it happen. It's always the same. Amelie will lock me away because she'll have no choice; she must try to keep the secret, and it will take me a very long time to die, because I am so very old." He shook his head. "Doesn't matter. Not now. All that matters is that you go home, child, and never come back. I can't imagine I would have the unexpected strength of will to refuse such a lovely warm gift twice."

It was stupid. She didn't like Myrnin, she *couldn't*. He was scary and strange and he'd tried to kill her not just once, but at least twice.

So why did she feel like she wanted to cry?

"What if we use the crystals?" she blurted. Myrnin's eyes narrowed. "I learned, when you had me take them. What if we use them now? Both of us? Would that help?"

He was already shaking his head. "Claire, it's a fool's quest. Even if we continue research on the cure, there's not enough time—"

"The cure to your disease!" She felt a sudden surge of hope as she dug through her backpack and came up with the shaker of crystals. "Isn't this what you've done so far?"

"It is. Clever of you to discover that. But the point is, it's taken years to develop it, and it's at best only a temporary measure. Even a large dose will wear off in a few hours for either one of us, and the consequences for you . . ."

"But if we can come up with a cure, a real cure?"

"It's naïve to think that we could perfect such a thing in mere hours. No, I think you had better go. I have been quite noble today. You really should let me enjoy it while I can." He looked at the shaker in her hands, and for a second she thought she saw a spark of that quick interest that had driven him so hard in earlier meetings. "Perhaps—if I show you the research, you could carry that part of it onward. For the others."

"Sam said you were all sick. Even Amelie."

Myrnin nodded. "As I am, so shall they all be. Every vampire who lives will suffer this in the next ten years, unless it is stopped."

Ten years! No. Not Michael.

She couldn't stand by without trying to stop it, at least for him.

"Amelie brought us to Morganville to buy us time, to find a way to ensure our survival. She believed— she believed that humans might hold the keys to this plague, and she also believed that we could no longer afford to live as we had, preying in the night or hiding. She thought that humans and vampires could live in cooperation, and find the solution to our illness together. That quickly became impossible, of course; she realized, after telling the first few vampires, that they would go mad knowing what was to come, that they would kill indiscriminately. So it became a secret, a terrible secret. She told them part of the truth, that she was seeking a cure to what makes us sterile. Never the rest."

"So—Morganville's a kind of lab. She's trying to find a cure, and protect all of you at the same time."

"Exactly so." Myrnin rubbed his hands over his face again. "I'm getting tired, Claire. Best give me the crystals."

She poured out a few in his hand. He met her eyes.

"More," he said. "The disease has advanced. I will need a large dose to stay with you, even for a while."

She poured about a teaspoon out. Myrnin popped it into his mouth, made a face at the bitterness, and swallowed. A shudder went through him, and she actually saw the weariness and confusion fade. "Excellent. That really was an amazing discovery. Too bad about the doctor; really, he was very bright." Oh dear. Myrnin was swinging toward the manic now, thanks to the drugs. That was dangerous. "You're very bright. Perhaps you could read through the notes."

"I—I'm just *now* starting advanced biochemistry—"

"Nonsense, your native ability is clear." He pointed toward the shaker of crystals in her hand. "Take it."

"No. It's your medicine, not mine."

"And it will help you keep up with me, because we have very little time, Claire, very little." His eyes were bright and clear, like a bird's, and with about as much affection. "There are two ways you can assist me. You can take the crystals, or you can help me extend this period of clarity in other ways."

She sat back on her heels. "You said you wouldn't."

"Indeed. But you see, the disease makes me a sentimental fool. If I am to find an heir to my knowledge, *and* find a cure for my people, then I can't be burdened with such considerations." His gaze brushed over her, abstract and hungry. "You burn so very brightly, you know."

"Yeah," she muttered. "You said." She hated this. She hated that Myrnin could change like this, go from friend to enemy in the space of a minute. Which one was real? Or was any of it?

Claire shook half a teaspoon of the crystals into her palm.

"More," Myrnin said. She added a couple, and he reached out, took the shaker, and poured a heaping mound of it into her hand. "You have a great deal to learn, and you are operating from such a disadvantage. Better safe than sorry."

She didn't want to take it—well, she did, a little, because the strawberry smell of the crystals brought back flashes of the way the world had looked: diamond clear, uncomplicated, *simple*.

Hard not to want that.

Myrnin said, "Take it, or I will have to take you, Claire. We have no more moves on our chessboard."

She poured the crystals onto her tongue and almost gagged from the bitterness. The strawberry flavor was overwhelmed by it, and the aftertaste was rotten and cold on her tongue, and she thought for a second she might throw up. . . .

And then everything snapped into hot, sharp, *perfect* focus.

Myrnin no longer looked strange and pathetic; he was a burning pillar of energy barely contained by skin. She could see that he was sick, somehow; there was a darkness in him, like rot at the heart of a tree. The room took on a fey glitter. *Neurotransmitters,* she thought. Her brain was rushing a million miles an hour, making her giddy and breathless. *My reaction time must be ten times faster.*

Myrnin bounded up to his feet, grabbed her hand, and dragged her to the shelves, where he began frantically pulling down books. Notebooks, textbooks, scraps of handwritten paper. Two black-bound composition books, the same kind Claire used in lab class. Even a couple of the cheap blue books she used for essay tests. Everything was crammed with fine, perfect handwriting.

"Read," he said. "Hurry."

All she had to do was flip pages. Her eyes captured things, like cameras, and her brain was so fast and efficient that she translated and comprehended the text almost instantly. Nearly two hundred pages, and she paged through as fast as her fingers could go.

"Well?" Myrnin demanded.

"This is wrong," she said, and flipped back to the first third of the notebook. "Right here. See? The formula's wrong. The variable doesn't match up with the prior version, and the error gets replicated going forward—"

Myrnin gave out a fierce, sharp cry, like a hunting hawk, and snatched the book away from her. "Yes! Yes, I see it! That fool. No wonder he sustained me only for a few days. But you, Claire, oh, you are different."

She knew she ought to be afraid of the slow, predatory smile he gave her, but she couldn't help it.

She smiled back.

"Give me the next one," she said. "And let's start making crystals."

When it wore off, it hit Myrnin first. He took more, but she could see it wasn't really working this time. Diminishing returns. That was why he'd only taken a few crystals last time, to prolong the effects even if the change hadn't been as dramatic.

This crash was like hitting a brick wall at ninety miles an hour.

It started when he lost his balance, caught himself, and knocked a tray off the lab table; he tried to catch it in midair, a feat he'd been more than capable of an hour before, and missed it completely. He stared at his hands in frustration and viciously kicked the tray. It sailed across the room and hit the far wall with a spectacular clatter.

Claire straightened up from spreading the crystals out on the drying tray. She could feel the effects, too—her brain was slowing down, her body aching. It had to be worse for Myrnin, because of the disease. *It was wrong to do this,* she thought. Wrong, because his manic phase always led to dementia, and he'd wanted so badly to be himself again.

But the crystals drying on the tray could change that, or at least, she hoped they could. It wasn't that Myrnin had been wrong, but that his last assistant had made mistakes; whether deliberate or not, Claire couldn't tell. But the crystals in the tray would be more effective, and longer lasting.

Myrnin could stabilize again.

"It isn't a cure," Myrnin said, as if he were reading her thoughts.

"No, but it buys you time," Claire said. "Look, I can come tomorrow. Promise me you'll leave these here, all right? Don't try to take them yet; they're not ready. And they're more powerful, so you'll have to start with a small dose and work up."

"Don't tell me what to do!" Myrnin barked. "Who is the master here? Who is the student?"

This was familiar, and dangerous. She lowered her head. "You're the master," she said. "I have to go now. I'm sorry. I'll come back tomorrow, okay?"

He didn't answer. His dark eyes were fixed on her, and she couldn't tell what he was thinking. Or even *if* he was thinking. He was right on the edge.

Claire took the shaker of the less effective crystals and stuffed it in her backpack—there wasn't that much left, but enough for one more dose for them both, and if he did something to the crystals during his manic phase, they might need it. She needed to ask Amelie for some kind of strongbox where she could store things. . . .

"Why?" Myrnin asked. She looked up at him, frowning. "Why are you helping us? Isn't it better for humans if we waste away and die? By helping me, you help all vampires."

Claire knew what Shane would have done. He'd have walked away, considered it a win all around. Eve might have done the same thing, except for Michael.

And she . . . she was helping. *Helping.* She couldn't even really explain why, except that it seemed wrong to turn away. They weren't all bad, and she couldn't sacrifice people like Sam and Michael for the greater good.

"I know," Claire said. "Believe me, I'm not happy about it."

"You do it because you're afraid," he said.

"No. I do it because you need it."

He just stared at her, as if he couldn't figure out what she was saying. Time to go. She shivered, shouldered her backpack, and hurried for the stairs. She kept looking behind, but she never saw Myrnin move. . . . Even so, he was in a different place, closer, every time she looked. It was like a child's game, only deadly serious. He wouldn't move while she was looking at him.

Claire turned and walked backward, staring at him. Myrnin chuckled, and the sound echoed through the room like the rustle of bat wings.

When her heels hit the steps, she turned and ran.

He could have caught her, but he didn't. She burst through the doors of the shack into the alley, breathing hard, sweating, shaking.

He didn't follow. She didn't think he could, past the steps. She wasn't sure why—maybe the same way that Morganville itself kept people in town, or wiped their memories, kept Myrnin confined in his bottle.

She felt the hair on the back of her neck stir, and then she heard a voice. Whispering and indistinct. Shane? What was Shane doing here?

He was inside. He was inside and he was in trouble; she had to go to him. . . .

Claire found herself reaching for the door to the shack before she knew what she was doing. .

"Myrnin, stop it!" she gasped and pulled away. She turned and ran down the alley toward the relative safety of the street.

It was only when she got there that she saw it was already nightfall.

Eddie wouldn't come for her after dark, and she was a long way from home. Too far to walk.

Claire was about to dial Michael at home when she spotted a police car cruising slowly down the cul-de-sac. Not a vampire squad car—this one had only light tinting on the front windows, although the back was blacked out. Claire squinted against the harsh brightness and waved. The effects of the crystals were ebbing fast, and she felt clumsy, strange, and exhausted. All she wanted to do was sleep. She'd have taken a ride with Satan in his big red handbasket if it had helped her get off her feet for a few minutes.

The cruiser pulled to a stop, and the passenger-side window rolled down. Claire bent over to look inside.

Officer Fenton. "You shouldn't be out by yourself," he said. "You know better. Everybody's looking for you. Your friends called you in as missing."

"Oh," she said. That hadn't even occurred to her. She hadn't realized how long she'd been away. "I just—can I get a ride home? Please?"

He shrugged. "Hop in." She did, gratefully, and buckled herself in. Everything ached now—her head, her eyes, every muscle in her body. And she had the feeling it was going to get worse before it got better. "Speaking of your friends, how are they? Heard about that thing with Shane. Damn shame."

"He'll be okay," she said.

"And the other one? Michael?"

"Yeah, he's fine," she said. "Why?"

"Just checking. Probably good to keep an eye on him, since he was the target of the hit in the first place," Fenton said. He turned the patrol car in a slow, crunching circle and headed back out, away from the alley. "Since the guy was looking for him, specifically."

Claire's head hurt too much for conversation. "I guess," she agreed faintly. And then some last flash of cognitive clarity put together strings of chemicals, and she felt her heartbeat jump and hammer harder. "How did you know that?"

"What?"

"I mean, about Sam not being the real target? He was unconscious when you found him. He couldn't have said anything."

"Unconscious, crap. He was dead."

"But anyway, he couldn't have said—" Things clicked into place, and the pattern looked bad. Very bad. "You were there before the sirens."

"What are you talking about?"

"When we first looked out, we saw you parked behind Sam's car and we just thought you'd found him there. But you didn't just find him lying in the street—"

Officer Fenton pressed the gas pedal, and the cruiser shot forward at a high rate of speed. He turned on the lights. She heard the harsh clicking sound they made, and the night was flooded with flashes of blue and red strobes.

"Where are you taking me?"

"Shut up."

Claire put her hand on the door handle, but they were going so fast she knew she couldn't jump. She'd be badly hurt, at the very least. "If you hurt me, the Founder—"

"That's what we're counting on," Fenton sneered. "Shut up."

Shane would have totally gotten off on the whole vampire-killer-secret-society thing. Claire just wanted to go home. Badly.

In addition to Officer Fenton, the group that gathered in the shed behind the photo processing store included Fenton's wife, the unpleasant nurse who treated Claire as though she were carrying some totally disgusting disease. She even wore latex gloves to tie Claire to the chair.

Claire barely recognized the others. One was a maintenance worker from the university; she'd seen him a few times. One was a bank teller. One was the smooth-faced, unremarkable guy who'd delivered Amelie's note to her that afternoon. He'd killed her courier, Claire found out. He spent a lot of time tracking down who worked for Amelie and trying to find out where she stayed.

He was the one who leaned over into her space, hands braced on the arms of the chair, and said, "We don't much care for collaborators. Even little underage ones."

Claire's mouth felt foul and dry, and she was shaking now with the aftereffects of the crystals. Myrnin had been right: the consequences weren't going to be pleasant. "Captain Obvious, I presume," she said.

He laughed. He had nice, white teeth, no sign of vampire fangs. "Aren't you the clever one. Living up to your reputation, I see." He tapped a finger on her gold bracelet. "Not too many breathers have ever seen the Founder, much less become her pet. Sam Glass was the last one, before you. Did you know that? This is his bracelet you're wearing. Probably sized down a little, though."

She squirmed a little, but the ropes were too tight. "What do you want with me?"

"Leverage," said Officer Fenton. "Vamps seem to like you."

"Not all of them," Claire said. If they asked Oliver to come running to her rescue, it wasn't too likely he'd so much as yawn. "And if you think Amelie's going to sacrifice herself for me, you're crazy." Amelie had already sold her down the river, by sending her to Myrnin with the clear expectation that Myrnin would . . . eat her. The fact that he hadn't was just Claire's good luck. "In fact, I don't think any of them would raise a finger—"

"Michael Glass would," Captain Obvious said. "And he's the one we want. She knows that, of course. She's done everything she could to keep him away from us." He flipped open the phone and pressed something on speed dial. "Tell him where you are."

Claire glared. "No." She clamped her lips shut as she heard Michael's distant *hello* on the other end. *I'm not going to talk; I'm not going to make a sound. . . .*

The door at the back of the shed opened, and someone came in. Thin, greasy, dressed in a black leather jacket with a hole in the pocket. Crazy eyes. Fang marks on his neck.

Jason.

He took the phone from Captain Obvious. "Hey, Mikey, it's Jason. Just shut up and listen. I've got

Claire, and I'm thinking about all the things I can do with her until you get here. Better hurry."

"No!" Claire blurted, and realized it was a mistake. She'd just confirmed that she was there, and now Michael wouldn't have any choice, would he? "Michael, *don't*!"

She could hear the sound of Michael's voice, but not what he was saying. Jason put the phone back to his ear and listened. "Yeah, that's right. You've got half an hour to show, or I'll bring her home in pieces. Oh, and it's not a trap; it's a business proposition. You walk in alone, you both walk out alive." Pause. "Where? Oh, come on, man. You know where. The captain's waiting."

He snapped the phone shut, tossed it in the air, and caught it, smiling. His eyes never left Claire.

Michael wouldn't do it. He just wouldn't be that stupid, right? But Shane was in the hospital. He didn't have anybody he could turn to for help except the other vampires, and they wouldn't lift a finger to save Claire. She wasn't sure anymore that Amelie would bother, unless she was just saving her as Myrnin's midnight snack.

The door to the shed opened again, and both Captain Obvious and Jason turned to look.

Detective Travis Lowe stepped inside and closed the door, and for a second Claire felt a wild jolt of relief and satisfaction, but it faded just as quickly. Lowe looked at Jason and Captain Obvious as though he was expecting to find them there, and when his gaze moved to Claire, he didn't react except to seem angry and harassed.

Oh God. He was one of them. Whoever *them* might be.

"Could you screw this up any more?" he asked, low and vicious. "I told you, Glass isn't important. We don't need to do this."

"He's the youngest. He's a symbol, man," Captain Obvious said. "And he was one of us. He's a traitor."

One of us? Did he mean—no, he couldn't mean that. He couldn't mean that Michael *knew* these people, that he'd been part of this skanky little conspiracy . . . but Jason had acted as though Michael knew where they were.

Nurse Fenton destroyed that hope by saying, "We've already been over this. Michael knows too much. If he decides to talk, we're all dead. We can't take the risk. Not anymore." She shot her husband a dark look. "If you hadn't screwed up—"

"Don't blame me! Vampire car pulling out of the vampire's house, how was I supposed to know it wasn't him?"

Of course. No wonder that had bothered her all along—the house had woken all of them up not because of the threat to Sam, but the threat to Michael, its owner. Even though Michael wasn't there, it was reacting to intent.

Officer Fenton hadn't been the first man on the scene; he'd been the one who staked Sam and left him to die, then pretended to be Johnny-on-the-spot. If Richard Morrell hadn't shown up to scoop and run, he would have succeeded.

Claire swallowed hard and focused on Detective Lowe. "I thought you were a good guy."

Something weary and painful passed across his face. "Claire—" He shook his head. "It's not as simple as that. Not in Morganville. You don't just get to be one thing around here."

"It's not his fault," Jason said, and grinned like a wolf. "If he wants his partner back, he's not going to do anything stupid."

Detective Hess. They had him. No wonder she hadn't seen him for days—and no wonder Lowe had been acting weird. She looked more closely at Officer Fenton, and found he had a dark bruise on his left cheek that matched the scrapes on Detective Lowe's knuckles. He'd been in the house, maybe with Detective Hess, and Lowe had taken a swing at him.

Lowe's eyes were dark and full of misery, and he looked away from Claire. "The kid has nothing to do with this," he said.

"The *kid* hangs with the top-shelf vampires," Nurse Fenton shot back. "How many humans do you know with access to the Founder? She doesn't even let her own kind get close! Of *course* she's got something to do with this. Probably a lot more than you know."

Truer than Nurse Fenton knew. Claire thought about what she'd learned from Myrnin—the vampire sickness, the wormhole doorways through town, the network of Founder Houses—and realized that she knew enough to destroy Morganville.

She did her best to look scared and clueless. The first part, at least, wasn't much of a stretch.

When Jason sauntered over and put his hand on Claire's shoulder, she flinched. He smelled like a garbage heap in the summer, and she caught a lingering hint of blood from his coat. *He stabbed Shane.* And he'd smiled about it, too.

"Get your hands off me," she said, and turned to stare right at him. "I'm not afraid of you."

Lowe grabbed Jason by the arm, swung him around, and slammed him face-first into the rough wooden wall of the shed. "Me neither," he growled. "And I'm not tied to a chair. Leave her alone."

"Big hero," Nurse Fenton said bitterly. "You and Hess, you're both pathetic."

"Am I?" Lowe twisted Jason's arm painfully high. "I'm not the one raping and killing girls for fun."

"Jason's not the one doing it, either," Fenton said. "He just likes to talk about it."

Claire said, "Then how'd he know about the one in our basement?"

They all looked at her. "I never saw a report about any body in your house," Lowe said. "Just the one in the alley."

Jason laughed, a dry crack of sound. "They moved it. Hey, Claire, you ever think that maybe it wasn't me? Maybe it was one of your two boyfriends *inside* the house. Shane, he ain't too stable, you know. And who knows about Michael these days?"

She wanted to scream at him, but she saved her strength. She had thin wrists, and Captain Obvious hadn't done a very good job of tying her; she could feel a little give in the ropes, and she wouldn't need much slack to slip at least one hand free. The rough surface of the rope sawed at her skin, but she kept pulling, trying not to make it too obvious, and felt a sudden sharp pain in her wrist as the cut Jason had given her broke open again, sending a slow trickle of blood down her wrist.

It helped, along with the sweat running down her arms. She coughed, and at the same time pulled, and her right hand slipped free of the ropes with a fiery scrape. She kept it behind her back and started working on the knot holding her left hand to the crossbar of the chair.

"So what are you?" she asked, to fill the silence and keep them from noticing what she was doing. "Vampire hunters?"

"Something like that," Officer Fenton said.

"Not that I've noticed," Claire sniffed. "Shane's dad blew into town and killed all the vampires that I know about. What have *you* done?"

"Shut up," Nurse Fenton said flatly. "You've been here months, if that. You have no idea what this town is like to live in. When we're ready, we'll act. Frank Collins had the right idea, but he wasn't much of a planner."

"So you're planning a revolution," Claire said. "Not just random attacks."

"Would you *stop* telling the prisoner our plans?" Captain Obvious snapped. "Jesus, don't you watch movies? Just shut up!"

"She's not going to tell anybody," Officer Fenton said, in such an offhand way that Claire's heart sank.

They didn't intend to keep any promises to Michael. No way were they letting Michael, or her, walk out of here alive.

Don't do it, Michael. Don't come for me.

But fifteen minutes later, the door burst open and a vampire rushed in, wrapped in a heavy blanket. The greasy smell of cooking flesh filled the shed, and then the vampire kicked the door closed and collapsed against it, gasping. Smoke rose up from him in a thick, choking cloud. In a few places, Claire could see blackened skin beneath the covering.

"About time," Fenton growled. Then he picked up a black stick from a crate next to him and drove it into the vampire's chest. For a second Claire thought that it was a stake, but then she saw sparks, and the vampire went down in a tangle of blankets and smoke.

He'd been Tasered.

Captain Obvious brought out a wooden stake and rolled the vampire over. Claire screamed. Somehow, she'd been avoiding thinking of him as *Michael,* but the flash of golden hair and the pale shape of his face were unmistakable.

His blue eyes were open, but he couldn't move. There were burned patches on his hands and arms, but he was alive. . . .

Captain Obvious positioned the stake.

Claire lurched to her feet and spun to her right. Her left hand was still tied to the crossbar of the chair, but the momentum helped her swing it with bone-breaking force right into Captain Obvious's back. He crumpled against the wall. Claire grabbed the chair in both hands and used it as a shield as Officer Fenton jabbed the Taser at her, knocking it aside, and managed to hit him in the gut with at least one of the chair's legs as she screamed for help. He stumbled backward.

Travis Lowe cursed and flicked handcuffs onto Jason's wrists. "Sit," he ordered, and pulled his gun. He looked strained and grim, but determined. "Back up, Fenton. You too, Christine. Turn and face the wall."

"You can't do this," Officer Fenton said. "Trav, if you cross us—"

"I know. You'll get me. I'll try not to pee all over

myself in terror." Lowe nodded to Claire, who was undoing the last of the knots holding the chair to her left hand. "Put the cuffs on them. I'll cover you." He tossed her an extra two sets, and she fumbled the unfamiliar weight in her numbed fingers. As she bent to pick them up, Captain Obvious—down, not out—reached over Michael's still body, grabbed her foot, and yanked. Claire cried out and fell, and Captain Obvious dragged her backward.

Lowe spun, aiming his gun, but it was too late. Captain Obvious had a knife, a big, wicked thing, and he put it to Claire's throat, right under her chin. It felt cold, then hot as it pressed into the tender skin. "Put it down, Jeff," Lowe barked. He took a threatening step forward. "I mean it; I will put you down."

He got Tasered in the back. Claire watched him convulse and fall, and felt panic well up inside. *They'll kill us now. All three of us.* Four, counting Joe Hess, who was being held prisoner somewhere else.

She heard a sharp, loud crack, and a pale strong hand exploded through the boards beside Captain Obvious's head, grabbed him, and pulled. The entire section of boards broke away, and Captain Obvious was yanked backward. Claire felt the knife slide along her neck, but it didn't have any force behind it. He dropped it, flailing for balance, and then he was outside in the bright, dusty sunlight, and there was a dry snapping sound.

Dressed in a black leather trench coat, a black broad-brimmed hat, and black gloves, Oliver stepped into the shed. He gave them all a vampire smile.

"Well, that was refreshing," he said. He reached down and pulled Michael up to a sitting position next to Claire, then stepped in front of them.

"Could've come sooner," Michael whispered. He was shaking all over, but he was coming out of his paralysis. Claire hugged him. He fumbled in his pocket, came up with a handkerchief, and pressed it to Claire's neck. She hadn't even realized she was bleeding.

Oliver ignored them and walked toward the Fentons, who tried to get to the door. He flashed ahead of them with that easy snakelike speed vampires could display when they wanted, and Claire shuddered at the looks on their faces.

They knew what was going to happen to them.

"Don't worry," Oliver said. "There'll be a fair trial. Since Samuel didn't die, and you didn't succeed today, you won't burn for what you've done." He reached for Christine Fenton's wrist, ripped her sleeve, and exposed her silver bracelet. It fit tightly around her wrist, but he slid a finger underneath the metal and it split along an invisible seam. He dropped the bracelet in his pocket, then did the same to Officer Fenton.

The places where their bracelets had been were sickly pale, and Christine kept rubbing hers, as if the shock of open air on the skin was painful.

"Congratulations," Oliver said. "I release you from your contracts."

And then he grabbed Christine. Claire had a glimpse of his fangs flashing down, silvery and sharp, and then he slammed the woman against the wall of the shed and bit.

Claire hid her face against Michael's chest. He put his hand on her hair and held her there, turned away from the sight of Christine Fenton dying.

She heard the woman's body hit the floor and then Oliver, his voice thick and dark, say, "Your turn now."

A sharp, snapping sound, and another body hit the floor.

When Michael let her go, Claire didn't look at the bodies. She couldn't.

She looked at Oliver, who was staring down at Travis Lowe. The detective was just starting to stir. "What about this one?" he asked. "Friend or foe?"

He wasn't waiting for an answer. He grabbed Lowe by the collar and lifted him off the ground.

"Friend! Friend!" Claire blurted frantically, and saw

Lowe's eyes close in relief. "His partner's missing. I think they were holding him somewhere."

Oliver shrugged, clearly not interested. He dropped Lowe back to the ground and turned a slow circle. "There was another one," he said. "Where is he?" He pulled in a deep breath, then let it out with a disgusted cough. "Jason. Well, well."

Sometime while Oliver had been busy killing the Fentons, Jason had escaped out the door, and Michael hadn't stopped him. Maybe too weak, maybe just worried for Claire. But anyway, Jason was long gone.

"I'll find him," Oliver said. "I've been tolerant, so long as he didn't threaten our interests, but enough." He glanced down at Michael and Claire. "Go home." He stalked away, out into the sun, without a backward glance. Three dead bodies, and he didn't even pause.

Travis Lowe managed to pull himself to a sitting position, groaning, and rested his head in his hands. "I hate Tasers." He looked up and fixed his bloodshot gaze on Claire. "You're okay? Let me see your throat."

She moved the handkerchief. There was just a thin smear on the cloth. Her wrist was worse; she tied the cloth around it as a makeshift bandage and thought, *I'm going to have to buy Michael some new ones.* Though why she thought of that now, she had no idea. Maybe she just wanted to imagine normal life.

Because this definitely wasn't normal.

Michael stood up and helped Claire to her feet, then Lowe. He pulled keys from his pocket and tossed them to Lowe. "Pull the car in with the trunk facing the door," he said. "Open it and honk when you're ready."

Lowe nodded and went outside, into the blinding sun. Michael put both hands on Claire's shoulders and looked down at her, then cupped her cheeks in his palms.

"Don't do that again," he said.

"I didn't do *anything*. I got a ride from a cop, that was all—"

"Not that," he said. "Myrnin. Don't do it again. You can't go back. He'll kill you next time."

He knew where she'd been. Well, she supposed it hadn't been hard to figure out.

"You shouldn't have come," she said. "You knew it was a trap; what are you, crazy?"

"I called Oliver," Michael said.

"You didn't!"

"It worked, didn't it?"

She looked around at the dead people in the shed. "Yeah."

He looked ill for a second and started to say something, but then the horn honked outside, and he changed it to, "Ride's here."

She nodded, and walked out into the dazzling glare. Something brushed by her, moving fast, and then the trunk of the sedan slammed closed before she'd taken more than two steps.

Claire trudged to the passenger side of the car. Exhausted and aching, and feeling a stupid need to cry, she said nothing at all on the ride home.

13

Joe Hess was in the run-down house on Spring Street, locked in a closet, filthy, with a broken arm and two broken ribs—Lowe had called with the news of his rescue two hours later. Claire tried to be happy, but the crash that had started for her before she left Myrnin's just kept driving her down. She felt sick and weak and hollow, and she couldn't even summon the energy to go to the hospital to see Shane. Michael told Eve that she was sick, which wasn't much of a lie; Claire stayed in bed, shivering, wrapped in layers of blankets even though the room was warm. Everything kept shifting in her head, from dull gray fog to glittering icy clarity, and she didn't know how long it was going to last. She developed a knife-sharp headache sometime during the night, and by the time she finally slept, it was nearly morning.

Her cell phone rang at two p.m. on Sunday. She'd gotten up to visit the bathroom and grab a bottle of water, but no food, and her whole body felt weak and abused. "Where are you?" the voice on the other end demanded. Claire squinted at the clock and scrubbed a hand through her matted, oily hair.

"Who is it?"

A sigh rattled the speaker. "It's Jennifer, idiot. I'm waiting at Common Grounds. Are you going to show or what?"

"No," she said, and then tried again. "I'm sick."

"Look, I don't care if you're dying; I've got a midterm tomorrow for half my grade! Get your ass down here *now*!"

Jennifer hung up. Claire threw the phone down on the nightstand with a clatter and sat—or fell—onto the bed. *I can't. I just want to sleep, that's all.*

Someone rapped gently on the door, and then it creaked open. Eve was standing there, with a cracked, much-abused plastic tray in her hands. On it was a frosty glass of Coke, still fizzing, a sandwich, and a cookie.

And a red rose.

"Eat," she said, and slid the trap onto Claire's lap. "Man, that's one hell of a hangover."

"Hangover?" Claire looked at her oddly, and sipped the Coke. It went down sweet and cool, and that helped. "I'm not hungover."

Eve just shook her head. "Been there, CB. Trust me on this. Eat, shower, you'll feel better."

Claire nodded. She did feel a spark of hunger, distant as it was, and managed to take two bites of the sandwich before weariness overtook her again. She tried the cookie in between.

The shower felt like heaven, and Eve was right about that, too; when she finally got dressed and finished half the sandwich she felt almost alive.

Her cell phone rang again. Jennifer. Claire didn't even let her get started yelling and threatening. "Ten minutes," she said, and hung up. She didn't want to go, but staying in bed didn't seem to be doing much for her. She took the tray downstairs, washed up, and grabbed her backpack on the way out.

"Where the *hell* do you think you're going?"

Michael. He was standing in the hallway, blocking the door, looking like he was guarding the gates of heaven itself. His hands looked raw and pink—still healing from the burns. She thought about that, about how important his hands were to him, because of the music, and felt a sharp stab of guilt.

"I'm meeting Jennifer at Common Grounds," she said. "Tutoring. For money."

"Well, you're not walking, and I can't take you until dark."

"I can," Eve offered. She joined Claire in the hall. "I need to go into work, anyway. Kim didn't show again; they called a little while ago. Hey, overtime pay. Gotta love it. Maybe we can afford tacos."

Michael looked exasperated, but it wasn't as though there were a lot of choices. He nodded and stepped out of the way. Eve stretched up on her toes to kiss him, and that went on for a while before Claire cleared her throat, checked her watch, and got her moving to the car.

It was a short ride to Common Grounds, but not exactly a comfortable one, because the first thing Eve said was, "Is it true? Oliver killed the Fentons and Captain Obvious?"

Claire didn't want to talk about it, but she nodded.

"And Michael? Michael was there?"

Again, the nod. Claire looked out the window.

"He got hurt. I saw the burns." This time she didn't even try to answer. Eve let the silence stretch for a few seconds, then said, "Don't shut me out, Claire. The four of us, we're all we've got."

Except that what Claire had couldn't be shared. Not with Michael, not with Eve, and certainly not with Shane.

She was alone, carrying an ugly weight of knowledge she didn't want and couldn't use. And every time she thought about Oliver's icy smile, about him ripping out Christine Fenton's throat, she felt sick. *I'm helping him, if I keep working for Myrnin and Amelie.* But she was also helping Michael. Sam. Myrnin.

Eve seemed to sense it wasn't time to push; she pulled to a stop in front of the coffee shop and said, "Stay inside until dark; Michael will come get you."

"I'm going to see Shane," Claire said. "But I'll get a ride home."

"Claire, dammit—" Eve sighed. "I can't stop you. But if you wait, you and Michael can go together. I'll see you guys tonight. Tacos for dinner, right?"

Nothing sounded very exciting to her right now, but Claire nodded. She got out and walked into Common Grounds, which was a sea of noise and conversation—packed, as always, with college students and a few locals. She was getting used to picking out the gleam of ID bracelets.

Jennifer was sitting at the same table Monica favored, sipping a drink that Claire bet was the same thing Monica always had, wearing an outfit that was probably Monica's hand-me-downs, or at least copied from the same designers. She looked angry and scowled at Claire as Claire dropped her backpack on the floor and slid into her chair. "You look like crap," Jennifer said. "Sick sick, or hungover?"

"Does it matter?"

"Hungover," Jennifer said, and grinned. "And here I thought you were all underage Goody Two-shoes."

The smell of coffee was making her feel queasy, but Claire went to the counter and ordered a mocha anyway. Oliver wasn't on duty, and she didn't know the two working as baristas.

When she turned around, somebody else was sitting at Jennifer's table in the previously empty third chair.

Monica.

Crap. I can't deal with her. Not now. She felt horrible, and the last thing she wanted to do was match wits with the witch queen.

Monica gave her the X-ray scan, looked at Jennifer, and did an over-the-top hand to the forehead. "I thought the homeless look died in the nineties."

"Shut up." Claire slid into her chair, mocha in hand. "I'm tutoring Jennifer, not you."

"Bitch, I wouldn't *let* you tutor me. You'd probably give me all the wrong answers."

Which was a totally good idea, and Claire saw the fear flash into Jennifer's expression. She sighed. "I wouldn't," she said.

"Why not?"

"Because—because this matters. School." They both looked at Claire as though she were a lunatic.

"Never mind. I just wouldn't. You want my help or not?"

Jennifer nodded. Claire reached for her notebook and flipped to the notes she'd taken in Economics, and started explaining. Jennifer was trying, at least; Monica kept sighing and fidgeting, but Jennifer seemed to be kind of following along. She even got a couple of the formulas right, when Claire pop-quizzed her. It took about an hour to get her to the level of a solid B, but that was good enough. Jennifer wasn't interested in As, and Monica couldn't have cared less.

Claire's mocha was making her nauseated. She tossed the half-full cup and went to the bathroom. She picked up her backpack and brought it along; half out of an entirely reasonable expectation that Monica and/ or Jennifer would do something mean if she left it at their mercy.

She was standing at the mirror staring at her sallow face with its raccoon-bruise eyes and pale lips when the second of clarity hit again, a flicker of unforgiving beauty in a world that seemed drowning in gray.

Maybe a little. Just to get through the day. There wasn't that much left, anyway.

She didn't let herself think. Her head was pounding, her mouth dry, her muscles aching, and she needed to feel better. Because right now, she didn't know if she could make it through the day.

She shook about ten measly crystals out into her palm. The strawberry scent teased her, and she shifted them around, watching the light glint on the sharp edges. It looked like candy.

It's a drug. She was finally admitting it to herself. *It's not even for you. It's for Myrnin. What are you doing? It's making you sick.*

But it would also make her well.

She was in the process of dumping the crystals in her mouth when Monica shoved open the bathroom door.

Claire swallowed and choked and quickly wiped her hand on her pants. She knew she looked guilty. Monica, who'd been heading for the stall, stopped and looked at her.

"What was that?" Monica asked.

"What was what?" Wrong answer, Claire knew it as soon as she said it. Why not, *aspirin for my hangover*? Or, *breath mints*? She was a terrible liar.

She couldn't help but drag in a shocked breath as the crystals raced their chemical message through her nerve endings, ice in every vein, and the whole world turned sharp and bright and—for the moment—painless.

And Monica was way too savvy. She looked at the hand Claire was convulsively rubbing against her blue jeans, then gave her the X-ray stare again, and slowly smiled. "Man, that must be good stuff. Your pupils just dilated like crazy." Monica edged up next to her and checked her makeup. "Where'd you get it?"

Claire said nothing. She reached for the shaker, which was sitting on the edge of the sink, but Monica got there first. She looked it over and shook a crystal out in her hand. "Cool. What is it?"

"Nothing. It's not for you."

Monica pulled the shaker back when she reached for it. "Oh, I think it is. Especially if you want it so bad."

Claire didn't think; she just acted. Her brain worked so fast that she moved in a blur, slamming Monica back against the wall, then twisting the silver can out of her hand. Monica didn't even have time to yell.

Monica straightened her clothes and tossed back her hair. There was a crazy light in her eyes, and a glow in her cheeks. She *liked* this.

"Oh, you stupid bitch," Monica breathed. "That was such a bad idea. So, it makes you faster. And I'm betting it's something from the vamps. That makes it *mine*."

"No," Claire said. She'd screwed up, she knew that, but talking was only going to make it worse. She put the shaker in her backpack and zipped it up, shouldered the load, and turned to go.

Her hand was on the doorknob when Monica said, "Shane's still in ICU." There was something about the way she said it. . . . Claire turned slowly to face her. "That means he's not out of the woods yet. Funny thing, people can have all kinds of setbacks. Maybe he gets the wrong meds or something. That can kill you. They did a story about it on the news." Monica's smile was vicious. "I'd hate to see that happen."

Claire felt the wildest, coldest impulse that had ever come over her—she wanted to lunge for Monica, knock her head into the wall, rip her apart. She could *visualize* it. That was terrifying, and she pulled herself back with a snap into sanity.

"What do you want?" she said. Her voice wasn't quite steady.

Monica just held out her finely manicured hand, raised an eyebrow, and waited.

Claire put down her backpack, pulled out the shaker, and handed it over. "When that's gone, I don't have any more," she said. "I hope you choke on it."

Monica poured some of the red crystals into her palm. "How much? And don't be stupid. You OD me, and it's your neck, not mine."

"Don't do more than half of that," Claire said. Monica scraped half of the crystals off her palm, back into the container. It looked about right. Claire nodded.

Monica dumped it into her mouth, licked the residue from her palm, and Claire could tell the exact second that the chemicals hit her—her eyes went wide, and her pupils began to grow. And grow. It was eerie, and Claire felt her skin crawl as Monica began to shake. *This is what it looks like.* It looked awful.

"You're pretty." Monica sounded surprised. "It's all so clear now—"

And then her eyes rolled back in her head, and she fell down and started to convulse.

Claire screamed for help, jammed her backpack under Monica's head to keep her from knocking it against the tile floor, and tried to hold her down. Jennifer ran in and screamed, too, then came at Claire, swinging. Claire moved out of the way of the punch—it seemed slow to her—and shoved Jennifer out of the way. "I didn't do it!" she yelled. "She took something!"

Jennifer called 911.

This wasn't how Claire had intended to end up at the hospital. Worse, by the time they'd gotten there, Monica had stopped breathing, and the paramedics had to put a tube down her throat. They were hooking her up to machines now, and the mayor was coming, and half the cops in town were converging on it.

"I need to know what she took," the doctor was saying. Claire tried to look over his shoulder; she saw Richard Morrell coming through the parking lot doors. The doctor snapped his fingers in front of her face to get her attention. "Your pupils are dilated. You took something, too. What is it?"

Claire silently handed over the shaker. The doctor looked at the red crystals, frowned, and said, "Where did you get these?" He was wearing a bracelet, silver, with a symbol she didn't recognize. "Look, I'm not kidding. That girl is dying, and I need to know—"

"I can't tell you," she said. "Ask Amelie." She held up the bracelet. She felt numb. Even though she'd wanted to kill Monica, she hadn't really meant to *kill* her. Why had this happened? It was the same dose Claire had taken, and she knew the crystals weren't contaminated. . . .

The doctor gave her a look of cold contempt, and handed it to an orderly. "Lab," he said. "I need to know what this stuff is, right now. Tell them it's priority one."

The orderly left at a run.

"I want you in the lab, too," the doctor said, and grabbed a passing nurse. He rattled off tests, talking faster than even Claire's heightened brain could process, though the nurse just nodded. *Blood tests,* she thought. Claire went without complaint. It was better than waiting for Richard Morrell to hear that she'd poisoned his sister.

As soon as the nurse was finished drawing her blood, Claire went to ICU. Shane was awake, reading a book. He looked better, and his smile was warm and relieved. "Eve said you were sick," he said. "I figured maybe you were just sick of seeing me here."

Claire wanted to cry. She wanted to crawl into the bed with him and be wrapped in his arms and not have all this guilt and horror bearing down on her shoulders, just for a minute.

"What's wrong?" he asked. "Your eyes—"

"I made a mistake," she blurted. "I made a terrible mistake, and I don't know how to fix it. She's dying and I don't know how—"

"Dying?" Shane struggled to sit up. "Who? God, not Eve—"

"Monica. I gave her something, and she took it and she's dying." There were tears sliding cold down her cheeks, and she could feel every icy pinprick. "I have to do something. But I don't know what I can do."

Shane's eyes narrowed. "Claire, are you talking about drugs? You gave her drugs? Christ, what are you thinking?" He grabbed her hand. "Did you take something, too?"

She nodded miserably. "It doesn't hurt me, but it's killing her."

"You have to tell them. Tell them what you took. Do it now."

"I can't—it's—" She knew what it would mean, saying this. She already knew how it would change things between them. "I can't tell because it's something to do with Amelie. I can't, Shane."

His hand tightened, then released. He let go and looked away. "You're going to let a human die because Amelie told you not to say anything. Not even Monica ranks that low. If you don't do something—" He paused and took in a long, slow breath. His voice wasn't quite steady when he went on. "If you don't do something, that means that you put the vampires first, and I can't deal with that, Claire. I'm sorry, but I can't."

She knew that. Tears continued to burn in her eyes, but she didn't try to talk him out of it. He was right, she was wrong, and she had to find a way out of this; she had to. Enough people were dying in Morganville, and some of them had died because of her.

The notes. The notes I left at Myrnin's. Those could tell the doctor exactly what the crystals were, and how to counteract them. She could start reconstructing them now, since her brain was still working at high speed, but she could already feel things starting to fade at the edges.

"Shane," she said. He didn't look at her. "I love you." She wasn't going to say it, but she knew that she might not come back. Ever. And as if he knew that, he grabbed her hand and squeezed it. When he did finally look at her she said, "I can't tell them anything, but I think I can help her. And I'm going to."

His brown eyes were tired and anxious and understood way too much. "You're going to do something crazy."

"Well," she said, "not as crazy as what you'd do, but . . . yeah." She kissed him, and it felt terrifyingly good, the perfect way his lips fit to hers, the way time seemed to stop when they touched. "I'll see you," she whispered, and stroked her fingers down his cheek.

And then she escaped before he could try to talk her out of it.

"Wait!" he called after her. She didn't.

Claire left the hospital at a run, moving faster than anyone could react to stop her, and headed for the last place on earth she wanted to go.

It was deathly silent inside Myrnin's lab. Claire came down the steps very slowly, very carefully, listening for any hint of his presence. All the lights were burning, oil lamps flickering, and a couple of Bunsen burners hissed under bubbling flasks. The whole place smelled of strawberry and rot, and it felt strangely cold.

If I hurry . . . Myrnin had a bedroom somewhere

down here, right? Maybe he was asleep. Or reading. Or doing something normal.

And maybe he's not.

Claire picked her way across the room, moving very slowly and taking care not to tip over any of the leaning books, or crunch on any broken glass. At the back of the lab she saw that the tray where she'd put out the red crystals for drying was empty. There was no sign of the crystals themselves, but the notebooks were stacked neatly on one corner.

As she picked them up, Myrnin's voice came from right behind her shoulder. She felt his breath cool on the back of her neck. "Those don't belong to you."

She whirled, backed up, and overturned a stack of books that slithered into another, like stacks of dominos crashing.

"Now look what you've done," Myrnin said. He seemed very quiet, but there was something wrong in his eyes.

Badly wrong.

Claire backed up, glancing behind her to be sure the way was clear; in that instant, Myrnin was on her. She shoved the notebooks between them, and his claws tore into them, shredding them. "No! Myrnin, *no!*"

She threw him off, mainly because his knees slipped on fallen books, and she scrambled away, panting. Somehow, she remembered to hold on to the damaged notebooks. Myrnin snarled and tried to follow, but the debris made for uncertain footing, and his jump went wrong. He crashed into a bookcase, and it toppled over on him, raining volumes.

Claire tried to get to the stairs, but there was no way she was going to make it. He was already flanking her, angling to cut her off from any hope of rescue or escape.

She was going to die, and Monica would die, too. And so would Myrnin, because he was too far gone now. She hadn't seen any flicker of recognition left, not even for an instant.

She backed up, and her shoulders hit the hard stone wall. She slid, trying to put herself in a corner, but there was a leaning bookcase in the way. When she fell against it, it slid sideways, revealing the door that Myrnin had shown her before.

The heart-shaped lock was hanging open.

Unlocked.

Claire gasped and grabbed it, ripped it away, and swung open the door.

She felt Myrnin's claws catch in her hair, but she pulled free and fell forward . . . into the dark.

No, no, this showed me my house; it led to the living room. . . .

It didn't now. Myrnin had changed the destination, and this was no place she recognized at all. It was dark, damp, and it smelled like a combination of sewer and garbage dump. She blinked, and her eyes adjusted much more quickly to the darkness than they should have—the crystals, still doing their job. She was feeling an ache in her extremities now, working its way in. Once it reached her core, she'd be into withdrawal again.

She had no idea how bad it would be this time, but she couldn't afford to wait.

Claire whirled, and the doorway was still there, right where it had been.

Myrnin was framed in it, staring at her.

She couldn't go that way. She had to find another path.

Claire ran into the dark. There was just enough light filtering in from very narrow, very tall windows, that as her eyes adjusted, she realized she was inside a prison—a filthy, horrible prison, with very little light.

And some of the cells were full.

It took her a while to realize it, because they were all so *quiet*—pale, quiet things, one to a cell, that flashed to the bars like ghosts as she ran past. That changed, the farther she went. A sound went up—a whisper at first, rising to a howl. She heard metal rattling.

They were trying to get out.

Claire was gasping, and she was getting tired, and Myrnin was behind her.

This is where she keeps them. The ones who can't be fixed.

It was where all the vampires would end up, one after another. Left to die in the dark, alone, trapped, and starving.

Amelie let that happen.

It got quiet suddenly, and that was worse than the howling and rattling. Claire glanced over her shoulder and saw that Myrnin was slowing down, then stopping. There was only the sound of her feet hitting the stone floor, until she skidded to a stop, too.

"Claire," Myrnin whispered. "What are you doing here?" He sounded confused, but at least he knew her name. He fumbled at his pockets, found some kind of small silver box, and opened it. Red crystals spilled out into his palm, mounded up, and, choking and retching, he forced them into his mouth.

The effects sent him staggering. He braced himself with one shoulder against the wall of the hallway and moaned. It sounded like it hurt. A lot.

"Not much time," he said. His voice was barely there at all, but in the cold silence, she heard every word. "The notebooks. You need them?"

"I—I made a mistake. Somebody else took the crystals. I need to give them to the doctors."

"Someone else took the crystals?"

"Yes."

"Most die," he said, as if it didn't matter. "Maybe you can find a way from what you wrote; I don't know. I never tried."

That meant that when he'd given her the crystals that first time, he hadn't even known if they would kill her.

God. And she'd thought he actually cared.

He sounded very tired. "You understand how to use the doors now?"

"No."

"All you have to do is find a doorway, then concentrate on your destination. Mind you, it's the rare human who has the mind to manage it even once, never mind on a regular basis—and the doors have a subtle go-away to anyone not invited to use them. You can go to any Founder House, or to seven other doorways in town, but you must have a mental picture of where you are going first. If you fail to do so, you end up"—he raised a hand with effort, and gestured feebly—"here. Where she keeps the monsters." Myrnin smiled faintly, but his smile looked broken. "After all, I ended up here, didn't I?"

Claire fought to still her heartbeat. "How do I get back? Back to your lab?"

"That way." Myrnin looked down at his hand, as if it seemed odd to him. He turned it this way and that, examining it, and then pointed. "Stay to the right; you'll find it. Don't go near the bars. If they grab you, you must not let them pull you close enough to bite. And Claire . . ."

She clutched the notebooks tight to her chest as he met her eyes. He still seemed rational, but even that massive dose of crystals hadn't driven the beast completely back.

"I need you to do me two services," he said. "First—promise me that you'll continue to work to find the cure. I'm no longer able to carry it forward."

She swallowed hard, and nodded. She'd have tried, anyway. "I can't do it alone," she said. "I'll need help. Doctors. I'm going to give them the notes and see if we can find something."

Myrnin nodded. "Just don't explain what it does." He looked around. On the far side of the wall was an empty cell, with its door standing open. There was a decaying bunk, but nothing else.

He took a breath, let it out, and walked into the cell. Then he turned and firmly closed the door behind him. Claire heard the lock engage with a thick, metallic *clank*.

"Second thing," Myrnin said, "do bring me some

books, when you visit. And perhaps more crystals, if you're able to produce more. It's so nice to think clearly again, even for a few moments."

She felt as though he'd punched into her chest and ripped out her heart. She felt hollow, light, and empty.

And very, very sad.

"I will," she said. "I'll be back."

When she looked back, Myrnin had settled himself on the edge of the bunk, staring at the floor.

He didn't look up when she said, "I won't just leave you here. I promise. I'll come see you."

She hesitated, and thought she heard something whispering to her. A voice.

Her mother's voice.

"You should go," Myrnin said tonelessly. "Before we both have cause to regret it."

She ran.

Nothing got her on the way back to the door, although a lot of the sick vampires reached out mutely to her, or screamed; she covered her ears and ran, heart pounding, feeling sicker and more terrified all the time. The relief of seeing the open door ahead was like a warm blanket after the cold. The doorway was black, just black; she couldn't see Myrnin's lab on the other side. Couldn't see anything.

Think! Myrnin had said she had to focus, visualize where she wanted to go. Of course, he'd also said that she probably wouldn't be able to do it. *No, don't think about that. If you want out of here, you have to focus. Hard!*

Nothing. Nothing at all.

She closed her eyes, even though it was terrifying to do it here, in this place, and slowed her breathing. She thought about the lab, about the confusion of clutter, the books, the bottles, the new and the old. She *smelled* it, like a breath of home, and when she opened her eyes she could see it on the other side of the door.

Claire took a deep breath, stepped over the threshold through a slight tug of resistance, and turned to close the door as soon as she was through.

When she turned back, Amelie was waiting.

She stood in the center of the room, hands folded. Her ancient, smooth face was untroubled by any kind of expression, but there was something bitter in her eyes.

"He's gone," Amelie said. "Where is he?"

"I—the prison."

"You took him below." Amelie frowned slightly. "*You* took him below."

"I think he wanted to go there. He—put himself in a cage." Claire struggled to keep her voice steady. "How—how can you leave them like that?"

"I have no choice." It would never occur to Amelie to explain, of course, and it would probably get Claire nowhere to demand it. "If he is truly lost, then it's over. The experiment is ended, and there is no cure. No way to save my people." She sat down in one of the thread-bare armchairs, shoving books out of the way as she did. It was the first ungraceful thing Claire had ever seen her do. "I thought—I never thought we would fail."

Claire came a step or two closer. "I have the notebooks," she said. "And—Myrnin must have left more stuff here I can read. You haven't failed yet."

Amelie shook her head, and a wisp of hair broke free from the coronet. It made her look young and very fragile. "I must have someone trusted to maintain the machines, or it will all fail, anyway. And only Myrnin could do that. I had hoped that you—but he told me only a vampire could. And there is no one else."

"Sam?"

"Not old enough, and nowhere near powerful enough. It would have to be someone near my own age, and that would mean—" Amelie looked at her sharply. "I can't give such power to my enemy."

Claire didn't like the thought, either. "What else can you do?"

"End it." Amelie's voice was so soft Claire barely understood the words. "Let it all go. Destroy it."

"You mean—let everybody go?"

Amelie's gaze locked with hers, and held. "No," she said. "That is not what I mean at all."

Claire shuddered. "Then—why not let Oliver in? You've been fighting so hard to keep him out. Why not try this first? What do you really have to lose?"

Amelie's pale eyebrows slowly rose. "Nothing. And everything, of course. But you should fear that we would succeed, Claire. Because if we do, if the vampire race is not doomed to die, where does that leave you? An interesting question, for another day, perhaps." She nodded at the notebooks in Claire's hands. "If you intend to save the Morrell girl, you should hurry," she said. "Use the portal. I will send you directly to the hospital."

There was a portal to the hospital? Claire blinked and looked back at the closed and locked door. "Um—are you sure it won't open to—"

"To below?" Amelie shook her head. "I have no intention it should. If you do not, then it will do as we say. Myrnin could only make the doorway work to below, never back here. So only you and I have such abilities, for now."

Claire thought about something, with a sickening wrench. "Are you sure?"

"What do you mean?" Amelie looked up, slowly, her eyes fierce and bright.

A rush of images flitted through Claire's mind: Oliver, grabbing her in her own house. The dead girl in the basement. Jason appearing and disappearing from Monica's party, and reappearing near Common Grounds.

Oh no.

"Can you tell?" Claire asked. "If somebody's using the portal?"

"Myrnin could, I suspect, but I cannot. Why?" Amelie stood up, and this time the frown was definite. "What do you know?"

"I think you've got a traitor," Claire said. "Somebody showed Oliver, and Oliver showed Jason. And

Captain Obvious and his friends probably knew, too. Jason must have shown them—"

"Impossible," Amelie interrupted with a flash of impatience. "My people are beyond suspicion."

"Then how did Jason bring a dead girl into Michael's house without permission? Because you said he'd have to be invited in. And he wasn't."

Amelie froze, and her eyes went cold and flat. "I see," she said, and then whirled toward the small door that led into the narrow, overstuffed library, and the door that Claire had once used to come in from the university. "You seem to be proven right. Someone's coming in. Go, take the doorway. *Hurry.*"

Claire opened the door. Beyond it, air rippled, and shifted . . . her living room. A stranger's house. A quiet white room with a stained-glass window.

"Now!" Amelie said sharply. "That's the hospital."

Claire stepped through. As she looked back, she saw Oliver walk into Myrnin's lab, look around, and focus on Amelie. Jason was right behind him, grinning, clearly Oliver's new pet. Or maybe, Oliver's pet all along.

"Interesting," Oliver said, and then turned his head to look at the open doorway, and Claire. "And unexpected."

She slammed the door between them, heart pounding, and it vanished on her side. That didn't mean it couldn't reappear, but at least she was safe for the moment. She didn't think Amelie would let Oliver follow her.

She hoped.

She flipped pages in the notebooks. Myrnin had clawed them, but only the last one, and only at the back. The rest were intact.

She left the white room and found that she was standing in the hospital's nondenominational chapel— more of a meditation room than anything else. It was empty, except for one person kneeling near the front.

Jennifer. She scrambled to her feet when she saw Claire, and blurted, "What are you doing here?" Her eyes were red, and she sniffled and swiped angrily at her eyes, smearing mascara and ruining what was left of her makeup. She had freckles. Claire had never known that.

"Saving your friend," Claire said. "I hope."

It took three days for the lab to work out a counteragent, but once they did, Monica came off the ventilator within hours. Or so Claire heard from Richard Morrell, who dropped by on Wednesday night, as the four of them—Shane being finally released from the hospital—were sitting down to dinner.

"I'm glad she's going to be okay," Claire said. "Richard—I'm sorry. If I'd known—"

"You're lucky that stuff didn't fry you, too," he said, but without any real heat. "Look, my sister isn't the best person I've ever met, but I love her. Thanks for helping."

Claire nodded. Michael was nearby, seeming to be just lounging but, she knew, ready to step in if Richard went postal. Not that Richard would. So far, he was the best-adjusted Morrell she'd met.

"Don't come by the hospital," Richard continued. "I'm trying to convince her you weren't out to kill her. If you show up, I may not be able to keep a lid on things. As it is—" He shifted uncomfortably and looked away. "Just watch your back, Claire."

"She doesn't need to," Eve said, and put her arm around Claire's shoulders. "Tell your sister, if she messes with Claire, she messes with all of us."

Richard's expression went deliberately bland. "I'm sure that'll terrify her," he said. "Night, Claire. Eve." He nodded to Michael. Shane hadn't gotten up from the table, partly because hey, gut wound, but also he wasn't about to put himself out for any Morrell, even Richard. Claire had the impression Richard was just as happy not to have to make nice.

Claire saw Richard out the door, locked it, and came back to fight over who would get the last taco. Which, of course, turned out to be Shane. "Wounded!" was his new comeback, and it was one they couldn't really argue with, at least for a couple of weeks. He happily loaded up his plate, and Claire sat back and felt, for the first time in days, a little of the tension relax. Shane was even being civil to Michael again, especially after she'd explained to him how Michael had raced to her rescue. That mattered to Shane, in ways that other things didn't.

When the knock came on the front door, the four of them froze, and Michael sighed. "Right. My turn to play doorman, I guess."

Claire nabbed some meat off Shane's plate. He pretend-stabbed her hand, and ended up licking Claire's fingers for her, one at a time.

"Okay, that's either gross or hot, but I'm thinking gross, so quit it," Eve said. "If you're going to be licking each other, get a room."

"Good idea," Shane whispered.

"Wounded!" Claire shot back mockingly. "And anyway, I thought you wanted to play it safe."

"Dude, I live in Morganville. How exactly is that playing it safe?"

Michael came back down the hall with a very odd expression. "Claire," he said. "I think you should come."

She pushed away from the table and went after him. He opened the door and stepped aside.

Her parents were standing on the step.

"Mom! Dad!" Claire threw herself into their arms. It was stupid to be so cheered by the sight of them, but for a second she enjoyed being stupid, through and through.

And then the dread hit her, and she backed up and said, "What are you doing here?" *Please say you're dropping something off. Please.*

Her mother—dressed in pressed blue jeans and a starched blue work shirt and a Coldwater Creek jacket, even in the heat of summer—looked taken aback. "We wanted to surprise you," she said. "Isn't that all right? Claire, you *are* only sixteen—"

"Nearly seventeen," Claire sighed, under her breath.

"And really, we ought to be able to come see you when we want to, to be sure you're safe and happy." Claire's mom gave Michael a distracted, nervous smile. "All right, then, I'll tell you the truth. We've been very worried about you, honey. First you had that trouble in the dorm; then you were attacked and ended up in the hospital—and someone told us about that party."

"What?" She sent Michael a look, but he looked just as surprised as she felt. "Who told you?"

"I don't know. An e-mail. You know I can never figure those things out; anyway, it was some friend of yours."

"Oh," Claire breathed, "I really don't think it was. Mom, look, it was—"

"Don't tell us it was nothing, honey," her dad cut in. "I read all about it. Drinking, drugs, fighting, destruction of property. Kids having sex. And you were at this party, weren't you?"

"I—no, Dad, not like—" She couldn't lie about it. "I was there. We were all there. But Shane wasn't stabbed at the party; it was after, on the way home." She realized as soon as she said it that neither one of them had mentioned anything about Shane. And it was too late to take it back.

"Stabbed?" her mother echoed blankly, and covered her mouth with her hand. "Oh, that is just *it*. That's the last straw!"

"Let's talk about all this inside," her father said. He looked so grim now. "We've decided we had to make a change."

"A change?" Claire echoed.

"We're moving," he said. "We bought a nice house on the other side of town. Looks kind of like this one, maybe a little smaller. Even has the same layout to the place, I think. Good thing we did. Clearly, things are much worse than we thought."

"You're—" She could *not* have heard that right. "Moving *here*? To *this* town? You can't! You can't move here!"

"Oh, Claire, I was so hoping you'd be happy," her mom said, in that tone that Claire dreaded. The *I'm-so-disappointed-in-you* tone. "We've already sold our old house. The truck with the furniture should get here tomorrow. Oh"—she turned to Claire's father—"did we remember to—"

"Oh, for heaven's sake—yes," he rumbled. "Whatever it is, yes, we remembered."

"Well, you don't have to be—"

"Mom!" Claire interrupted desperately. "*You can't move here!*"

Michael put his hand on her shoulder. "Just a second," he said to her parents, and pulled Claire a few feet back. "Claire, don't. It's already too late. If the Council hadn't wanted them here, they wouldn't be here, and they wouldn't have a Founder House. If it looks like this house and has the same layout, that's what it is, a Founder House. That means Amelie wants it to happen. She probably made it happen."

That didn't exactly make her feel any better. She was shaking all over now. "But they're my *parents*!" she whispered fiercely. "Can't you do something?"

He looked grim and shook his head. "I don't know. I'll try. But for now we'd better just make nice, okay?"

She didn't want to. She wanted to drag her parents out to their car and *make* them go.

How could Amelie do this to her? No, that was obvious: it was easy. Her parents were just another way to force Claire to do whatever the vampires needed. And now that she knew so much, now that she was their only hope of working with Myrnin on a cure, they'd never let her go.

"Hello?" Claire's mom called. "Can we come in?"

Michael kept his expression blank and friendly. "Sure. Everybody inside." Because it was getting dark.

Claire's mom and dad stepped over the threshold.

As Michael started to swing the door shut, a third person stopped the door from closing with an open hand and stepped through. Claire had no idea who he was. She'd never seen him before, and she was sure she'd have remembered. He had thick gray hair, a big gray mustache, and huge green eyes behind thick, fifties-style eyeglasses.

Michael froze, and Claire knew instantly that something was very, very wrong.

"Oh," Claire's mother said, as if she'd forgotten all about him. "This is Mr. Bishop. We met him on our way into town; his car was broken down."

Mr. Bishop smiled and tipped an invisible hat. "Thank you for the kind invitation to enter your home," he said. His voice was incredibly deep and smooth, with an inflection that sounded like Russian. "Although I really didn't require one."

Because he was a vampire.

Claire backed slowly away. Michael looked like he couldn't move at all as Bishop walked into the house.

"I don't want to upset your nice family," Bishop said in a lower tone, focusing on Claire, "but if Amelie isn't here to talk to me in half an hour, I'll kill everyone breathing in this house."

Claire involuntarily looked after her parents, but they were already moving down the hall. They hadn't heard.

"No," Michael said. "You won't touch anyone. This is my house. Get out now, or I'll have to hurt you."

Bishop looked him up and down. "Nice bark, puppy, but you don't have the teeth. Get Amelie."

"Who are you?" Claire whispered. There was menace boiling off this old man like fog. She could almost see it.

"Tell her that her father's come to visit," he said, and smiled. "Aren't family reunions nice?"

About the Author

In addition to the Morganville Vampires series, Rachel Caine is the author of the popular Weather Warden series, which includes *Ill Wind, Heat Stroke, Chill Factor, Windfall,* and *Firestorm.* Her sixth Weather Warden novel, *Thin Air,* was released in August 2007, and she is currently at work on the seventh in the series. Rachel and her husband, fantasy artist R. Cat Conrad, live in Texas with their iguanas, Popeye and Darwin, a *mali uromastyx* named (appropriately) O'Malley, and a leopard tortoise named Shelley (for the poet, of course).

Please visit her Web site: www.rachelcaine.com; and her MySpace: www.myspace.com/rachelcaine.